MC #3

COMPANY OF SINNERS MC

PREZ

LISA J HOBMAN

This is a fictional work. The names, characters, incidents, places, and locations are solely the concepts and products of the author's imagination or are used to create a fictitious story and should not be construed as real.

PRIVATE MOMENTS PUBLISHING & BOOKS, LLC
PO Box 16507
Denver, CO 80216
www.privatemementspublishing.com

ISBN13: 978-1-63112-184-5 ISBN10: 1-63112-184-7

PREZ. Lissa Jay

Cover Credit: Viola Estrella

First Edition 2016
PRIVATE MOMENTS PUBLISHING AND BOOKS, LLC.

For every biker-loving, bad-boy-adoring, tattoo-worshiping reader I've met, and those I've yet to meet.

CHAPTER ONE

Ellie

I hated myself.

That was all there was to it. I had lowered myself to *their* level. The *bikers*. The greasy, violent, foul-mouthed engine monkeys. The way I had berated their President, Colt, when he was visiting my best friend Chloe in the hospital, was totally uncalled-for, and I had *never* felt so ashamed of myself.

Regardless of how much I *hated* them—and boy *did* I hate them—I wished I could suck the words back in as soon as they had fallen from my big, stupid mouth. Even after I arrived home, the whole debacle kept on playing over and over like a horrible Candid Camera reel.

I was pissed already that day as my on/off boyfriend had dumped me, claiming not to be ready for a serious relationship. Asshole might as well have said, "It's not you, it's me." So I had stomped up to Chloe's hospital room in a snit, ready to spill my angst out on my best friend. But as I approached, I heard Colt's voice—the President of Company of Sinners MC in case you were wondering—and ironically *he* was talking about *respect*. The thug who had caused endless heartache in our small town was talking about something he clearly had *no clue* about.

I just flipped.

How the hell *dare he?*

Stepping into the doorway of the room I laughed derisively. "Respect? That's a frickin' *joke* if I ever heard one. You could give Jerry Seinfeld a run for his money with material like that. And you want to know the really funny part? I bet you can't even *spell* respect never mind knowing what it means. If it weren't for you and your stupid club, Chloe wouldn't have gotten mixed up in all this shit. And she wouldn't be in the goddamn hospital!"

I glanced over at Chloe, who was now drained of all color, mouth open.

She gasped. "Eleanor Cassidy. *Please,* would you just *stop* with the hostility."

The blonde, tattooed bimbo I'd heard referred to as Delilah was there too, she stood and stepped toward me with a sneer of violent intent on her face like a little pet pitbull.

Oh, bring it on honey. Bring. It. On.

Colt grabbed her arm and fired her a warning look and like a good little pooch, she heeded her master and sat back down with a huff. However, the narrowing of her eyes told me *this* wasn't over.

Fine by me, bitch.

Moving my focus again I discreetly trailed my gaze over the huge hulk of a man. His long, black hair was tied back in a ponytail, and his steel grey eyes held a kind of fierce fire that would no doubt intimidate the strongest of men. Never mind the bulk of his biceps where they bulged out in all their tattooed glory from the leather vest sleeves of his cut. Tribal tattoos wrapped around his arms and the glimpses of some kind of winged beast were visible from the neck of his T-shirt. From what I had heard, he was an older guy. Around thirty-eight or forty, but he hid it well. No doubt the tattoos and beard covered any of the usual signs of aging, and only a couple of grey flecks peppered his facial hair. If I hadn't been looking so closely, I would no doubt have missed those. Yes, he definitely *didn't* look his age.

Then it hit me like a ton of bricks. I was checking him out. *What. The. Ever. Loving. Frick?*

Reminding myself that I *hated* him and everything he stood for, I turned my attention to the girl I was most concerned about; and whom I cared about deeply. The one who had been innocently caught up in *their* sordid motorcycle gang war.

I stepped toward her. "Chloe, I'm only speaking the truth. You're my best friend, and I *hate* to see what you go through because of these... these *animals*." I gestured wildly in the direction of the two Company of Sinners bikers who were sitting there. Apparently they were staking their claim on *my* friend.

Chloe's cheeks flared a bright pink, and she opened and closed her mouth as if searching for the right words. Was she about to throw me out? Had I overstepped a mark? Were *they* suddenly more important to her than *I* was?

In a move that took me completely by surprise, Colt stood, towering over me at what I guessed must have been six foot four or more. He held out his hand. "Miss Cassidy? Is that right? *Eamon* Cassidy's daughter?"

I snapped my aggressive stare up to the eyes of the low-life before me and then glanced down at his hand. *What a strange gesture from someone I've just insulted.* Bewildered, I reached out and slipped my hand into his where it was immediately swallowed up.

He squeezed gently and lightly ran his thumb over the back of my hand sending a shiver of awareness along my arm. My pulse quickened in an unwelcome reaction to the contact and I swallowed, hoping my sudden heartbeat spike was due to anger; but knowing deep down that it *wasn't*.

I snatched my hand back like I'd been stung and shook my head to dislodge the ridiculous sensation and accompanying thoughts that he had caused.

Lifting my gaze back to meet his I stiffened my spine. "That's right. What of it?"

He smiled to show a row of perfect white teeth and rubbed at the stubble on his angular jaw as he dropped his gaze sheepishly. "I've spent the odd night at your father's hotel when my wife kicked me out." He lifted his chin again and locked those grey eyes on me once more.

Angry at myself for noticing *details* about him. *Personal* details about his appearance, I snapped, "Sounds to *me* like your *wife* is a sensible woman."

He lowered his head briefly and nodded. When he lifted his face once more a distinct impression of pain clouded his eyes, *and* his brow crumpled. "She *was*. Sadly Maria passed away four years ago now."

Oh, shitty shit. Oh God. What the hell do I say? Ground swallow me up, please. "Oh... I'm... I didn't mean... I'm sorry, I..."

He held up his hand dismissively. "Don't sweat it, Red. You weren't to know."

My stomach flipped. *He called me Red. No-one's ever given me a nickname before. Why did my stomach flip?*

Okay, I'm leaving.

I refocused my attention on my only friend in the room. "Chloe... I think I'll come back later. I'm... sorry for my outburst. *Really* I am." And as soon as the words had left my lips I turned and high-tailed it out of there.

Once I was outside the hospital building, a wave of dizziness washed over me and I leaned on a bench to catch my breath. A mixture of guilt and something else I couldn't quite allow myself to acknowledge swirled around my head and I just wanted to get home.

CHAPTER TWO

COLT

Losing Maria to her fight with breast cancer had almost broken me. She was my *life*. My *heart*. How the hell do you come back from losing the *one* person you were meant to be with forever? The walls I had built up around my heart ever since were impenetrable, and I'd made sure to keep it that way. I didn't *need* a woman to nag me and hold me back. Maria had *never* done that and I knew that there was no-one else out there as perfect for me as her.

Anyone else would simply pale into insignificance.

Nah, the truth was I was *done* with love. But fucking? Oh, I liked fucking a *whole* lot. And for some reason unbeknownst to me, the women at the club liked fucking *me,* too. So there was an endless supply of willing pussy for me to get my fill of —if you pardon the pun.

Things been changing around the club lately, and both my VP and his best bud had found themselves long-term relationships, meaning that my wingmen were seriously out of action. I guess at thirty-eight I maybe should have known better than to be chasing ass, but I couldn't help myself. It should've been me settling down but if I'm honest, the thought of doing that just didn't appeal to me. I'd had my forever *stolen* from me, and I was never going to get that back, so I was planning on growing old disgracefully with as many tats as my body could take and as much sex as my dick would cope with.

One thing that continually pissed me off was the attitude that the local folks had about the club. Company of Sinners were seen as a force of evil; a group to do more harm than good in the community. And yeah, okay, we were notorious for getting shit done and taking the law into our own hands, but let's be straight here, sometimes the law by itself just wasn't sufficient. I mean, don't get me wrong, in the past we did get involved in drugs and guns and the stuff that people expect of a club such as CoSMiC, but you know, we had to bring in the dough somehow. And okay maybe I *was* a known criminal, but that was my past and I had fucking feelings too.

That was never truer than when I lost Maria.

At only a couple years younger than me she was the toughest bitch you were ever likely to meet. After the shit she had been through she was afraid of nothing. And I mean *nothing*. Not even death. She had this long black hair. A mass of curls that shimmered almost blue in the sunlight.

I met her when I was taking some time out and traveling the West Coast. Things happened fast between us, but regardless of *that* fact, they lasted ten years.

She was the typical Italian goddess. Curves in all the right places, luscious full lips and dark eyes. She was in an abusive relationship with some dumb fucker who didn't know how good he had it, when I met her. Around the time I was twenty-four, she was twenty-two and working in a diner that I frequented. In spite of fixing her hair in different styles, her bruises didn't go unnoticed. Not by me. I knew the signs, since I'd witnessed that shit before on my travels, and the more I saw her covered in marks, the more I wanted to kill the son of a bitch who had put them there.

One night I was sitting at the counter in the empty diner eating the best scrambled eggs I'd ever had in my life when my wish became a real-life opportunity. The douche bag showed up intoxicated and threatening to do all kinds of bad shit to her when she got off work.

It transpired that she had plucked up courage and left his ass, and he hadn't taken too kindly to it. I sat there, gritting my teeth and clenching my fists trying to stay out of it, as he hurled abuse at her, figuring she didn't know *me* from Adam, and it probably wouldn't help for me to intervene. Well, that was all fine and dandy until he *slapped* her. Her head ricocheted to the right, and she cried out. There was no way on God's earth I was staying the fuck out of *that* shit.

In two rapid steps, I was behind him. I had him in a choke-hold as I informed him through gritted teeth, "You lay a fucking finger on her again, my friend, and I swear I will rip your goddamn arms from their sockets. You hearin' me?"

He struggled and flailed, gasping for the scant amount of air that I would allow him. And when I glanced up at the black-haired young woman before me and locked eyes with her, that was it.

I was done for.

Lost.

The dark chocolate hue of her irises penetrated me. She was the most beautiful woman I had *ever* laid eyes on, and I wanted her. To *protect* her from bastards like the guy in my grasp.

Realizing I still had her ex in my grip, I growled into his ear, "You're gonna leave here, and you're *never* going to bother her again. You hear me? And if you think I'm joking when I say I'll tear you limb from limb if you don't leave, then you are *very* much mistaken. I *don't* joke when it comes to a guy abusing a woman. And just so you know, you're getting off lightly here so I'd take this chance and get the fuck out of Dodge. Just sayin'." I released him and shoved him toward the door he stumbled and almost lost his footing, but when he righted himself, he turned around.

Snarling at me, he gave a humorless laugh. "Yeah? And who the *fuck* do you think *you* are?"

Doing a 180-degree turn so that I faced him full on, I stepped forward and raised my eyebrows. "Oh, did you not *see* my patch? My sincere apologies... here." I turned my back to him and glared at him over my shoulder as I gestured to the logo on my leather cut. "Heard of these guys?"

The color drained from his face as he read the words *Company of Sinners MC Nomad* and when his eyes met mine again, I couldn't help grinning at the way he seemed to shrink by several inches right before my eyes.

I chuckled. "Oh, I see you *have* heard of us? Well, I'm guessing now you *know* I'm serious you'll be on your way, huh?"

Without further words, he made a dash for the door and yanked it open so hard I thought I was gonna be carrying out door repairs.

Once the dick-weed was out of the way, I turned to check on the Italian beauty and as I did, she launched herself into my arms. "Thank you. Oh, thank you so much. You have no idea what you've done for me. Honestly, you can't possibly know."

That first embrace will stay with me forever.

As will our final one.

————

Six had met a beautiful erotic dancer at *The Fox Hub*, a strip joint in town. Her *stage* name was Nina, and he became obsessed pretty much as soon as he laid eyes on her. No wonder, considering she was stunning. Turns out the real her —Chloe—was sweet too. Six had fallen hard in spite of trying not to. He had fought to keep her safe when a rival gang— Loki's Legion—decided to target *her* to get at him—well to get at *us*.

Keeping her safe even entailed him choosing to push her away so that she would keep her distance from the club and all the violence surrounding the club war. It turns out the heart wants what it wants and he failed miserably at staying away from her. I mean the guy was head over heels in love with her, and as the President of Company of Sinners MC, it was *my* remit to ensure the safety of my VP. The problem was, Loki's Legion were hellbent on seeking revenge for shit they had no right being pissed over. And Six was slap bang in the middle of the revenge attacks.

When all hell broke loose, and Chloe was kidnapped by a former Legion puppet, it was me that accompanied Six right up to the building where she was being held against her will. Six was shot in the process of Chloe's rescue. I thought I'd lost him, and my fucking heart broke. Six has been like a brother to me for so long I'd almost forgotten I actually *had* a brother by birth. An *identical twin* brother in fact.

But more about that another time I guess.

Anyway, I felt the need to protect Chloe while Six was in the hospital undergoing surgery, and during his recovery. But the main issue I had was with one fiery redhead who just happened to be the best friend of my new charge.

My God, if looks could kill I swear the rest of the club would have been buying funeral attire and weeping over my fucking grave. My encounters with Ellie Cassidy had been anything but civil, and it burned me that she hated me so much without having anything to base her misguided opinion on.

Okay, maybe it wasn't *exactly* misguided, I mean she *did* have stuff to base her opinions on, if I thought about it logically. But surely the best way to judge someone was to actually take the time to get to know them personally. Shame *Red* didn't see things that way.

The way she barged into Chloe's hospital room and fired insults at me with her AK-47 mouth wasn't exactly indicative of a happy future relationship. I could see I was going to have trouble getting her to 'make nice' with the club, but I had to figure out a way to keep her sweet, or she was going to make my life a living hell.

I stood to face her and held out my hand to introduce myself properly. I hoped that way she would see that I could behave like a civilized human being even if *she* couldn't. I was momentarily distracted as her sexy, fresh, floral scent infiltrated my senses and I found myself stroking the silken skin on the back of her hand with my calloused thumb.

Sadly, the silence that fell between us didn't last, and she began to shoot her mouth off again. This time, my deceased wife was dragged into the situation, and the knot in my stomach returned with a familiar heaviness that reminded me I was alone. And at that moment, I hated the redhead. How dare she speak of my wife in such a way that made me remember that deep ache?

I decided there and then that she and I were *never* going

to be anything even *close* to friends. She was so judgmental she couldn't see past the end of her fucking cute, freckled nose. Her opinion of me would possibly never change but I was a stubborn-ass man too, and she would quickly discover that if she pushed me. It would be a cold fucking day in hell before I would let a woman rule my life or get under my skin.

I don't care how fucking amazing she smelled.

CHAPTER THREE

Ellie

As I arrived home from my embarrassing encounter at the hospital, I found my dad sitting at the dining table with his head in his hands. All thoughts of tattooed bikers temporarily disappeared from my mind as I walked over to him.

I kissed his head before I sat. "Hey, Daddy. What's wrong?"

He lifted his head quickly, eyes wide. But no sooner had the shock registered on his unshaven features than it vanished in a blink of my eyes.

"Oh hey, sunshine. Oh, I'm okay. Just a little headache. Mom thinks I need my eyes checked."

I scrunched my brow and tilted my head. "Come on, Dad, why do I get the feeling you're not telling me the truth here?"

He chuckled and smiled widely. "Ah, my little ray of sunlight, always putting everyone else first. Honestly, sweetheart, I'm good. Just the old eyes. I swear." He made a little cross sign over his heart and held his fingers up in a Boy Scout salute.

I relaxed a little as his loving gaze lit up with mirth. His smile was always contagious to me, and I returned it with one of my own. "Okay, well you'd better get yourself an appointment made with Doctor Alonzo. Promise?"

He nodded and saluted me once more. "Scout's honor."

I eyed him with a suspicious grin. "Were you ever *actually* a Boy Scout?"

He leaned in conspiratorially. "Shh, don't tell your mom but no. I taught *myself* everything I know." Tapping the side of his nose he winked, and I giggled just as I used to as a kid. I loved my parents to the moon and back. They were the center of my universe and as an only child, I was the center of theirs.

At almost twenty-three years old I still lived ridiculously close to home. So close in fact that I could stride from the hotel—where my folks lived—across a gravel driveway to my own place. My one-bed apartment over the garage block was small but perfectly adequate for me, and it meant I was there to help out whenever the hotel was busy. It wasn't exactly the career I had envisaged for myself, but I had given up on the dream of college when—just after my eighteenth birthday— my mom got sick, and Dad needed help running the family business.

The hotel had been in my family for three generations up to that point, and I wasn't about to let my parents down by pursuing my dream of being a journalist. I made the hotel my primary concern until I was twenty and needed to separate my work and home life. That was when I got the job waiting tables at Hank's all night café and met my best friend, Chloe.

At around the same time as I started working for Hank, I started volunteering at the Rose Acres Rag on the weekends, and that certainly helped to sate my desire to be a roving reporter. Although I guess who won the best burger competition in the town's annual cook-out wasn't maybe as exciting as what the Hollywood celebrities were doing—or *who* they were doing more's the point.

I left my dad to relax and helped my mom with dinner. I was fortunate to have her still in my life and certainly counted my blessings. Spending time with her was never a chore. She loved to cook, and I made a point of having dinner with them at least once a week.

As we stood loading the dishwasher, I watched her with interest. A crease had appeared between her brows, and she had been quieter than normal.

I had bitten my tongue for longer than I cared to and decided I had to break the silence. "Mom, is everything okay?"

She lifted her face to meet my gaze. "Hmm? Oh yes, sweetie. I'm just tired."

"How come?"

She sighed. "Your dad has been a little restless. He's not sleeping and so, of course, I don't sleep when he doesn't."

"He was telling me about the headaches. Do you... do you think it's something else maybe?"

Her frown deepened, and she twisted the plate she was just about to place in the rack. "Something else?" Her voice was hesitant and wavered as she spoke.

I shrugged. "Like stress maybe?"

She placed the plate in the washer and closed the door. "Oh no. He just needs to get his sight checked, honey. That's all. Nothing else." She shook her head and smiled.

I wasn't buying it. There was something going on, but I wasn't about to cause a scene. I resolved to wait until they both felt able to discuss whatever it was but decided that I would be keeping a close eye on things.

After eating dinner with my folks, I walked across the driveway to my apartment over the garage. As I climbed the steps I could hear arguing coming from the side fire exit of the hotel, but in the dim light, I couldn't make out who the culprits were.

"You said *fifty*," a male voice hissed.

"That was before what just happened," a female voice replied in a high pitched whine. It wasn't often that such situations arose at Cassidy's as the clientele were of a reasonably high class and so I shook the uneasy feeling off deciding it was probably a lovers' spat.

Once inside my home I flicked on the TV and kicked off my shoes. I was ready to chill out and watch whatever crap there was to offer, but my cell rang. After rummaging around in the bottomless pit of my bag I grabbed my phone in a fluster and was relieved to see Chloe's number lighting up the screen.

"Hey, Chloe... I'm glad you've called because—"

"Ellie, if you're going to apologize don't. I know you only have my best interests at heart, and I'm sorry if you felt I didn't have your back."

I rolled my eyes in spite of the fact she couldn't see me. "Are you *kidding* me? *You*'re apologizing to *me* after I barged in there and insulted your friends?"

"They could be *your* friends too if you gave them a chance you know."

I sighed heavily. "Honey, it's never going to happen. I'm sorry. They're just... we're too different." I immediately regretted the choice of words that made me sound like a snob.

"They're human beings, El. They have feelings too. They really do care about me *and* about keeping me safe. All the stuff you said about them causing me harm is just plain wrong."

I disagreed. But I decided to bite my tongue and change the subject. "So, when are you getting out?"

"I know what you're doing, El. And I'll let it slide for now.

But we're not done on this subject, just so you know. They've said I can come home in a couple days."

"Great. Well let me know and I'll bring food over."

"Well that's the thing… you see… um…"

My stomach sank. "That *Colt* dude is bringing you home, isn't he?"

She sighed, and I knew she could sense the disappointment in my voice. "Yeah. Do you think you can at least *pretend* to be civil?"

I huffed like a sulking teen. "Is he going to *stay* for dinner?"

"Ellie, I thought it would be nice to at least invite them. They've been great, you know."

It was clear, I was fighting a losing battle, and so I relented, albeit reluctantly. "Fine. I'll bring enough Chinese food for the three of us."

She cleared her throat. "Ahem… four."

Oh great. "That *Delilah Doberman* too huh?"

She snickered. "Hey, that's not nice."

I couldn't help giggling. "She *does* act a little bit like a guard dog though. You have to admit it."

"Ellie, you're terrible. And I'll admit no such thing. Now I'm going to sleep. Say hi to your mom and dad for me. Goodnight."

"Night, honey. Sleep well."

I ended the call and slumped back into my seat. Her mention of my parents and the bikers in the same conversation had set the hairs on my neck prickling, and I had no clue why. All I *did* know was that a knot of dread was tightening at my gut, and I didn't like it one bit.

CHAPTER FOUR

Colt

That fucking redhead was preying on my mind. After the incident at the hospital, I was pretty sure that she and I would never see eye to eye. It was a good thing that I didn't have to deal with her often. Even though she was Chloe's friend I was relieved to know it didn't mean I would run into her. Or at least I hoped it didn't.

Thinking about Maria and the emptiness inside of me since I lost her had kept me awake most of the night and I blamed the redhead. Okay so I already knew Maria was gone, but I had been coping with it. Or rather I had been pushing it to the back of my mind.

I dragged myself out of bed and took my naked ass over to the mirror in the bathroom. I looked like shit. More flecks of grey were appearing in my beard and at my temples, and the lines around my eyes were looking far too prominent for my liking. Maria had always said my specks of grey were distinguished-looking. She'd sidle up to me on the bathroom countertop as I combed through my hair in the morning and take the comb from my hands. Then she'd lovingly, slowly and sensually trail the comb through the long strands. God that woman could turn me on with the most normal of tasks.

My dick would strain at my boxers almost every time and on most of those occasions we'd end up fucking right then and there. I say fucking, but it was love. Real, honest, deep-to-the-bone love. That woman knew every little way to make me feel like a king. Like I was the most important thing in her life. Well, the truth of it was that she was the most important thing in mine.

Closing my eyes, I rubbed my hands over my face and sighed. Reminiscing never did me any good. I leaned in and turned the shower on and waited for the room to fill up with steam, and once it had, I climbed under the torrent of hot water. I reached for the shower gel and squirted a generous amount of the clear liquid into my palm.

Just one more memory. I'll allow myself one more for today then that's it.

I drifted back to a time when Maria and I had gone up to Baylor's Point after a huge fight. Apparently *I* had been in a pissy mood, even though it had been Maria—not me—that had been damned crabby. She had waved her arms around like some kind of berserk windmill, and I'd stood there, arms folded across my chest, brow crinkled as she hurled abuse at me. The dumb thing was that I loved it when she went crazy on my ass. She gave me a hard on when she got that fire in her eyes. And as she ranted at me all I could think about was tying those fucking flailing arms up and fucking her.

A sly smile crept along my lips, and I couldn't fight it. She glared at me and told me to stop fucking grinning or she'd slap it off my face.

Bring it on, baby.

Bring. It. On.

In one step I was in front of her. Her eyes widened at the speed with which I dragged the cord from the bathrobe she was wearing and tied her hands with it. I left her naked body on show, put her over my shoulder, carried her to the SUV and deposited her in the passenger seat locking the door behind her. She had screamed and shouted at me, calling me every negative name she could come up with and I had just laughed in her face. She had squirmed and wrestled with the cord, but she was good and tied. I'd made sure of that.

I drove us out to Baylor's Point and parked the car in our usual spot. She had gone silent and was refusing to answer me or acknowledge me. Stubborn-ass woman. But it just made me love her more. There was never a dull moment. Being with her was like constantly driving into a cyclone. I took a blanket from the trunk and laid it out by a little tree stump before going back to fetch her. I was still getting the silent treatment, but that was going to change.

I pulled her out of the car and again flung her curvy body over my shoulder, and once I reached the blanket I laid her down. I grabbed the tie that was still in place around her wrists, raised her hands above her head and tied it around the little tree stump.

"What the hell are you doing, Colt? Take me home *right now*."

"Shut the fuck up, woman." She hated it when I called her that and so I did it on purpose to rile her.

"Colt, what are you *doing*? People *walk* this trail. I'm *naked*. Colt!"

I dropped to my knees before her and slipped her silky thighs apart. She eyed me with intrigue and didn't fight.

"Na-uh, you have on a robe, baby. Anyway, I thought that the best way to get us *both* out of *our* apparent pissy mood would be a nice open-air fuck." I raised my eyebrows and pulled my lip in between my teeth.

Her eyes widened, and her chest began to heave. "We can't. It's too... exposed." But her body betrayed her, and I watched with a sly smile as her pupils dilated and her nipples peaked.

Oh, she *wanted* me alright.

I tugged off my T-shirt and watched as her nostrils flared and her eyes raked over my tattooed chest. Another thing I knew about her. She *loved* my ink.

She licked her lips until they were glistening. "C—Colt... what are you—"

I swooped down and dragged my tongue up the center of her pussy in a long, lingering lick. She moaned and writhed.

I couldn't help the grin that tugged at my lips. "Feeling less pissy now, huh?"

"Colt, please..."

"Please what, baby? Want me to stop?"

She gazed up at me and pulled her bottom lip between her teeth as she slowly shook her head no.

Needing no further encouragement, I dove straight in. Tongue first. *God*, the taste of her. The smell of her. It was like a drug to me, and I couldn't get enough. I swirled my tongue around the little nub of flesh that had swollen with her arousal, and she gasped as she thrust her pelvis into my mouth. I slipped my tongue inside her body and groaned as she tensed her muscles around me. But it wasn't enough. I needed so much more of her.

Pulling myself reluctantly away I gazed down at her where she lay, and my heart almost burst with the love I held for this beautiful, frustrating-as-hell woman. The robe had slipped down off her collar bone, and her chest rose and fell rapidly. Her pink, tight nipples stood at attention as if begging me to touch them, to squeeze them, to *bite* them. I stood and slipped off my jeans and boxers before lowering myself between her thighs and obliging the little buds with my tongue and teeth.

As I nibbled at her, she rocked her hips, rubbing her wet pussy along my shaft, and it was almost too much. Too good. With one pull back and a thrust forward, I connected with her; my cock gliding effortlessly deep inside of the woman I adored. An appreciative rumble escaped from my chest as I worshiped her nipples one at a time, biting and sucking as I withdrew and slipped my rigid flesh back inside.

"Oh God Colt, I *need* you... I *need* you so much," she breathed into my hair as I took a nipple between my teeth and bit down. She gasped and thrust her pelvis up so that I sank deeper still.

"You *have* me, baby. *All* of me. And I don't plan on letting you go. Come for me, Maria... come for me, baby. I wanna hear you." Her core began to tighten around my cock, and I knew she was close.

"Come with me," she moaned, and my movements increased in fervor.

I repositioned myself so I could gaze into her eyes and I pulled out and sank back in deep once more. She began to moan my name over and over as her back arched, and her nipples brushed my chest.

"Baby, I'm so fucking hard for you. Only you. Only you, Maria." The muscles low in my groin tightened, and she cried out as she began to spasm in quickening pulses around my cock. And in a split second, I followed her into the abyss.

———

Chloe was coming home from the hospital, and Dee and I had

decided to collect her and bring her home. I had anticipated an argument from her, seeing as she liked to be completely independent and made sure we all knew it. Fortunately, the stubborn little dancer hadn't argued after all. Call it progress, call it capitulation. I don't care. I was just relieved not to have her fighting me on the matter.

Once I had secured the patient in the back of my black SUV—with many protestations from said patient I might add about how she could look after herself and that she wasn't some fragile little doll—I climbed in the driver's seat and slammed the door.

Her easy-going manner had been short-lived after all.

I decided a change of subject was needed. "So, CD, you hungry after that crap they fed you in there? Should we maybe call for take-out on the way back to your apartment?"

Dee climbed in beside her in the back seat, and I suddenly felt like a goddamn chauffeur.

Chloe's response was bright and breezy once again, and I got the impression that getting out of the hospital was the reason. "Oh, no need to do that. Ellie's grabbing some food for us all. In fact, she'll probably be there when we arrive."

Hearing Chloe mention the *redhead* caused a sinking sensation in my gut. I rolled my eyes, thankful for the fact that I was facing front. "Oh... *great*."

Dee laughed. "Jeez, Colt, you could sound even *less* happy if you tried hard enough." I turned and glared at her over my shoulder, and she bit down on her lip evidently trying to stifle her outpouring of humor at my discomfort. I made a mental note to deal with her later.

Chloe chimed in. "Look, Colt, you guys can just drop me home if you can't face an evening with Ellie. I totally understand after last time. But she's just looking out for me, you know? Just like you guys."

The disappointment in her voice caused my stomach to knot, and I knew I was being an ass. The redhead was her best friend after all, and we were—for all intents and purposes—her newly acquired family. We should at least *try* to get along.

I shook my head and shrugged. "Nah. It's fine. *I* don't have an issue with Ellie. I think *she's* already decided she fucking hates *me*. Well, *us* in fact." I gestured toward Dee, feeling the need to drag her down with me.

Chloe leaned toward me. "No. No, she doesn't *hate* you... it's just... she just... umm..."

"*Detests* me?" I asked with a chuckle. I glanced through the rear view mirror to find Chloe's brow scrunched and the distinct shadow of guilt in her eyes.

She broke my gaze and fiddled with the cast on her wrist. "It's just that *hate* is a *very* strong word, Colt." Her voice was fragile and quiet.

"Hey, CD, don't sweat it. She'll come around. I'll just use my masculine charms and my deathly good looks to win her over."

Dee almost choked on fresh air. "Oh yeah. That'll work if you have cosmetic surgery first."

I busted out laughing. "Fuck you, Delilah."

"Yeah, *you* wish." She laughed too.

When I cast a glance at Chloe in my rear-view again, her furtive gaze was darting between Dee and I. She was clearly taken aback by our harsh banter.

"Hey, CD don't fret. Dee loves me really. She just likes busting my balls."

A sweet smile appeared on Chloe's lips, and she visibly relaxed. I guess some people just don't get that a guy and a woman can have such a platonic, teasing relationship. But that's just what Delilah and I had. There was no attraction between us and never had been. She was like my kid sister. And besides she'd only ever had eyes for Cain Somers.

Poor bitch. But that's a whole other story.

All too soon we arrived at Chloe's apartment and Ellie, the feisty redhead, opened the door to us with a wide smile. As soon as she locked eyes with me, however, her jovial mood disappeared, and she became icy until she quickly turned to focus on Chloe.

She gave a dumb, girlie squeal. "Hey, sweetie. It's so good to have you out of that hospital," she told her friend as she pulled Chloe into her arms.

Chloe hugged her back. "Urgh, I can't *wait* to sleep in my own bed. Those hospital beds are like sleeping on wooden planks."

The delicious aroma of Chinese spices floated through from the kitchen, and my stomach gave an extremely loud appreciative growl. Three pairs of eyes turned on me all at once and after a shocked second of silence, they all busted out laughing at me. Three fucking hysterical women. Jeez. For what may have been the first time in my *life,* I felt my cheeks glowing with embarrassment.

Fucking great timing, inner workings of my body. Thanks for that.

Trying to hide the color of my face, I pushed my way past the giggling females and stormed into the living room. "How cute does a guy have to be to get fed around here?"

"A hell of a lot cuter than *you,* dog-face," Dee called after me, her insult resulting in more laughter at my expense.

Me and my big mouth.

"I've laid out the table in the kitchen. The plates are warmed, and everything's good to go," Ellie announced as she made her way through the living room, and we all followed.

Now, I'm not sure whether it was done on purpose, but I

ended up seated straight across from my arch nemesis. She avoided eye contact as she opened the cartons of rice, chicken and noodles. I grabbed and opened a beer bottle that was nearest to me and took a long pull, eager to give my mouth something to do.

I glanced up to find Red watching me. A sideways glance uncovered the fact that Chloe was watching *her*. The woman clearly had something to say. I just hoped it wasn't another barrage of insults and anger.

It wasn't the time nor the place.

Red opened her mouth to speak, and I found myself holding my breath. *Here we go...*

She cleared her throat and her cheeks colored up a bright pink. *Kinda cute really if she wasn't so fucking sour-faced.*

"Colt... I... I want to apologize again for what I said about your wife at the hospital. I felt terrible when I left, and it's plagued me ever since. I really should learn to think before I speak."

I shook my head. My gaze locked firmly on hers giving no quarter. "Like I said, Red, don't sweat it, you didn't know. It's a long time ago that I lost her, so it's not as raw as it once was."

She nodded slightly. "Well, I'm *very* sorry for your loss. No-one should have to go through losing someone so close to them."

It was the nicest she had been so far, and I wondered if this chink in her armor was something to do with a personal experience. There was a huskiness to her voice, and I watched as the pink in her cheeks spread across her chest. She swallowed, and I could have sworn her pupils dilated as I fixed her with an intense stare. She was clearly uneasy about my attention, but I was trying to read her mind—to gauge her level of animosity toward me. What I *didn't* expect was to recognize something akin to *lust* shining back at me.

If the truth be told, I couldn't fucking *stand* the woman. She was snooty and judgmental and irritating as fucking hell. But for some reason, my dick had *other* opinions. I felt the need to adjust myself in my jeans where my erection was rubbing uncomfortably at the denim. A lack of laundry had left me commando, and it was only *now* that I was regretting it.

Chloe coughed loudly, and I snapped my focus onto her. "So how is everyone enjoying the food?"

I nodded, happy for the distraction. "Yeah... yeah it's good. Good choice." I shoveled a huge chunk of chicken and noodles into my mouth.

When I glanced over at Red again, all signs of lust were gone. She was eyeing me with disgust as I chewed extra loud... on *purpose*. The last thing I needed was for her to be *wanting* me and vice fucking versa.

The *last* thing.

CHAPTER FIVE

Ellie

What the hell was that?

Something had crackled in the air between me and the dark-haired biker. Luckily he seemed as unhappy about it as I was, and he ate his food quickly. In around twenty minutes he made his excuses and took his little guard dog, *Delilah*, with him, and they left.

I breathed a silent sigh of relief, but once I had collected the dirty dishes up and placed them in the sink, I turned to find Chloe staring at me knowingly. There was an unmistakable glint of awareness in her narrowed eyes.

Oh great. Just what I need.

"Okay, Ellie, what the *hell* was *that* back there with you and Colt?"

I made a totally unladylike snorting sound. "What? *What* back there? I don't know what you mean."

"You shared a *moment*."

Shit, shit, shit. "Oh *please*. Seriously? Come on, Chloe. You know me better than that. I was simply offering my condolences. The guy's *wife* died." I lifted my wine glass to my lips and took a big glug.

She shrugged. "If you say so." Annoyingly, the sly smile on her face told me that this conversation was *far* from over.

I needed to deflect her train of thought from the crazy tracks back onto the line for sensible-ville. "What? You think I'm *hot* for the guy? Is *that* it?" *Yeah well done, Ellie. Way to sound convincing. Not protesting too much at all.*

She pursed her lips as her smile threatened to widen.

I had to try again at the deflection thing. "Well, I can tell you one hundred percent that old guys are *not* my thing. Okay? They just don't do it for me. And old guy bikers are *so* far from being my thing that I... Urgh, I can't even believe you'd think that. Jeez. You *know* my opinion on *those* people. Shit, Chloe, do you know me at all?"

She picked up the wine bottle and topped up her glass. "Oh come on, I'm only teasing, El. Don't get so touchy. Anyway, what's new around here? How are your mom and dad?"

Relieved that she had *finally* changed the subject, I slumped back into my chair, and my mind drifted back to the conversations I'd had with my folks. "I'm not sure. Things seem... strained."

She leaned toward me. "Strained? How?"

I waved my hand dismissively. "It's probably nothing. But... When I got home the other night, my dad was sitting in the dining room with his head in his hands. He said it was just a headache but when I asked mom she was really evasive too. I don't know... it feels like something's going on. I just don't know what."

Voicing my fears really made things seem real to me and I left Chloe's apartment with a heavy feeling in my chest.

Colt

The fact that I was wide awake at stupid o'clock in the morning pissed me off. But the fact that there was a certain redhead haunting my dreams when I *did* drift off to sleep pissed me off even more.

The dreams were so damn vivid.

It was the way she peered up at me through hooded, lust filled eyes and begged me to fuck her hard as she gripped my ass, pulling me deeper, that got to me most. I mean, come on, she was the *last* person I would choose to fuck. And I liked sex as much as the next guy. I *hated* that my mind had conjured up the feeling of her tight, wet pussy clenching around my cock, and the smell of her perfume and was toying with me and teasing me. That and the sight of stiff, rosy pink nipples on her pert tits that were just big enough to fill my greedy hand. Shit, I had a wicked imagination. But why was it working overtime on *that* pain in the ass?

Eventually, I got up and took a shower with the temperature as cold as I could take it before my balls would re-ascend and cause me major problems.

After my shower, I walked back through to my bedroom and caught sight of my stunning wife Maria smiling at me from the photo on my nightstand.

As I rubbed a towel over my hair I picked up the frame and let my gaze trail up the chocolate brown hair that draped in waves over her shoulder to meet the familiar brown eyes twinkling back at me.

I sighed heavily and shook my head. "Why did you have to fucking leave me, huh? You died and everything went to shit, baby. I swear I'm losing my fucking mind. I *must* be, if that annoying redhead is getting under my skin. How do I get her out of there? Huh? If only you were here none of these things would even matter. I'd be holding *you*, dreaming about making love to *you*." I clenched my jaw as a wave of excruciating sadness began to tighten my stomach. "God I miss you, baby. I miss you *so* much. Moving on is too damned hard. I don't *want* to leave you in my past. Why is life so fucking unfair, huh?" A lump began to form in my throat, so I quickly placed the picture back and rubbed the towel over my face.

Come on asshole. Pull yourself together. You haven't done this in a long while.

I inhaled deeply but in my mind's eye, I could see Maria running away from me through the long grass as I chased her. The chimes of her laughter ringing out and dancing on the air. Okay, it *was* a cliché like some fucking romance movie, but it *did* actually happen. The best part though, was when I eventually caught her, and we made love out in the warm summer sunshine, amongst the long waving strands of pale green. God the way she *looked*. How she *felt* beneath me and around me and how her whole being captured and held me fast, body, mind, and soul. We fit together like two carved, flawed pieces that somehow made one perfect whole.

I'd *never* have that again.

After spending so long convincing myself that I'd had my one shot at love, I was becoming a cynic where real relationships were concerned. But deep down I knew that those little shards of negativity were born of jealousy.

I saw people in love and silently, if only momentarily, I hated them and their happiness. The way their lives continued together when I was back to being a broken half of myself.

Deciding I'd spent too long wallowing, I dressed and made my way downstairs to the bike. I'd forgone the Harley and chosen a Ducati as my main mode of transport. The SUV only came out on the necessary occasions. Collecting my charge from the hospital today had been one such occasion, but I felt the need to get outside into the warm morning and feel the wind and rays on my face. The sun was just starting its ascent, and I knew just the spot to watch the colors change as it rose.

Once I was on the bike and the engine had revved to life, I took off at speed along my block. I stayed in my little house—the one that had belonged to Maria and I—at every given opportunity. The clubhouse wasn't my home. And anyways, I needed time away from the crazy partying. I wasn't getting any younger after all.

As I rode past Cassidy's hotel, a movement caught my eye. I slowed down when I spotted Eamon pacing up and down with his hands in his hair. What the hell was he doing outside so early? And why was he looking so stressed? I figured that infuriating daughter of his had something to do with it and without stopping to find out, I sped up and rode off toward my destination. I certainly didn't need to be getting any more involved with that chick than I already was.

CHAPTER SIX

Ellie

It took far too long for me to fall asleep. And with insomnia comes thinking. And thinking isn't always a great pastime. Thinking can be catastrophic.

Along with the concerns about my parents that were taking up residence in my head, were images flashing through my mind of a muscular, tattooed biker. I *hated* that he was lodged in my subconscious. He was so unwelcome there. I *didn't* want him in spite of what Chloe thought.

He just... *irked* me.

He *bothered* me.

His arrogance. His ridiculous cartoon-like angular jaw that was stubbled with not-quite-a-beard. Those damn muscles that he *clearly* worked too hard to maintain. *Vain bastard.* And ugh... those tattoos. What possessed someone to get another human being to permanently scrawl all over their skin like that? Just the thought of being scratched with needles made a shiver of anxiety travel up my spine and a wave of nausea bubble up my esophagus.

The thing that had stuck in my head was how he'd surprised me at the meal. He'd been... *sociable... nice* even. But don't get me wrong, my opinion of him *still* resided somewhere in the gutter with the rats. That wouldn't be changing any time soon. After all, you know what they say about leopards, right? And *he* was the king cat in his little screwed-up jungle.

And ugh... the way he'd locked his gaze on mine like he was undressing me with his eyes. As I remembered his ravenous stare my nipples peaked, forcing me to pull the covers higher on my body. I was almost definitely coming down with something. I mean, it's not like it was cold inside the apartment so why else would my nipples stand to attention?

Okay, so that was a rhetorical question that I didn't want *nor* need to dwell on.

I rolled over and snuggled down into the mattress...

Just as I began to drift off, the security light out on the driveway woke me. After a few moments, everything went dark again but as I watched it illuminate once more, my heart began to beat rapidly and fear set in. Was there an intruder on the premises? I climbed out of bed to go to my window and once I had pulled back the curtain I could see a figure pacing around down there.

It was too dark to see who it was, and when the security light kicked in, the glare forced me to avert my eyes. The figure eventually stopped pacing, and I tried hard to focus on it as I reached for my cell phone from the side table. With shaking hands, I dialed my dad's cell.

The figure began to pace again and rummage around in what I guessed were pockets.

"H-hey, sunshine. W-what are you doing up so early?

Can't sleep, huh?" The figure on the driveway turned and gazed up at my window; a hand raised in a wave.

I opened and closed my mouth, but words didn't form. The figure was my *dad*.

What the hell is he doing out there at this hour? "Daddy? Why are you outside? I saw the security light and got scared."

"Oh... oh nothing. Just a headache. I came out for... for some fresh air. Fresh air's good for my headaches."

A headache again? "Did you make an appointment with Doctor Alonzo?"

"I did, honey. I did. I'm going tomorrow... well later *today* actually."

My heart ached, and the little seed of worry that was planted earlier began to gestate. "Okay. Can I get you anything? Can I *do* anything?"

"Aww, no sweetie. You go back to sleep. I'll be fine. Promise." He ended the call, and I allowed the curtain to fall back into place. Something was definitely wrong. But how could I get him to stop being so evasive and tell me the truth?

Although I crawled back into bed, I couldn't rest. Too many worries stomped around my head, making relaxation an impossibility. In the end I grabbed the romance novel I'd been reading and opened it up.

———

Colt

Red, pink, violet, blue.

I watched, mesmerized, as the sky set alight before my eyes. The rocky precipice that overlooked what I guessed was a small meteor crater gave me the best view point I could wish for. It had been a favorite place for Maria and I to come.

You wouldn't think it to look at my bulky, muscular, tattooed exterior, but I had a softer side. However, it was a side that only Maria knew how to expose. Sitting here with her all those times had formed so many wonderful memories. Although, now those memories were tinged with sadness and pain it didn't stop me replaying them over and over.

My cell vibrated in my pocket, dragging me back from my daydream. Pissed off at the ill-timed interruption, I yanked it out of my pocket and answered with a gruff growl. "What?"

A familiar chuckle traveled down the airwaves. "Well, *that* was a helluva charming greeting, Prez." Then a silent pause. "Fuck! Oh shit, did I *wake* you? These goddamn time differences get me every time. Seven hours is a bitch, huh?"

"Hey, Cain… I mean *Cameron*. Nah I'm just up at Baylor's Point. How are you doing bro?"

Another pregnant pause. "*Baylor's?* Shit, is everything okay, man? You only go there when—"

I tried to lighten my tone of voice. "It's all good. I'm fine. Just watching the sun come up. Is there a reason for this early morning alarm call?"

"Um… yeah… I kind of… did something amazing. I *proposed!* Annnd… She said *yes.*" The excitement in his voice grabbed me by the heart and squeezed tight.

"Yeah? Wow, that's *great*! Congratulations to you both. Hey, I hope we get an invite to Scotland for the wedding. Even if you are a gazillion miles away these days, we'll still wanna be there."

"Hell *yeah* you will. It won't be for a long while. You know we gotta save some dough and plan it all. But… well I'm just happy she said yes."

I couldn't help laughing at the surprise in his voice. "Fuck, dude, she *does* know you're a crazy-ass right? I mean… I know she's some kind of *mind doctor* but does she know you can't be fixed, huh?"

Ca...*meron*—shit the new name was taking some getting used to—responded with a deep belly laugh. "Colt, my friend, all she knows is I'm crazy in love with her, and that's how it's gonna stay."

Another way to wind him up sprang to mind. "Is she gonna make you wear one of those *skirts?*"

"If you mean a *kilt* then yeah, maybe. I'd fucking *rock* one of those bad boys. I've got great legs. You're just jealous."

"Yeah, you keep thinking that about your scrawny little chicken sticks, buddy."

I could hear his grin even though I couldn't see it. "Whatever, Colt, whatever. Anyways, I'd better go. We're out to lunch over on the mainland. A little pub near Arisaig. It's fucking *beautiful* in this place. Scotland forever, baby! Woohoo!" His loud exclamation reverberated through my ear drum.

I pulled the phone away from my head. "Douche bag." I shook my head and grinned. "I'm happy for you, Cam. *Really* happy. Can't wait to see your old lady in her wedding gown. Phew, now *that*'ll be a sight for sore eyes. Give her a kiss from me but hey no tongue, okay? She's gonna be *married* you know. Shame her future husband is an asshole."

He laughed and relayed the message to his fiancée. "She says you can't afford her and her husband-to-be has a *fine* ass thank you very much. Bye, Colt. Say hi to everyone from us and tell them to keep checking the mail for their invites."

The call ended and I gazed out into the distance with a smile tugging at my mouth. I was happy it worked out for them, after all the shit they went through. And I just hoped they were set to have many happy years ahead of them. I hoped beyond everything that they got plenty of time. Something Maria and I'd had cut short.

So there was gonna be a wedding in the MC, huh?

CHAPTER SEVEN

Ellie

Against my advice, Chloe had gotten back together with Six. His head was all shaved at the sides following the awful incident they had been through and there was a new tattoo on his scalp of a wolf. Apparently it was some reference to Chloe's initial opinions on the guy. Kinda sweet I guess. Although he looked even *more* unapproachable than he had before, and that's saying something. But the more I got to know him, the more I began to like him. And for once in my life I began to wonder if I'd been *wrong* about the bikers—or at least *some* of them anyway.

Now Chloe and Six were head over heels in love all over again, and he was treating her so well. Whenever I saw the way they just gazed at each other, a tiny twinge of envy tugged at my insides. I wanted to be loved like that. But maybe I somehow didn't deserve it.

My dad had finally seen the doctor and had been diagnosed with stress related migraine and high blood pressure.

There was no wonder really. He worked too damn hard at the hotel and as much as he loved the place I was thinking that maybe he *should* sell it. Although I hadn't had the guts to express this to him directly.

I was biding my time on *that* one.

Saturday evening arrived and I was getting ready to go on my first date in ages. I wasn't exactly filled with enthusiasm, but I hated being single when love was in the air all around me. I decided I needed to get back out there, and so I had agreed to a date with a colleague from the newspaper. Simon was a guy I'd met when I was volunteering at the Rose Acres Rag. He was cute but a little too clean cut and wholesome, and after what had happened to Chloe I had become incredibly suspicious of men in general. I suppose the good thing with a tattooed biker was that you kind of knew what you were getting from the start. Not that I wanted that for *me*. It was great for Chloe. But it wasn't a road I was intent on traveling.

I buttoned up my pale green silk blouse and tucked the hem into the waist of my skinny jeans. My curly hair was as tamed as it could be but I chose to wear it down. Simon had commented on the fiery color of my locks, and so I figured he'd like to see it natural seeing as I usually wore it pinned up at the paper.

I applied a thin layer of lip shimmer and spritzed my chest and wrists with my favorite floral perfume. After giving myself a final surveying glance in the mirror, I decided I would have to do and then right on time, seven in the evening, there was a knock on my door.

―――――

It was a shame that the date with Simon didn't go well. It didn't go *horribly,* don't get me wrong. We had plenty to talk about, and he was a really nice guy. He listened as no guy I had ever met, but I kept on apologizing for hogging the conversation. He was cute and funny too. But there was just no... *spark,* and he didn't make my panties melt. It was clear he felt the same when he dropped me home so early and said he'd see me at the office. There was no request for another date. Not that I would have accepted anyway but it would have been nice to be asked, right?

We didn't hug or kiss when we parked up on the street outside the hotel, and so I climbed out of his car and waved as he drove away up the road. Heaving a sigh of disappointment that I was destined to sleep alone again, I turned to walk toward my apartment. As I rounded the first tree on the driveway, I heard scuffling and my heart skipped a beat.

I stopped dead.

In the dim evening light, I could make out that some guy wearing dark clothing had my dad pinned up against the wall by the neck and was growling words that I couldn't quite make out.

My dad's hands were held up in surrender, and I could hear him pleading, "N-no... no *please* leave Eleanor out of this. She has *no* involvement. You hear me? *Please.*"

Hearing my name mentioned caused my heartbeat to hammer at my ribs so hard that I feared I may collapse. The attacker's voice got louder and his grip around my father's throat seemed to tighten as I heard him choking.

The man's voice boomed in the dimming light. "You know what I'd *like* to do to sweet Ellie, don't you huh? I think I may have mentioned that." There was a deep, dark laugh before he continued. "And you know what I *will* do to her if my plans all go to shit, right, Eamon? I don't make idle threats old man. You know I'll do it. Don't you?"

I leapt forward from my hiding place ready to launch my own assault on my father's assailant, but something grabbed me from behind and a hand covered my mouth. I tried to scream, but my captor's hold tightened. Tears sprang from my eyes, and I wriggled and fought hard, as whom I presumed to be the monster's accomplice held me against my will. My fists clenched, and my legs flailed wildly, trying to make contact with a shin bone, a kneecap or whatever other part of the bastard's anatomy that I could get to.

Hot breath hit my ear, and someone spoke in a low whispered hiss. "Hey, Red. I suggest you stop with the fucking squirming. I'm *not* gonna hurt you, but you need to calm. The fuck. *Down*."

Colt? What the hell?

A small squeak left my throat but didn't get much further thanks to the huge hand clamped over my closed lips. My breath heaved rapidly through my nose, and I could no longer see through the fog of tears.

His voice came again but this time, it was more soothing. "It's okay, Red. It's okay, shhh. Look, I'm gonna move my hand, and you and me are going to hide here in the bushes for a while. I'll explain later, 'kay?" I nodded. "Good. Now promise me you won't scream or do anything dumb. *I'm* not the enemy here."

If *he* wasn't the enemy, then what the hell was going on? A million different thoughts and emotions scrambled around my brain but panic mixed with fear, and I figured I had no other option but to trust him. After all, he'd been good to my friend. That was something... *right*? I nodded again.

His hand loosened and he spun me around to face him. I could just make out the sparkle of his wide eyes as the emerging moonlight highlighted his rugged features. He held his finger up to his lips in a shushing motion. Why the hell was someone as tough as *him* hiding in a bush while my father was attacked? What kind of lily-livered, cowardly bastard was he anyway?

He pointed toward the man who held my father, and I turned my face to see that a group of men were now crowding around with violent intent. Okay, so Colt was *very* much outnumbered. I could forgive him for not diving in fists first, but who *were* they? Why did they have my father? What did they *want* from him?

The assailant spoke again. "Okay, now we'll leave you to mull over our little... *proposition*. You know where we are, so when you've made the *right* decision, you'll be in touch. *Won't* you, Eamon?" My father nodded, and the ring leader slapped his face three times patronizingly. "Good little man."

The group turned and began to walk away like zombies down the other side of the curved driveway. All at once the air was filled with the roar of motorcycle engines and gas fumes and one by one the men revved and sped off down the road.

My heart still hammered in my chest and I was shaking so much my teeth were chattering. I turned to face Colt. "W-what the hell?" It was a rhetorical question... I think... although answers *would* have been good. But right then all I wanted to do was get to my father and see if he was all right.

I turned and tried to move, but Colt grabbed me again. His voice was a barked whisper. "Wait, Red. You *can't* go. Your dad can't know that you saw *any* of that."

I responded in the same tone through clenched teeth. "*What*? *Why*? I need to check he's okay. He may need to go to the emergency room. He's suffering from stress. His heart—"

He sighed. "Because if Loki's Legion get the *slightest* hint that you saw any of that, you're *dead*. That's why."

"But you were supposed to have dealt with the Loki problem, Colt. Why are they still hanging around?"

"I don't know, but believe me, you don't want to get in the middle of it. They *will* kill you. If you think my crew is bad—and we both know that you *do*—then those animals make my crew look like the fucking bingo club."

Not satisfied with his response, I sneered at him. "Why are you even *here,* prowling around my home without invitation? What the hell is *wrong* with you?"

He scowled as if I'd slapped him. "I was out on the bike, and I saw some of Loki's Legion riding up the driveway. I didn't know if you were in and I wanted to check on what they were going to do."

"But *why*? What has it got to do with *you* anyway?"

He shook his head, and an expression of defeat settled over his features. "Nothing. Absolutely nothing. Call me sentimental, but you're the friend of a friend and the thought of you winding up dead didn't sit easily with me."

My heart tripped over itself and dizziness overwhelmed me as I heard him refer to me dying again. My legs began to buckle as stars danced before my eyes. My stomach rolled almost giving up the meal I had not long since consumed and I felt myself crumbling.

I was aware that my feet were no longer on the floor and the cool evening air was caressing my skin as my head rested against something firm. The next thing I knew we were inside, and I opened my eyes to familiar surroundings.

Confusion washed over me as I gazed up into narrowed eyes. "How... how did you get into my apartment?" He gently placed me down on my couch.

Colt stepped back and held up my keys making them jingle as he waggled them. "*These* were in your hand." He raised his eyebrows as if to say *D'uh, stupid.*

"Oh."

He chuckled. "You thought I picked the lock didn't you?"

I shrugged. "I don't think I'm *capable* of cognizant thought right now, to be honest."

He stepped closer and loomed over me. "Do you have any alcohol?"

I scrunched my face as anger bubbled up inside of me. "Are you *kidding* me? My dad was brutally attacked by a gang of thugs, and you want a *drink*?"

He slumped onto the couch beside me and ran his hands through his straggly hair. "What the *fuck* did I do to create such a low impression of myself, Red?" I just glared at him as he continued. "I wanted the alcohol for *you*. To calm your nerves, okay? You've had a fucking nasty shock tonight. That's *all*. Look I'll go. I sense I'm not wanted here." He stood to leave.

Guilt needled at me, so I reached out and grabbed his arm. "Wait!" He clenched his jaw as he peered down at me and I pulled my bottom lip between my teeth. "I'm sorry I jumped to the wrong conclusion, Colt."

He shrugged easily out of my grip. "Don't sweat it, Red. I'm kinda getting used to being *judged* when I'm with you."

Ouch. Am I that bad? "I... I don't *mean* to judge you. I just... I only *know* the bad stuff. The rumors. The bad shit that happened to Chloe. You've got to admit it doesn't cast a great light on the MC *or* you, seeing as you're the boss."

He stayed silent for a few moments, and I wasn't sure whether to fill the void in the conversation, but eventually he spoke. "Look, I'm gonna go. It's getting late, and I don't think it would be a good idea for your dad to find me here after the evening he's had. But... keep what you saw tonight to yourself okay? What we witnessed *can't* go any further. Not right now.

I know it'll be hard but... it's safer that way for you *and* your family."

My stomach knotted as images of my father being held by the throat and his panicked demeanor assaulted my frontal lobe again. "W-what do you think they want from him, Colt?"

"Honestly? I have *no* idea. And it's not *my* place to go poking around to find out. I've dealt with enough shit from Loki's Legion to last me a goddamn lifetime. Whatever it is lies between Eamon and *them*." He turned and walked toward my door.

Overcome with exasperation and disbelief at his apparent nonchalance, I pushed myself to a standing position. "So that's *it*? You're not going to help? You're just going to *leave* here and forget about what happened?" I couldn't hide the incredulity from my voice. After all, he had cared enough to follow them onto the hotel premises.

He stopped and glanced over his shoulder toward me but didn't make eye contact. "None of my beeswax, Red. Like I said."

His hand was on the doorknob, and panic once again gripped me. How the hell could *I* deal with Loki's Legion? I was *one* woman. And not one accustomed to the under-handed ways of biker gangs. Six was still healing, and I didn't really know *any* of the other members of Company of Sinners —not that they would help me without the President's say so anyway. Colt was the *only* one who could help me.

Remembering the way he had looked at me with hungry eyes when we'd been at Chloe's I dashed toward him, all self-respect and thoughts of what I was about to do pushed down... deep down. "I *need* you, Colt. I need your *help*," I pleaded.

He rubbed his chin and eyed me with a grin that was

either salacious or filled with sick amusement at my expense, but he was so damn hard to read.

He chucked his chin at me. "Oh yeah? And why would I want to do that, huh? Why would *I* want to help *you*?"

I took a step back and began to unbutton the pale green silk blouse I was wearing until my flesh colored lace bra was exposed. With a shaking, small voice I told him, "I can offer you... *me*... I mean... my *body*."

CHAPTER EIGHT

Colt

I watched in bemusement as Ellie unbuttoned and discarded her silky shirt, letting it swish to the floor. I was confused but mesmerized simultaneously. I was unable to look away even though something deep inside of me was telling me I should. She reached around her back and unclasped her bra, allowing that to fall too.

Her beautiful, alabaster skin was completely exposed to my greedy stare. Pretty pink nipples stood to attention atop pert rounded mounds of flesh, begging for my touch. My appreciative cock stirred to life, and a familiar sweet ache began low in my groin. I inhaled a deep, ragged breath and swallowed hard in the hope of calming my hammering heart, but when I lifted my chin, instead of seeing the slightest hint of lust in her gaze, I was greeted with fear-filled, teary eyes and anger began to burn in my veins.

Why the hell was she doing this? It was clear she didn't want me anywhere *near* her let alone inside of her. I had *never* been made to feel less than a man by *any* woman, but right then I knew what she saw in me and what she *thought* of me.

To her, I was a monster.

I disgusted her.

I stepped forward and gripped her chin hard enough to sting, covering her mouth viciously with mine and pushing her against the wall. My hand slipped roughly down her chest until it was filled with one of her firm, pert tits, soft and so feminine and I squeezed.

I *hated* that I was turned on. Hated that she smelled so fucking good. Hated that my body had reacted to her in this way.

She gasped and stiffened her spine as she grasped at my shoulders whimpering. It wasn't clear if she was fighting with *me* or with *herself* as her breaths came faster and faster. But as soon as she began to yield to me and relax, I pushed away from her and stepped back.

"Is *that* what you think I want? To *fuck* you like you're some hooker paying me in sex for coming to your aid? Jeez, you really *do* have a low opinion of me, huh?" My chest heaved, and my jaw began to ache through repeated clenching as I glared at her. A flush of pink tinged her cheeks and spread all the way down to her chest, and her lip began to tremble as she lifted her arms and crossed them defensively over her naked breasts.

What the hell did she take me for? "You think that you can fucking *bribe* me with your tits and pussy into helping you?" I shook my head in disbelief and pulled my mouth into a grimaced smile. "My God, I can't quite figure out if you have a stupidly *high* opinion of yourself for presuming I'll take you up on your offer, or a damn *low* one for offering yourself so easily like that, Red." I stepped toward her again so that my nose almost grazed her cheek. "But believe me, when I say this. *If* I *ever* fuck you—and after tonight, that's a big-ass if— it'll be because it's something we *both* want. Not because you're trying to convince me to serve you like some fucking bodyguard. You're *not* a prostitute so don't fucking *act* like one. Now put your clothes back on, you stupid girl."

I didn't bother looking back as I gripped the handle and yanked the door free, slamming it hard behind me as I left.

Once outside her apartment I stomped down the driveway as quietly as my angry footsteps would allow. The last thing I needed was to alert the rest of the hotel to my presence. When I arrived at the bottom of the lane, I rounded the corner to where I had left the bike and stopped. I ran my hands roughly through my hair and breathed deeply in an attempt to calm my raging heart and breathing when all I wanted to do was smash stuff.

Talk about being misunderstood. I should have been plenty used to it, but for some reason, what *she* thought of me, in particular, stung like a bitch.

The more I thought about it, the more the realization of her desperation sank in. She was a young woman. I figured no more than twenty-two, twenty-three years old, and there she was so desperate to protect her family that she was willing to throw herself sexually at the mercy of someone she couldn't stand. And I had verbally abused her. She had been willing to give herself to me, and I had treated her like shit.

Way to go at improving popular opinion, asshole.

———

Ellie

The door slammed, and I slid down the wall until my ass hit the floor with a thud. What the *hell* had I been thinking? I had *never* thrown myself at *any* man in my life. Let alone one I didn't even *want* or find attractive. He had been right in accusing me of prostituting myself, and as I replayed his words in my mind my stomach rolled. I sat there on the floor for what seemed like hours letting hot tears stream down my face and drop onto my bare chest. Why was everything beginning to fall apart around me? And why was I acting so ridiculously out of character?

My mind raced as I tried to come up with something... *any*thing that would allow me to eradicate the Loki's Legion problem from my father's life. But there was *no-one* I could turn to. If I told Chloe, she would tell Six, and he was in no fit state to help me after what he had been through.

No, I needed to face this head on. Maybe I needed to contact Loki's Legion myself and find out what they wanted with my family.

I didn't see any other option.

————

COLT

I dumped the bike in the lot at the clubhouse and slammed through the entrance door. I had no clue who had decided that a party would be a fucking good idea, but I was kind of glad one was going on. I needed a drink, and I needed to forget what had happened tonight.

Dee was standing behind the bar dancing away to the Pearl Jam track playing over the sound system, and when she spotted me, she scrunched her face and immediately poured me a double JD. *She* knew me well.

She placed the glass of amber liquid down before me.

"What the fuck happened to you, Colt? You look pissed as hell and ready to commit murder."

I picked up the drink and downed it in one, enjoying the burn of the alcohol as it made a trail to my stomach.

I gestured for another and sat on one of the bar stools. "Fucking *women*, Dee. What the hell is it with you people? One minute you hate us and the next..."

Initially, she appeared affronted by my generalization but then she frowned. "And the next *what*? And who are you talking about?" She handed me another full glass.

This time, I took a sip and then shook my head. "Never mind. I really can't be bothered rehashing the whole goddamn thing."

Someone slid their hand up my arm and I turned to find Bonny, one of the club's hangers-on biting her lip and pouting at me.

"'Sup, Bonny?" Okay so I may be a man of few words sometimes, but I was still too wound up to make conversation.

Her red hair was scooped over one shoulder and her low cut top displayed the curves of her large—but obviously fake—tits. She ran her hand down and back up my arm again, but this time she didn't stop until her fingers were in my hair. "I haven't seen you around much, Colt. Where ya been, babe?"

I fought the urge to roll my eyes and instead tilted my mouth in a half smile. One that I knew got her going. "Well, sweet cheeks, I've just been busy. You know how it is? I am the President after all." *That* was why she wanted to fuck me so badly. The *status*.

She pouted again and stepped into the space between my thighs. "You look tense. Want me to help you relax?" She fluttered her eyelashes and pouted suggestively.

For a few seconds, my mind was forced back to the proposition I'd received earlier, and I clenched my jaw. But fuck if I was going to let Ellie take up room in my head. Like I said before, cold day in hell and all that jazz.

Turning my attention on the busty redhead beside me, I fixed her with a determined stare. "Hell yeah I do."

Her eyes lit up like the fourth of July, and she grabbed my hand. "The end room is free, come on."

I allowed her to lead me up the stairs and along the corridor to the bedroom that MC members used when they stayed over. Or when they were fucking someone they didn't want their old lady to know about.

She opened the door and backed in, keeping her eyes locked on me. "What do you wanna do?" She tilted her head to one side and smiled.

"Right now... I just want to fuck. Is that okay with you?"

"Hell yes, it's okay. I've wanted you to fuck me for so long." She began dragging her clothes from her body and my cock hardened at the sight of her naked curves. She was more shapely than Ellie. Her hair was straight whereas Ellie's was curly. But I just needed to come. And if using my imagination would help get the frustrating woman out of my system then so be it.

She launched herself into my arms and kissed me desperately. Her tongue was invading my mouth as she moaned and tugged at my hair. I kissed her back but was reminded of the kiss I had forced on Ellie earlier in the evening. She'd fought me at first but then she'd acquiesced and slipped her tongue along mine. It was at that point I had pushed away from her.

"Colt? You drifted off there for a moment, baby."

"Huh? Oh... yeah sorry." I shook my head in a bid to dislodge the *other* redhead from my thoughts, as Bonny let her feet meet the ground again and she began undressing me. I watched her as my dick throbbed in my jeans. Bonny was a pretty woman that was for sure. Her pussy was shaved, and once again my thoughts darted back to Ellie. I had only seen her tits. I wondered if her pussy was shaved. Or if it was covered in hair the color that matched her auburn locks.

A jolt of pleasure shot through my body and I peered down to find Bonny on her knees with my cock sucked into her mouth, cheeks hollowed, eyes closed like she was devouring the best popsicle she'd ever tasted. She opened her eyes and glanced up at me with a smile, her mouth full of my rigid flesh. Her fingers gripped my thighs as I watched my cock slip out and be enveloped by her once again. I inhaled through my nose and closed my eyes. In my mind when I looked down again it was Ellie Cassidy's green eyes peering back up at me.

Why the fuck won't she just leave my damned head?

I reached down and gripped Bonny under her arms and pulled her to her feet. Crushing my mouth to hers again in a ferocious kiss, I knotted my hand in her hair as she clawed at my back.

She pulled away and pleaded with me. "Fuck me, Colt. Fuck me hard, *please*."

Willing to sate my needs *and* her wishes I carried her over to the bed and dropped her unceremoniously onto it. She spread her legs, and her chest heaved. Her pussy glistened with her arousal but once again Ellie was the one laying there begging to be fucked.

"Turn over," I ordered Bonny, and she smiled widely like I had just handed her the best gift ever.

She presented her ass to me and tilted her face so she could watch. I kicked my jeans the rest of the way off my legs and stepped forward. I dragged the nightstand drawer open, hoping to find what I needed in there. Relieved to find a box of condoms I opened one and stretched the latex down my cock. Then, gripping her hips, I yanked her body back to meet mine and slipped my fingers down to her wet pussy.

She moaned loudly. "Oh yes. Yes, Colt that's it. Make me come hard."

Gripping my cock, I slid it up and down between her ass cheeks until I was at her entrance. "You *sure* you want this hard?"

"Yes! Come on! Give it to me!" She almost squealed.

I rammed my cock into her body and growled at the sheer sensation of pleasure radiating from where her body tightened to grip me like a glove.

She gasped. "More... give me more, Colt." I closed my eyes, withdrew and slammed back into her as she reached down between her thighs and began to rub her clit. "Oh, yes. *Harder*." She cried again, and I obliged adding a quick spank to her round ass for good measure.

"Oh yes! Again!" she gasped.

I obliged, sending the fleshy mound a bright shade of pink before bending over her and cupping one of her tits, teasing the nipple between my thumb and finger eliciting another moan of delight. When I opened my eyes again, my eyes focused on the bad, scrawly tattoo on her lower back. A *tramp stump* if you will. And my jaw clenched. From what I had seen, Ellie's skin was perfect. Not a mark or blemish. Any tattoos she had would be stunning no doubt. Not like this badly drawn excuse for a flowering vine.

Ugh! There she is again! Ellie Cassidy was messing with my thoughts.

Closing my eyes once more, I withdrew and sank back in a few more times until the pressure began to build at the base of my cock, and I knew I was close to the release I so desperately needed.

Bonny was a screecher. A yeller. Her cries of "*Do me,*

Colt!", *"Harder, much harder, Colt!"* and *"Finger my clit, hard!"* were probably being heard way above the loud music and raucous atmosphere downstairs. At one point I had to hold back a laugh. I doubted that I would be engaging in any such acts with her again. I mean, I was glad she was enjoying it and all, but jeez, she was distracting me... and not in a good way.

One last time I imagined Ellie on all fours before me. Her red curls cascading down her back and her ass meeting my groin with a slap each time I thrust into her. Thinking of her that way did the trick, and I came *hard*. Waves of pleasure crashing over me as my body immediately began to relax. The tension was ebbing away with each pulsating throb. Bonny joined me before collapsing face down onto the bed, with me half on her back.

CHAPTER NINE

Ellie

After another restless night, I awoke in a cold sweat, and in desperate need of a shower. But even as I stood under the soothing cascade of hot water, enveloped in a blanket of steam, my mind was still whirring. Partly with the shame of what I had offered the biker the night before and partly through trying to come up with a way to find out what Loki's Legion wanted with my dad and what they were holding over his head to make him do their bidding.

I was due to be on shift for the day in the hotel, and I already knew it was going to be busy, as the booking diary was full. Once I was dressed smartly in my work attire, I left my apartment and made the short journey across the yard to say good morning to my parents.

Colt's instructions about keeping quiet sprang to mind. Gosh, that was going to be so difficult. But I could see *why* he told me to act like I had seen nothing. The last thing I needed was to exacerbate an already volatile situation.

Not until I knew more.

When I arrived over at the hotel, my mom was sitting behind the reception desk looking pale and drawn. I walked through the back and then around to the office to where she sat, and I kissed her head.

"Morning, Mom. Are you okay?"

She smiled, and her lip began to tremble. "Hi, sweetie. I'm... I'm..." She waved her hand dismissively. "Oh ignore me. I don't know *why* I'm so emotional today. Must be hormones." She dabbed at her eyes to catch the escaping tears. My heart ached for her and what they must both be going through and I was completely helpless to do anything. Although right then, in that moment, I decided that would have to change.

I know exactly why you're emotional, and it has nothing to do with hormones.

I squeezed her shoulder. "Well, I'm here now, so go and take a break, okay? I'll handle the desk." I hated to see her upset, but I couldn't say too much in case I gave the game away. Thankfully the phone began to ring, and I reached out to grab the receiver before my mom could get to it. I gave her a raised eyebrow glare which she must have understood as a repeat of my earlier instruction, and she tenderly kissed my cheek before leaving me.

I turned my attention on the call. "Hello, Cassidy's, how may I help you today?"

"Oh... um... hello there. My name is Mrs. Delores Spencer. My husband and I have a room booked for two nights this coming weekend but... I'm afraid I'll have to cancel. Will there be a fee?"

Oh great. "Oh, I'm sorry to hear that Mrs. Spencer. No, no fee will be charged as you've given more than twenty-four hours' notice. Would you like to rebook for another time perhaps?"

"No. No, thank you. That's okay."

I hated dealing with cancellations, but I plastered on a fake smile in spite of her being unable to see me and took the details of her booking, making sure to cancel it off the system. As soon as she could, she hastily ended the call leaving me a little bewildered and staring at the receiver.

Rude, much?

Throughout the day, there were four more cancellations which began to bother me. Why were people choosing not to come and stay? A worry niggled at the back of my mind that Loki's Legion had something to do with it, but I pushed it back. Figuring perhaps there had been a local event canceled or something. It was easier to think *that* than to try and figure out any other reasons why.

My mom brought me a sandwich while I was on the phone around lunchtime, and I passed her a pre-written note that told her I would work through, so she didn't need to cover my lunch break.

The day was long. In between taking calls and filing, I was updating the accounts software, and by the time darkness fell I was *so* ready to leave. My dad hadn't been in all day. But I was actually glad about that. At least I didn't have to pretend everything was fine when clearly he was hiding things from me.

After a twelve-hour shift, I handed over to Candace, who was taking the late shift. She'd worked for dad for three years and didn't seem to mind the anti-social hours. The hotel was locked, and it was a buzzer entry system, so I could return home, safe in the knowledge that things should be okay. But as I crossed the car park in the dimming evening light I caught movement in my periphery and almost jumped out of my skin.

My hand came to my mouth, and I gasped. "Shit!"

A dark figure stepped out from behind one of the larger

trees on the driveway. "Sorry, Red. Didn't mean to startle you."

"*Startle* me? Colt, you nearly scared the *crap* out of me. Jeez. What are you *doing* here?"

He tentatively stepped toward me. "I wanted to check you hadn't blabbed to your dad."

I snorted. "What do *you* care?" I turned to walk away, but he reached and grabbed my arm. I swung around and collided with the hard wall of his chest.

"I *don't* care. I just don't want any more fucking trouble. And *you*, little Red, *are* trouble."

I inhaled through my nose ready to go at him with both barrels but the scent of him scrambled my thought process. He smelled masculine and clean. The fact surprised me. *For chrissake get a grip, Ellie. So he uses soap. So frickin' what?* I yanked my arm free and stepped back but in the process, I stumbled and yelped as I careened backward toward the gravel. Once again he reached out and slipped his arm around me, somehow stopping my collision a split second before impact. My heart pounded in my chest and I was grateful that he had saved me from injury to my body—*and* pride.

He shook his head. "Trouble *and* fucking clumsy. Great combination." In the fading light, I saw him almost smile and I could definitely see the crinkle of humor in the corners of his eyes.

Once I was on my feet again, I tilted my chin and was suddenly caught in an intense stare. I was close enough to feel his hot breath tickling my lips, and his arm seemed to tighten around me. *What the hell?* He lowered his mouth until his lips almost touched mine and my pulse rate quickened. There was a distinct air of possessive lust in his eyes. I was *sure* of it. There was no way I could have imagined such intensity, surely? It was as if his gaze penetrated me and I shivered as a tingle of awareness rushed to the apex of my thighs. I may as well have been standing there naked in his arms.

But as if he was suddenly dragged back from a precipice he gripped my upper arms to steady me and stepped back. "You should watch your step, Red. You could fall into the *wrong* arms if you're not careful."

Once again I was left feeling foolish. I had been almost certain he was going to kiss me and some small part of me—a very small, *intimate* part of me—had wanted him to.

I huffed and crossed my arms over my flimsy blouse where my arousal was no doubt evident. I hated that my body reacted against the will of my mind. "Don't worry about that, *biker man*. I've learned my lesson." The acerbity of my tone even shocked me.

He sneered as he stepped further into the artificial light that illuminated parts of the driveway and nodded his head. "Yeah? *Good.*" His gruff voice was filled with disdain. "Now remember what I said about keeping quiet. Hopefully, Loki's crew will get tired of their little game and this whole shitty situation will just fade away."

God, I wanted him to be right on this. "Hopefully. Now if I were you, I'd get off this property before someone *sees* you and presumes the worst. I'm sure you don't want the cops on your tail *again,* and the last thing *we* need is to lose *more* bookings because of the riff-raff of the area."

Initially, a flash of hurt was visible in his eyes, but then he scrunched his brow. "*More* bookings? You've been losing bookings?"

I stiffened my spine and tried to appear nonchalant. "Not that it's any of your business but yes. Just a few. Only today. I'm sure it's a coincidence."

He rolled his eyes. "If you *really* think that then you're dumber than I thought. Let me know if it keeps happening."

How dare he pretend to care after I asked for his help and he refused? "I don't think so. We can manage fine without *your* interference thank you very much. All *you* people do is cause pain and terror in this town and I want *noing* to do with you. *Any* of you. Go home, Colt." I spat my words with as much venom as I could muster. He opened his mouth to respond but closed it again. "Well, well, the tough old biker has been rendered speechless by a helpless little girl." My snide comment dripped with saccharine, and his forehead crinkled in a deep, angry frown. I shook my head, turned and stormed away toward my apartment.

CHAPTER TEN

COLT

Back at the clubhouse, I stormed past everyone without a single word of greeting, and they let me. I could feel their eyes boring into my back as the room fell silent. Thankfully they knew when to stay quiet, and *this* was one of those occasions. I walked down the back corridor and flung open the door to the makeshift gym. Weasel was in there on the treadmill, earbuds in, but he clocked my reflection and immediately hit the stop button. As the machine slowed and eventually came to a halt, he kept his worried gaze fixed on me.

"You okay, Prez?" he panted as he tentatively walked toward me, sweat dripping down his face.

"Do I fucking *look* okay?" I asked through clenched teeth.

He held up his hands. "Shit, sorry. Just checking. I'll get out of your way." He backed toward the door.

"Probably a good idea. Make sure no-one comes in here, okay?"

"Sure thing, C." He closed the door behind him, and I turned to face my reflection once more.

Staring back at me was a man that barely resembled *me*. *This* guy was aging. The odd speck of grey hair was sneaking through amongst the others that were almost black. Wrinkles around my eyes added to the telltale signs that I was no longer a *young* man. Okay, so thirty-eight wasn't old. But it wasn't young either.

But *she* had called me old. *Old biker. Jeez.* The disgust in her eyes as I held her close to my chest to stop her fall had been like a blow to my solar plexus. I'd never suffered from the vanity thing before. But here I was taking a long hard look at myself and wondering what the fuck I'd become.

I'd started out life as a pretty decent kid.

My brother and I had been treated well. Loved and looked after like any kid should be. We'd been brought up in a small house in Daytona, Florida where my mom took care of us, and my dad worked fishing boats. Both parents had been present and very much involved in our lives. But then when we were thirteen our father was killed in a freak accident out in the ocean, and I guess I couldn't handle it. I went off the rails.

Had my first tattoo illegally when I was fifteen. It simply stated 'shit happens' and was very amateurish. Probably down to the fact that one of the kids in the gang I got involved in had done it with an old tat gun that he could barely control. When I was sixteen, I ran away north to Jacksonville and lived on the streets for a while. That is until I happened upon a tattoo parlor where I eventually got a job after forging documents to make me out to be eighteen. Turns out the guys there actually knew I was only a kid but they took me in, and I was grateful to them. I had the dumb tattoo covered and that started my fascination with *real* ink. Those guys were so fucking talented. I could watch them for hours.

A guy named Wrench McCormack was the owner of the

parlor and he was the President of Company of Sinners MC in Florida. He kind of took over the role of father figure and introduced me to his club. When I actually turned eighteen, I spent some time as a prospect and eventually was sworn into the MC.

Yeah, I got into trouble. Yeah, I did a little time. But it wasn't *all* bad shit. We were... how can I put it... caretakers of our community. If shit was happening, *we* dealt with it. And okay I hardened up and got into a fair few fights, but Maria was my saving grace. I never thought I would fall in love. Told myself I was too tough for all that bull, but she made me realize I could love her *and* still be a man. A *real* man. I looked after my own, and there's nothing wrong with that as far as I'm concerned.

After being with the CoSMiC charter in Florida, I went nomad and traveled around until I settled in Utah with my beautiful woman. After she died, I closed myself off. Got more ink to commemorate her. Caused plenty more fights. You get the picture. My nose has been broken more than three times. I stopped counting after the third. And I have scars from knife wounds covered by more ink. Make myself sound damned handsome huh?

So, anyway, what I'm getting at is that these days I no longer resemble the clean cut, sweet kid I once was. And I'm guessing my twin brother still looks the same as he always did. *He* was the one to toe the line. Keep his nose clean and every other fucking cliché that made *him* the good kid. The total opposite of me. And yeah, I do have regrets. I've written to my mom over the years, but I haven't visited. Except one time before I met Maria when I was traveling. My brother had moved out and gotten married. He was apparently working as a cop. A fucking *cop*. And there I was covered in a million tattoos, long hair, motorcycle and a

CoSMiC patch on my leather cut. Talk about chalk and fucking cheese.

So I guess the inferiority complex I was carrying—or you might call it the chip on my shoulder—had *some* reason for existence. I was the *bad* kid. The kid who people pitied my mom over. *"You can only do so much, Cora."*, *"At least you have another son who does respect you, Cora."*, *"Maybe one day he'll see sense, Cora."* were all platitudes I heard bandied around when I wasn't *quite* out of earshot.

I guess I always felt like I had let my mom down. So I did the best thing and left.

Being thought of as a bad seed had been something I'd lived with since my dad passed away. I should have been used to it. But for some reason, the way Ellie saw me got under my skin. The way she looked down her nose at me and called me *biker man*—like it tasted foul to say the words—really twisted at my gut. Why the fuck should it matter what *she* thought? I didn't even like the bitch. And it was clear that she despised me. Although the look in her eyes again when I was up close and personal with her seemed to contradict that.

Talk about fucking mixed messages.

The more I thought about it, however, the more I realized Ellie reminded me of someone. Feisty and opinionated, strong willed and stubborn. I just couldn't put my finger on exactly who that was...

Dragging myself from my melancholy regression, I stripped the jacket and shirt from my body and walked over to where the punching bag hung from the ceiling. Clenching my jaw, I balled my hands into fists and swung my right arm, grunting as I made contact with the bag.

Where the *fuck* had this seed of self-introspection sprouted from? And why, all of a sudden, did I wish I was someone else? Some*thing* else. My left fist collided with the bag, and I growled at the mild pain it caused.

Pain was good.

Pain made me feel alive.

Wrench had informed me many years ago that *that* was why I had so many tattoos. I enjoyed the pain. I'd laughed and told him he was spouting psychobabble bull shit. But looking back now I wonder if there might have been something in it.

The door to the gym opened and closed, but I kept on pounding the shit out of the bag. I didn't turn around, but I knew who had walked in.

"I said I didn't want to be disturbed, Dee," I growled as I slammed my fist into the leather bag once more.

"Yeah, I know. But you don't scare me when you're in one of your hissy fits, you big girl."

I glared at her over my shoulder as my chest heaved from the exertion. "Fuck off, bitch."

She laughed. "Oh, Colty-pie, just get it off your chest the normal way, huh? Instead of ruining your knuckles *and* the bag."

I punched the leather three more times with such ferocity that I was sure the thing was going to fall from its fixing. Gripping it, I stopped it from swinging and wiped the back of my hand across my sweat covered forehead.

"Women," I said to no-one in particular.

"Wo*men* or wo*man*? Plural or one *specific* female?"

She walked over and handed me a bottle of water. I grabbed it and after removing the lid, I downed the whole thing in one long pull. "You know me too fucking well, Dee."

She shrugged. "Yeah well you know what they say about bitches who live together and their menses synching."

"Again, fuck off."

"So. Who is she and what did she do?" She sat on the mat by the wall and patted the space beside her.

Reluctantly, I walked over and planted my ass beside her. "I don't know. That's the problem. Some woman has gotten under my skin for all the wrong reasons. She makes me feel like shit about who and what I am. But instead of putting me off it just makes me want to prove her the fuck wrong, you know?"

She smiled and shook her head. "You always *were* stubborn. Do I know her?"

I closed my eyes and rested my head back against the wall noticing how my heart was beginning to calm *until* I was faced with the prospect of saying *her* name. "Yeah, you know *of* her."

She clapped her hands together like an excited school kid. "Oooh cryptic. I like it. Should I guess? Oh fuck it's not Chloe is it? Please say it's not, 'coz Six will kill you and I mean that literally."

"What? No, it's not fucking Chloe, jeez." I sighed and rubbed my hands over my face in frustration. I couldn't believe I was about to admit this. "Ellie. Okay? Eleanor Cassidy. *Happy* now?"

She laughed. "Why are you acting like your crush is *my* fucking fault?"

I opened my eyes and turned my head to face her. "I'm *not*. I just... I didn't want to admit it out loud. And it's not a fucking crush. I can't stand her. She just... she gets under my skin is all."

Dee shoulder nudged me. "Yeah, instead of under your body in bed, huh?"

"It's not that... well, it's not *all* that. Yes, she's attractive... in a snooty, feisty, stubborn-ass, annoying-as-all-hell kind of way. But it's the way she looks *down* on me as if she's so much better, you know?"

Delilah looked thoughtful for a few moments. "I agree she *is* all those things. But why now? What happened recently to irk you so much?"

I couldn't help laughing at her choice of words but in all honesty, it was an attempt at a distraction technique. I wanted the subject closed. "*Irk* me? Jeez, Dee what are you? A fucking dictionary? *Irk...* shit." My shoulders jiggled as I chuckled.

Suffice it to say, the distraction was seen for what it was and it didn't work.

She nudged me again but this time harder. "You *know* what it means dumb-ass. Now come on. Spill it."

Under duress, I went on to explain the couple of recent occasions I'd encountered Red and the way she had offered her body to me, but I had refused both her offer of sex and to agree to her demands for help with the Loki's Legion situation.

"You... *refused* sex? *And* you refused to help her with the Legion assholes? What are you afraid of, Colt?"

Her question pissed me off even more—if that was possible. "I'm not fucking scared of Loki's fucking Legion for chrissake, Dee."

"I didn't mean that. Now don't get me wrong. I hate the fucking bitch, but it seems to me that you're scared to *feel*. If you fuck her, you might feel something. If you help her, it means she might think you're a decent guy. You want *neither* of those things. You're the master of avoidance when it comes to feeling. You know it, and I know it. But let's be honest here, you're *going* to help her. How can you let her deal with this alone? Because if you think about it seriously you know that's *exactly* what she'll try to do. You said it yourself she's feisty and stubborn. You leave her to handle this alone, and she *will* get hurt. Or worse. And I distinctly remember hearing a similar story involving a certain Italian woman who needed help. So I can understand why you're reluctant. But you don't have to fall in love with every damsel in distress, just so you know."

Then it hit me. Aside from the looking-down-on-me parts Ellie and her stubborn-ass ways reminded me of Maria.

Aww fuck.

Dee's damn right isn't she. And I hate it when I'm wrong. Shit!

CHAPTER ELEVEN

It was good to have time off. I needed to think. And being at the hotel didn't afford me that privilege. But as I was sitting down with my notepad and pen ready to plan out whatever the hell I was going to do about the awful situation my family was apparently in, there was a knock at my door.

For an instant and for reasons unbeknownst to me the first person that sprang to my mind was Colt. But when I opened the door to my smiling brunette friend I realized that I was relieved it *hadn't* been him.

I enveloped Chloe in a bear hug. "Hey, girlie. How are you? You're looking great."

She beamed at me. "Things are really good. I mean *really*, really good."

I held her at arm's-length and gazed into my friend's chocolate brown eyes. There was a sparkle there that had been absent for so long. And Six, the biker guy, had plenty to do with its appearance. "Six treating you okay?"

She sighed dreamily as she stepped into my apartment.

"Better than okay. He's amazing, Ellie. I just... I can't put into words how good he makes me feel." She snapped her attention back to me. "Oh, God listen to me. I'm like a lovesick teenager. I'm so sorry. I was here to visit you not talk about me."

"Fancy a glass of wine?" I asked her in my best attempt at a British accent, a big grin on my face.

"Always." Her attempt at Cockney made me giggle. This was more like it. More like us. Like old times.

She followed me into the kitchen where I uncorked a bottle of merlot and poured two substantial glasses full. We walked back through to the living room and sat down on my couch, but she immediately spied the open notepad and the pen beside it.

"Are you back to list-making?" she asked with a wry smile.

I wrote lists for everything in the past. It was a great way to make sure things got done. I hadn't written one in a while, and I was surprised she had even noticed that fact.

I cringed, wondering what the hell to say. "Kind of, yeah."

She tilted her head to one side, and I caught her concerned expression fixed on me. "What's going on Ellie? Something's been off with you for a few weeks now."

I shrugged, feigning nonchalance. "Oh, nothing. Just... work stuff, you know. Bookings and whatnot."

She eyed me with suspicion and took a sip of her wine. "You know that I can see right through you, don't you?"

I rolled my eyes, but a stinging sensation began to needle at them. *No, no, no, no don't cry, you stupid woman.* I faked a smile, but my lip began to tremble. "What? I'm *fine*. Just busy is all."

She reached out and squeezed my arm. "Ellie, honey, just tell me what's going on."

I placed my glass down and leaned forward resting my

elbows on my knees and my face in my hands. The tears I was trying to fight spilled over and left damp trails down my face. "I don't know what to do, Chloe. Things are just…"

She scooted closer to me. "Things are just what?" She slipped her arm around my shoulder and tugged me toward her. "Come on, start at the beginning."

I lifted my head and peered at her through my misty eyes. "I… I can't tell you."

She scrunched her brow. "Ellie, you can tell me *anything*. You know that. I won't judge you. I just want to help."

"No… it's not that. I… can't tell you because I don't want to involve you. You've had your fair share of shit with Lo…" *Oh no. Me and my big damn mouth.*

Her face paled. "Ellie, you're really worrying me. I may be adding two and two together and getting five here but… are you involved in some way with Loki's Legion?"

Wow, she was good. To draw the correct conclusion from my slip of the tongue like that. Wow. I really had to be more careful. Although maybe it was simply that she knew me better than anyone. But whatever it was the sense of relief that came over me was immense.

Finally, someone *knew*.

But as I nodded my confirmation, a sob left my throat as fear and realization of my mistake began to twist my gut. She wasn't *meant* to know. She'd had dealings with them that almost ended in her death and she didn't *need* any more. Hell, *I* didn't know exactly what was happening so there nothing I could tell her anyway. And, realistically, the fewer people who were involved, the better.

"Okay, you're going to tell me everything. And then we're going to tell Six and Colt."

I shook my head vehemently. "C-Colt already knows.

Well, he knows as much as I do which isn't much. But he... he *won't* help me."

She scrunched her brow, disbelief clouding her features. "What do you mean he *won't* help? You don't know until you ask, honey."

"He saw them—Loki's crew—coming up to the hotel and hid in the bushes to see if he could find out why they were here. When I arrived home, I saw them pinning my dad to the wall. I had to do something, but Colt grabbed me and stopped me from approaching them. Then... we heard them threatening *my* safety if my dad didn't co-operate and the fear in my dad's voice as he pleaded with them almost broke me, and I passed out. Colt took me home and... Oh God, Chloe, I'm so ashamed." I sobbed violently as the memory of what I had done came flooding back.

She gripped my chin and made me face her. "Ashamed of *what?* Just tell me!" The panic in her voice was clear.

"I offered to have *sex* with him if he helped me. Like a fucking hooker, Chloe. And the worst part was... he didn't *want* me. I made a complete ass of myself and he turned me down."

She cupped my face. "Now you listen to me. You are *not* a hooker. You did what you felt you had to do to get help. Anyone would have done the same."

"But... but I got him all wrong. I thought... I thought he was attracted to me. And I figured he was *that* kind of guy."

She cringed. "The kind of guy to do stuff in return for *sex?*"

I nodded. "Yes. I thought he'd use me for sex but at least *help* me. He didn't want to do *either* and now I can't think of any way to help my dad. I'm going to have to go up there to see Deak or whatever the Loki's Legion president is called... and I'm going to have to offer myself to *him* to get him to stop whatever it is he's doing to my dad." My stomach roiled and I retched as bile rose in my gullet.

"You'll do *no* such thing, Ellie. You're not the kind of girl who *does* that. You wouldn't be able to live with yourself if you did. And honestly, I doubt he would honor any agreement he made with you. The sick bastard would probably just relish your desperation. Or worse. You could get hurt. Colt *will* help you. And failing that, Six and I will..."

I gasped. "No! You've suffered enough because of them. No, I can't let you get involved."

Her nostrils flared. "You have no choice in the matter, Ellie. There's no way I'm letting you deal with this alone."

Before I could protest she was dialing a number on her cell.

Six arrived at my apartment in around ten minutes in his black car and I was ushered into the back seat. As we began to pull away I spotted a man in black walking zig-zag up the driveway toward the hotel. On his arm was a leggy blonde wearing a very short skirt and stiletto heels. Her large, fake breasts were almost spilling out of her skimpy tank top. Six pulled the car to a halt and killed the lights. We all watched as the couple stopped just before the entrance and the man fisted his hand in the woman's hair while his other hand disappeared up her skirt. With the engine now silent we could hear the woman gasping and giggling.

"So, Snake, let's get inside and see if what they say is true about what you got in your pants." Her whiny voice was sickly sweet.

"Oh sugar, fuck going inside. I wanna fuck you right out here. What do you say?"

"Outdoor fucking is extra, Snake. You know that. And anyway I need to pee first."

Delightful.

Six groaned. "Oh fuck. I think I may know what's going on."

Before he could explain further, another man approached them with a black haired girl wearing next to nothing. "You guys already sorted your room out? I've heard it's kinda busy in there tonight." The new guy chuckled darkly.

"Nah, we ain't got one yet so don't go thinking you're getting in ahead of us, douche bag. We're having the next room. I don't want no blue fucking balls man. You'll wait your turn," Snake informed the new guy.

The blonde woman reached out and took the new guy's hand and shoved it on her breast. "Maybe we could all play nicely together? I could go some foursome fun." She chewed on her lip.

The black haired girl grabbed the blonde's other breast, leaned forward and just about rammed her tongue down her throat.

"Okay, *now* we're talking. I'm gonna fuck you *both* first, and Dozer here can *watch*." Snake rubbed his hands together with salacious glee.

Six turned the key in the ignition and sped away up the road without speaking. The penny dropped and took my rolling stomach with it.

Loki's Legion were turning my father's family hotel into some kind of brothel.

CHAPTER TWELVE

Colt

I was sitting at the bar with paperwork scattered around me when the main door opened, and Six walked in. A split second later Chloe Dancer followed. But then the *real* fucking cherry on top happened—and I mean that with *every* ounce of sarcasm I can portray in black and white—Ellie followed behind them.

I rolled my eyes and shook my head but was greeted by a stern stare from Six. "Don't, Colt, okay? Just *don't*."

I held up my hands as if to protest my innocence. "What the fuck did *I* do?"

Six leaned in toward me. "Nothing *yet*. That's the point. Ellie needs a drink of something strong. Grab her one would you, huh?"

What the f— "Who the fuck *am* I? A bartender?"

Chloe stamped her foot like an errant teenager, gritted her teeth and glared at me. "Jeez, Colt, get your head out of your ass and do something *nice* for once okay?" Her tone shocked me and I stared open-mouthed at her for a moment before sliding off the stool where I sat and made my way behind the bar as requested.

Fucking feisty women everywhere.

I carried a double whiskey over to the table they were now seated at and placed the drink in front of the redhead. Her skin was pale and her eyes red. She was hunched over with her arms wrapped protectively around her body and it was clear she'd been crying. And come to think of it, she really did look like shit, which was a complete contrast to the well put together, stubborn-ass bitch I was used to.

I pulled out the spare chair and lowered myself onto it. "Anyone going to bother to enlighten me about what's happened?"

Six slammed his fists onto the table. "Fucking Loki's Legion. That's what happened." The two women jumped.

Chloe turned her evil stare on me once more, and I almost shrunk into my seat. Fuck, she was a fierce little thing. "And *you*. You selfish, spineless moron." I widened my eyes at her questioningly but stayed silent, and she continued, "And you know *very* well what I'm talking about before you dare to protest your innocence."

I flared my nostrils and clenched my jaw. My patience was thinning *rapidly*. "Why don't you *remind* me then, CD?"

"Ellie asked for your help, and you said *no*. You flat out refused to help her. I can't believe even *you* would do that."

I held up my hands. "Whoa, what the fuck? What do you mean *even you*? Ellie and her father's business are not my responsibility. So don't go fucking acting all high and goddamn mighty, Chloe."

Six stood and towered over me where I sat. "Don't you fucking talk to my woman that way."

Things were going crazy. The whole damn world was

going nuts. I pointed up at him. "Sit down, Six. You don't wanna start with me," I threatened.

His eyes widened, and so did his arms. "Oh really? You think I can't fucking take you, *old man*?" he spat.

I stood, ready to rumble but hands slammed on the table. "Stop!" We all turned to face Ellie. "Just *stop* with the fighting, please. Jeez, I just want to go home and see my dad. I *have* to help him. I don't even want to *be* here," she shouted at us.

I sneered down at her. "Well, that's *two* of us thinking you should go home," I growled, and Six grabbed the neck of my T-shirt. I glared at him and slowly stepped into his space. "I'm serious as fucking *death* right now, Six, you'd better let the fuck go, or I'm warning you..." Thankfully he released me with a shove and stepped back still grimacing at me, his chest heaving.

A sob escaped from Red's throat, and my heart squeezed. "Could someone take me home? *Please?* I'm clearly not welcome here. And I don't want to cause trouble between you. Please just... take me home."

Why the fuck was I feeling guilty? She was *nothing* to me. But either I was going soft in my late thirties, or she was good at the manipulation game.

I sighed heavily and rubbed my hands wearily over my face. "Aww fuck. Just stay. You can have the end room upstairs for the night. Get some sleep and we'll see what the fuck we can come up with in the morning. If Loki's crew are hanging near the hotel, then you'd probably better not go home."

"But... her *dad*?" Chloe sounded panicked.

"Look, CD, I don't run a safe house here. And I don't need the rival MC sniffing around this joint. If the bastards are getting what they want, they'll leave Eamon in peace. Let's just concentrate on formulating a plan, okay?"

I waited for her come up with more insults and protests but thankfully she just nodded. "Come on, Ellie, I'll show you up to the room."

Six and I watched as Chloe linked arms with Ellie and the two friends began to walk toward the stairs. Ellie stopped, turned and walked toward me. When she came to a halt only a foot away, I waited with bated breath to see what she'd say. I was expecting some comment about how I should have helped her when she asked—it's what I was thinking myself—but instead she placed her hand on my bicep, tiptoed and placed a gentle kiss on my cheek.

"I know you only tolerate me because of Chloe. And that you really don't want me here. But I want to thank you for letting me stay. If I'm honest, I was afraid to go back there tonight. This means..." Her lip began to tremble again. "Well, it means a lot. So... thank you, Colt." She squeezed my arm and turned away once more. I swallowed hard as I watched her ascend the stairs to the upper floor and wondered why—in that moment—I'd had the urge to hold her.

"I need a fucking drink," I told no-one in particular as I reached for the bottle of whiskey on the bar.

Seeing as the room upstairs was being used by my unwanted guest, and Six had gone back to Chloe's place, I sat up at the bar on my own until the early hours of the morning. My mind was a hive of buzzing thoughts as I tried in vain to formulate some kind of plan. I had to figure out what the hell Loki's Legion were doing using the hotel for their hook-ups. They had their own clubhouse so it made no sense to me at all.

"Can't sleep huh?" Ellie's voice startled me.

I turned my head slightly and shrugged. "Not even *tried* yet."

She slipped onto the stool beside me, and I glanced down to find her wearing a T-shirt that I had left in the end room. It was much too big for her, but even *I* had to admit she looked kinda cute. She must have noticed me eyeing her as she pulled at the hem trying to cover her slender, bare thighs.

"I... I hope you don't mind. I didn't have anything to sleep in, and I found this in the room. It... smells like you so I guess it's yours." I stayed silent as my gaze trailed up her body to where her nipples poked out of the greying fabric. "M-maybe I should've asked. I'm sorry, Colt."

"It's okay." My cock began to stir to life as I imagined the curves of her naked body underneath my shirt. The fact that she could smell me on the fabric and had still put it on lingered in my mind.

After a few moments of silence, she spoke again. "So, you're not going to bed?" she asked, dragging me from my lewd thoughts.

I shook my head both in response and in the hope that I could rattle the dumb thoughts free. "Nah. Anyways, you're in my room."

She knew this already yet she still gasped. "Oh... shit... look, you can go on up to bed, and I'll sleep on one of the couches. It's fine. I—"

I snapped my focus up to her face and frowned. "I didn't say it was a *problem,* did I?" My tone was hard and unnecessarily cold.

She chewed on her lip for a moment. "No... no you didn't but... I can sense..."

I sighed for about the millionth time since she landed in my fucking life. "Whatever you're *sensing* is wrong. What you *should* be sensing is that I don't give a crap okay?" *Shit, man.*

That was harsh. I faced front again, not wanting to see her reaction to my shitty attitude.

I heard her sniff, and I turned again to see glistening trails dampening her cheeks. *Aww fuck. Why did I have to go and do that?*

She cleared her throat. "Y-you can take me home. Or... or call me a cab. Really it's fine. I don't want to impose. And it's evident that you don't like me, nor do you want me here." Her voice wobbled as she spoke.

If she was *trying* to make me feel like shit, it was working, and I wasn't taking too kindly to the little guilt trip we were heading out on again. "Jeez. Shut the fuck up, Ellie, okay? I said you can stay, now just go back up to bed," I snapped and returned my focus on to the glass of amber liquid on the bar before me.

"Has anyone ever told you what a giant ass you are?" I guessed her question was rhetorical as she jumped down from the stool and headed back toward the stairs. I glanced over my shoulder and watched her retreating form. I was fascinated by the way the T-shirt skimmed over the pert curve of her ass and my cock stirred once again.

Damn my fucking dick

CHAPTER THIRTEEN

Ellie

I wanted to slam the door as hard as I could, but I was aware that other MC members were sleeping in adjacent rooms, and so I refrained. I walked over and angrily threw myself on the bed as hot tears began to flow. All I seemed to do was cry, and it wasn't like me. Every single sense and emotion was on high alert, and I hated feeling so damned fragile. It was like I was standing on a precipice and any minute now something would happen to knock me over the edge into oblivion. I really wasn't sure how much more I could take.

There was a light knock on the door and I quickly wiped the moisture from my face. "Who is it?"

After a few seconds of silence, I heard Colt clear his throat. "Umm... it's me. It's Colt. Can I come in?"

What the hell does he want now? "If you're coming in to be mean again don't bother. You've made your disdain for me blatantly clear. I'll leave in the morning and I won't be back."

The door handle turned, and I heard him step into the pitch dark room. "I didn't come to be mean."

I wished I'd locked the door and had no clue why I hadn't. "Then why *did* you come, Colt?"

I heard him step forward until I could see parts of him illuminated by the shafts of moonlight falling through a crack in the shades. "I came... to apologize."

Shocked by his words I leaned to the night stand, flicked on the lamp and gestured to him with open hands. "Go ahead." I wasn't about to make things easy for him.

He sat on the edge of the bed and focused his eyes on me. "Ellie, I'm sorry for being a giant ass. I'm sorry for making you feel unwelcome, and I'm sorry for refusing to help you before." There was a sincerity to his words *and* his demeanor that I didn't expect, and it disarmed me. Floored me.

I opened and closed my mouth a couple times before words would come. "Oh... okay... well thank you for your apology." He nodded and rubbed his hands over his face and my anger subsided. "You look exhausted."

A half smile tugged at his mouth. "Yeah, you could say that. Anyway, I'll leave you to sleep. Goodnight, Ellie. And... you can stay as long as you need, okay? We'll... we'll figure shit out." He pushed himself to stand and turned to face the door.

Before I could stop myself, I shouted out to him, "Wait. Look, why don't you come and sleep here. We're both adults. We can share a bed amicably." S*tupid, stupid woman.*

He turned his head slightly and peered at me over his shoulder. "Don't sweat it, Red. I'll go sleep on a couch in the bar."

I couldn't help the giggle that erupted as I envisaged that scenario. "You *have* seen how tall you are right? You won't fit. Then you'll be all grumpy tomorrow... not that that'd be any different to normal." I smiled in the hope that he would realize I was teasing. "Come on. I'll move over. It's a huge bed. And don't worry I can keep my hands to myself." Again, I was trying to lighten the heavy cloud that was constantly hanging in the air between us.

A hint of a smile ghosted over his lips, and my heart skipped. *What the hell?* Okay, he was kind of good looking... you know, if you liked older guys with tattoos... which I didn't... at all.

He walked back toward the bed and folded his arms across his broad chest. Eyeing me with suspicion, he asked, "You sure about this, Red?"

I nodded with maybe a little too much fervency. "Absolutely." I scooted over and patted the empty space beside me, immediately regretting the motion as he chuckled to himself and shook his head.

He grasped his T-shirt at the back of his neck, and I watched as he swiped the tight grey marl fabric from his body to reveal inked skin and rows of taut abdominal muscles. I swallowed a gasp and fidgeted as a twinge of something I didn't want to acknowledge spiked in my pussy.

Next, he unfastened his belt and the button fly of his jeans and then stopped dead. I lifted my chin and met his intrigued gaze. I realized then that I'd been staring, open-mouthed, at his body.

The left side of his mouth tilted up again. "You mind me getting comfortable? Can't sleep in my jeans. Too... you know... restrictive." As he said the last word, his eyebrows raised infinitesimally and I knew he was trying to get a reaction from me.

I decided I wouldn't give him the satisfaction, and shrugged nonchalantly. "I could care less. Just make sure you keep your boxers on. I sure as hell don't want to see your junk." Laying down, I turned my back to him. I heard his jeans fall to the floor and felt the bed dip as he climbed onto it.

He exhaled heavily, and I felt a light breeze as he lifted his arms and stretched out his long, lean body only inches from mine. I closed my eyes and willed myself to fall asleep but of course as soon as you try *too* hard to doze off there is no way you can.

"You still awake?" His voice vibrated through the mattress.

I huffed. "Yes, why?"

I felt him moving. "How was your dad today?"

I rolled to lay flat on my back. "I didn't actually see him."

"But you saw Loki's crew, huh?"

I nodded but then realized it was pitch dark. "Yeah." My voice broke as I remembered the nauseating conversation I'd had the displeasure to witness outside the hotel.

The bed moved again, and I felt Colt roll toward me. "Hey, don't get upset. We'll figure it out."

God what the hell happened to the strong independent woman I once was? "I honestly don't know how." Angry with myself for allowing more emotion to escape I lifted my hands and wiped at my eyes.

Colt gripped my wrist. "I promise you, Ellie. Those bastards won't get the better of me *or* my town. *Not* again." The determination in his voice tugged at my heart and sent a thrill through my veins. Hope for an end to the hellish situation my family was in began to blossom. Maybe I *could* trust this guy to help me after all.

I rolled to face him, not realizing just how close to me he was. I felt his breath on my face and the heat from his body radiating toward mine. "Thank you," I whispered.

A heavy, pregnant silence hung in the air between us, and all I could hear was his ragged breathing. I sensed something wasn't quite right. Maybe it was because the room was so dark. And I wondered why he was emanating such tension.

A rumble erupted from his throat. "Aw, fuck this," he

growled and before I knew what was happening his hand was tangled in my hair, and his mouth was crushed to mine. He drew the breath from my lungs in a kiss that seemed filled with desperation and urgency.

My mind screamed at me to stop him. To push him away and slap him. But in all honesty, I just wanted to feel *some*thing other than fear and dread. Even if it was a short time. So I gave in to my baser urges, gripped his shoulders and kissed him back. His tongue slipped into my mouth, and I moaned as my whole body sprang to life. My breasts ached for his touch, and my nipples grazed at his bare chest through my clothing.

One thing I knew was that sex didn't have to *always* be about feelings, emotions and love. Sometimes it was just a distraction. Just a way to release pent up tension. And boy was I pent up. I had no clue why this was happening and guessed that he didn't either. But it *was* happening none-theless.

He pushed me onto my back, and I instinctively opened my thighs for him to rest his body between my legs. His thick erection rubbed at my clit through my cotton panties, and I ground myself into him. Tingles shivered where we were touching, and I wanted more. His fingers slipped up inside the T-shirt I wore and roughly tweaked at my nipple as he moved to suck at my neck. The fact that I couldn't see his face meant I could fantasize about whomever I chose but try as I might it was still Colt's tanned, bearded face I saw in my mind as a hand slipped into my panties, and two thick fingers entered me.

"God, you *do* fucking want me. You're so wet, Ellie, and I feel you when you tighten around my fingers." His gruff voice only served to make me more wanton. What the hell was *wrong* with me? Why the hell was I allowing this to happen? His fingers began to slowly glide in and out of my pussy with tortuously slow movements as he grazed something inside of me that heightened the pleasure and I gasped, thrusting my hips so that the heel of his hand rubbed my clit. An appreciative groan rumbled from within him. "Yeah, you like that, huh? You like my fingers inside you... in your tight, wet pussy. You want more. I can tell you need more. You wanna come hard for me, Ellie, I can feel it."

No-one had *ever* spoken to me so crudely. But it did something to me, and I reached down to grasp his cock firmly in my hand but over his boxers. He was thick and rigid. A moan left his chest and so I began to move my hand up and down over the fabric.

He reached down and gripped my hand. "Like this." My hand was slipped under the fitted material, and he squeezed it around his taut flesh. As he desired I began to move, skin on skin, and he gave a pleasure filled groan. "So good... so... fucking... good." He maneuvered slightly to the side so we had better access to each other's bodies.

His fingers began to move faster, and his other hand tugged the T-shirt upwards just enough to expose my breasts to the cool air of the black room. He bent and sucked a nipple into the wet heat of his mouth, and I pressed my head back into the pillow as myriad sensations overtook me. His thumb began to circle my clit as his fingers continued their delicious assault and I tightened my grip on his cock.

"Yeah... yeah keep goin' baby... just like that... you're gonna make me come... Talk to me, Ellie... tell me what you feel..."

Oh hell no. I had *never* done the dirty talk thing. My mind began to race searching for sexy things to say. *What if I sound like a complete idiot?*

He panted, "Ellie... come on... fuck that's so good... talk to me."

Taking a deep breath, I began. "You're so hard, Colt... so thick... I love how you feel in my hand... I want you to come for me..." My voice was breathy and unrecognizable as my own.

But it seemed to work as he picked up the pace again and his breathing increased. "Oh yeah, baby, that's it..."

I was so close to my own release, but I didn't want to fall into the abyss so soon. It felt too good. "I wish your cock was inside of me. Tight and stiff in my pussy. I want to feel you there." What the *frick* was I saying? *Where* was it coming from?

He grunted with each thrust of his fingers. "Yeah... I wanna fuck you so hard... so fucking hard... I wanna hear you scream my name..."

My hand moved faster as I let his words work their magic and I found a few more of my own. "Colt... I'm... you're going to make me come..." I cried out as my body began to spasm around his fingers and a crashing wave of ecstasy hit me, almost making me dizzy with pleasure.

He growled, and I felt hot liquid pulse onto my stomach. "Oh yeah... oh fuck..." His chest heaved as he slowed the grind of his fingers, bringing me down from my orgasm and I exhaled a long shaking breath.

He suddenly jumped up from the bed and disappeared into the adjacent bathroom leaving me there, panting and bemused. Moments later he returned and clambered back onto the bed. He wiped my stomach clean and disappeared again. When he returned, he lay beside me once more but in total silence. I had no clue what the hell to say. In fact, I wasn't sure whether to speak or not.

And so I didn't.

CHAPTER FOURTEEN

COLT

I have no idea how long I laid there in the dark trying to find the right words before I eventually dozed off. *Thank you* sounded like she'd done me a favor. *Was that good for you* sounded desperate. And no other ideas sprang to mind. But when I awoke, Ellie was gone. I rubbed my hands over my face and huffed the air from my lungs in frustration.

Fuck. You fucking idiot. You should've said something. Jeez.

Although the night we had spent together had been finger fucking and orgasms and not all romance and flowers, I was sure Ellie would feel used and disgusted with me for not at least saying... shit... what *would* I have said, really? I was still at a fucking loss. *Thanks doll, that was great... Wow, you really know how to get a guy off... So when do we move on to fucking?*

The more I thought about it, the more I realized that there wasn't *any*thing at all that I *could* have said. Whatever had come out of my mouth after the event would have made me look even worse than I felt. But when I thought back to the way she handled my cock... sheesh... she was good. *So* good. And her body had been so responsive to my touch regardless of the fact that she allegedly couldn't stand me.

Then it hit me.

We'd been hand fucking in the *dark*. She was probably thinking of some *other* guy. A movie star maybe? As the thought entered my head, it was joined by a twinge of annoyance. I didn't want *any* woman thinking of someone else when it was *my* body giving them pleasure.

Fuck, no.

I heard shouting coming from downstairs and grabbed my clothes, dragging them onto my body as I made my way to the door. I yanked it open and jogged toward the stairs.

———

Ellie was screaming at the top of her lungs, "Everything is ruined! What will my dad do now? Oh God, *why* is this happening?" As I got into view, I could see Chloe trying in vain to calm her down. I walked over to Six who was holding a newspaper in his hands. His knuckles were white and his mouth was pursed into an angry snarl.

I stopped beside him. "What the fuck is going on? What's all the shouting?"

He thrust the open newspaper toward me, and I saw the headline.

Supposed Family Business Man Allows His Rooms To Be Rented To Bike Gang 'By The Hour'

There was a photo of Eamon Cassidy trying to shield his face, and beside that there was a grainy, yet graphic photograph of a naked woman with two guys in an upstairs window. At the bottom, there was an image of some of Loki's crew with scantily clad women making their way up the hotel driveway.

"What makes this shit worse is the article is written by one of her colleagues at the Rose Acres Rag," Six informed me.

I shook my head. "Shit. No way?"

"Yup. A guy she *dated* apparently." I glanced at the name *Simon Hardisty* and the thumbnail print of a smarmy looking dude was smiling up from the page. I immediately wanted to knock the fucking teeth from that cheesy grin.

"How could he report that shit without speaking to me first?" Ellie wailed.

She was damn near hysterical, and Chloe was having a hard time getting her to listen. I walked over and grabbed Ellie's arms. Before she could protest I lifted her, threw her over my shoulder like a rag doll and carried her up the stairs to the room where we had shared a night of bizarre sexual contact.

She screamed and hit my back as I carried her. Arms were flailing and fingernails scratched at me. "You *bastard*! Put me *down*! I *hate* you and your kind. You're all the fucking *same*!" Now I wasn't sure if she meant you and your kind as in *bikers* or you and your kind as in men in general. But I didn't much care for her rant, whatever the intention. Once we were inside the room at the end of the upstairs corridor, I unceremoniously threw her down on the bed.

She lashed out at me all red-faced and puffy-eyed. And in a kind of strange way she looked sort of cute.

I smirked at her, and she kicked her legs out. "Go fuck yourself, Colt! You complete and utter *asshole*! I *hate* you, and if you *ever* come near me again I swear I will fucking scratch your eyes out!"

I stood over her where she sat on the bed and crossed my arms over my chest. "You need to calm the fuck down, Ellie. I understand you're upset, but you're acting like a crazy bitch right now."

"Oh, *I'm* crazy? *Me?* I'm not the one printing lies about someone in a newspaper! I'm not the one refusing to help someone in a shitty situation. I'm not the one finger fucking a woman he hates and then saying *nothing* afterward! I'm not the one pretending to be a fucking tough guy biker. I think you will find, with the exception of the newspaper, those all relate to *you*! You cock-sucking, arrogant, pig-headed bastard!" She kicked out again and narrowly missed my balls.

That was it.

Fuse... lit.

Kaboom!

I pounced forward and pinned her to the mattress while she tried in vain to scratch and bite at me. But I managed to keep myself just out of reach while restraining her.

She struggled and squirmed. "Get *off* of me you shit head. I'll scream rape!"

I chuckled and shook my head as I held her down. For such a petite framed woman she was like a rabid bitch in heat. "Oh, so you'll scream rape, huh? Kind of dumb seeing as we're both fully clothed, and the door isn't locked. I'm not stopping anyone getting in here. If anyone does walk in here right now, they will clearly see I am trying to restrain a woman hell bent on ruining my family tree."

She gnashed her teeth and growled like a feral animal, eyes wide and hair wild. I have to admit to being a little turned on, and I had to fight with my dick to make it co-operate. The last thing she needed was to realize I was aroused at *that* specific point in time. Talk about fuel to her fire.

"Let me go!" she squealed.

"Not until you agree that my family jewels are safe from your cowboy boots."

Her chest continued to heave, and her nostrils flared for a few moments further until she seemed to realize she was fighting a losing battle. "Okay. I'll stop. Please just get *off* me."

I shook my head and laughed. "Yeah you sound *real* calm."

Her breathing was still heavy and rapid, and I happened to glance down to find her braless tits heaving beneath me through her shirt. It was *then* that I realized she was still wearing *my* shirt. I smiled at the discovery.

"Stop staring at my breasts, you old pervert," she snarled.

I decided to change tack. "Less of the *old* sweetheart. And you didn't mind the attention I was giving them last night."

She gasped, and her eyes widened. "You *disgust* me. How I *ever* let that happen is beyond me. You're old and dirty and... urgh!" she growled.

I lowered my face until my lips were dangerously close to hers and I could feel her panting breaths. "Ellie, you let it happen because deep inside you're attracted to me. Admit it to yourself. You may *hate* me as a person—although *that's* unfounded—and you *may* think that you don't want an older —but I prefer 'more experienced'—man but somewhere inside of you... some deep, dark little place—" I leaned down so that my mouth was at the crook of her neck. "That deep dark place I discovered last night—you *want* me." She gasped again. I had her attention, and she was calm. "You want me to *fuck* you hard but *hate* that you want it. You want me to help you but you *hate* that you *need* my help. You want someone to make all this shit go away, and you hate that the someone who can do that is *me*. I'm all you never wanted, Ellie." I placed a gentle, chaste kiss on her neck and watched as her skin flushed.

"You're right about *one* thing. I *never* wanted you. I still don't. You're all wrong for me and I... and I *hate* you." Her breathy, lust-filled whisper wasn't so convincing.

I nibbled at her neck, and she moaned, so I nibbled some more. "There *is* a physical attraction between us regardless of how much we dislike each other," I informed her.

"W-why do you dislike *me*? What did *I* do?"

I chuckled again at the disappointment in her voice. "You drive me fucking insane. And you have a *very* low opinion of me. Kind of a buzz kill." I told her in between suckling the skin of her neck.

"That's because you're a terrorizing bastard who breaks the law," she sighed as I released her arms and slipped one of my hands down to fondle her breast.

"Nope. Not broken the law for a *very* long time. And I like to think that the folks I terrorize deserve it." I licked up the side of her neck and sucked her ear lobe into my mouth. Slowly I moved my mouth down to her peaked nipple and sucked it through the fabric. I felt her squirm and try to squeeze her legs together.

"Stop... please stop... I have to go home..." she breathed.

I squeezed her other breast and toyed with her nipples some more. "Unless you stay a while and let me help you to relax," I mumbled into her tits and then glanced up at her.

She turned her face toward me, and our eyes met. "I can't, Colt. I have to go."

I rolled off her and held out my arm in a gesture that told her she could leave. She climbed from the bed and smoothed my T-shirt down her body. Her gaze dropped to the wet patch over her breast where I had sucked at her.

"Oh great. I can't go home in *this*. Could you help me to find my *own* shirt?" She started pacing around the room in search of her missing clothing.

I found it just under the bed and picked it up. "Looking for this?"

She grabbed it and turned her back to me as she dragged my T-shirt from her body. I could see her tits in the reflection of the wall mirror and my cock flinched at the sight of her pert, pale skin and tightened pink buds.

She caught me watching her and swung herself around. "You shouldn't be looking."

I held up my hands in surrender. "Hey, I'm a hot-blooded male what can I say?"

She rolled her eyes and stormed toward the door. When she reached it, she stopped and turned. "What happened last night. It can *never* happen again. I *don't* want you, physically or otherwise, in spite of the way my body reacts. I hadn't been touched for a long time, and *that's* why I reacted that way. You're not my type. At all. And you're wrong about my *deep dark desires*, Colt. Sorry to burst your bubble." And with that final snide blow she walked out of the room and slammed the door behind her.

Fucking stubborn bitch. Not worth the goddamn trouble. I can get pussy whenever and wherever I damn well please. I don't need her fucking shit that's for sure.

My inner dialog apparently wasn't heard by all the parts of my body and something that I acknowledged as disappointment twinged inside of me.

CHAPTER FIFTEEN

Ellie

How *dare* he presume things about me when he hardly knew me? Colt... whatever his full name was... was a frustrating, self-assured... old man. I stomped down the stairs of the clubhouse, and when I reached the bottom, I was greeted with half a dozen pairs of prying eyes.

I scowled around the biker collective. "What? Never seen a woman before?" I snapped before snorting derisively. "Oh sorry, I forgot you're all morons and haven't actually encountered one with more than two brain cells." My attention immediately turned to Chloe, and I cringed. "Not you, Chloe. You're not a moron."

"And neither is Six," she blurted huffily as the other leather-clad Neanderthals mumbled and chuntered.

Shit. Eleanor the idiot. "No... no you're *right*. In fact, I need to get out of here. Can you and Six take me home please?" I hoped that I hadn't overstepped the mark with my inappropriate, blanket insult.

"Make the bitch walk," came a barked voice from the bar.

I turned my head and saw Delilah sneering at me, and so I responded with a curled lip of my own. "I wasn't asking *you* for help."

"It's a good thing you're not, you ungrateful ho."

What the—? I snapped and yelled at her, "Who the *hell* do you think you are, huh? You stand there looking down your nose at anyone who doesn't fit in with your silly little biker crowd. Just because I don't sleep around and I'm not covered in scrawly patterns that don't wash off doesn't mean I'm less of a person."

"No. What makes you less of a person is the way you treat people like shit and make presumptions based on appearance before you even get to *know* them. If you'd bother to take the time you'd realize we're human beings too you self-centered, narrow-minded bimbo."

I scrambled around my brain trying to find a retort, but what she had said weighed heavily on my mind.

Shit, maybe she was right.

Chloe stepped into my line of sight and blocked my view of the blonde, inked rottweiler. "Come on, Ellie. Six and I will take you home right now."

Without digging my grave any deeper I followed Chloe out of the clubhouse with Six behind me as if he was expecting Delilah to pounce.

Once we were out in the parking lot, Chloe swung around to face me with her nostrils flared, and eyes narrowed. "You know you're going to have to stop being such a cantankerous bitch, Ellie. I can't support you when you start bad mouthing the people I care about." She pointed back at the building. "What you said in there was uncalled for, and I'm afraid Dee was right. You are *very* judgmental. And in spite of that fact, those guys have agreed to help you with the shitty situation you're in at the moment. And what's more, it's not as if *you're* squeaky clean. You've made your fair share of mistakes and bad decisions. Don't forget that."

I felt heat rise in my cheeks. I was thoroughly chastised and felt about two inches tall. Of course, she was right. I was going through my own version of hell with Loki's Legion, but I had no right to take it out on the people who could help me sort things out.

"I'm sorry, Chloe. I just..." I huffed the air from my lungs as every explanation about my ridiculous outburst evaded me. "I don't know. I guess... I guess I *fear* them. They're such a tight-knit unit and that makes me suspicious. Plus, the rumors I've heard. It makes it hard to have any other opinion than a negative one. And I think the best kind defense is... *offense.*" It was the best I could do.

"Yeah, well maybe you should stop listening to rumors, Ellie. Look at the one being spread around town about your family business."

Ouch.

As much as it hurt, she did have a good point.

In a tense silence, we all climbed into Six's car, and he set off toward the hotel. Once we pulled into the driveway and stopped outside my apartment, Six got out and checked that the coast was clear. He gestured to me that everything was okay, and I reached to open the car door.

"Chloe, I'm sorry for insulting your friends. I hope you can forgive me."

She sighed. "They could be *your* friends too if you'd just give them a chance."

I smiled and nodded before climbing out of the car. "Thanks for driving me home, Six."

He shrugged. "No sweat. And if there are any more issues you call okay? Don't hesitate."

"Thank you. I really do appreciate that. And... I guess I

don't exactly deserve it." I knew I didn't. And I was doubtful whether certain other members of the Company of Sinners felt the same way as Six did.

I watched them drive away before making my way over to my parents' living quarters. I heard the raised voices as soon as I opened the door and knew immediately what they were arguing about.

"We can't let it go on, Eamon. Our reputation... our livelihood... our family is all on the line here."

"You think I don't know that Maggie? You think I haven't tried my best to come up with a way to get rid of those damn bikers? The stress of all this is driving me insane."

Enough was enough. I wasn't prepared to stand by any longer and listen to my parents' marriage fall apart. I burst through the dining room door and slammed it behind me. "Stop it!"

They both snapped their attention on me, and a heavy silence fell on the room. My dad leaned his elbows on the table and rested his head in his hands, and my mom pushed the plate of food away until she could push it no farther.

"I know a way to help. But you have to trust me."

Dad lifted his head again and locked his worried gaze on me. His brow crumpled. "You've seen the newspaper article?"

I nodded. "But I knew before that."

"H-how? When?"

My lip began to tremble. "I saw the bikers attack you. And... and I saw some of them bringing their hos into the place, Dad."

"Aww, God dammit! I didn't want you involved Eleanor. I'm scared for you, sweetheart. Please stay *out* of this."

"Your father's right honey. They've already threatened to harm you."

My father slammed his hands on the table. "Maggie, jeez!"

"It's okay, Dad. I already knew that. But... I know people who can help. G-good people."

"Are their names Superman and Batman by any chance? Because they're the only people equipped to 'deal' with those bastards."

My mom gasped. "Eamon, language."

I held up my hands in the hope of halting the impending argument. "They're..." I sighed. "They know how to deal with Loki's Legion. Believe me."

Dad narrowed his eyes at me. "Wait a minute. The only human beings, if you can call them that, who'd know how to deal with a biker gang, would be *another* biker gang."

I nodded and cringed. "The Company of Sinners have agreed to help us."

My dad shoved his chair back and stood. "Oh no. No way, Eleanor. I don't want those people involved too. They'll want payback. I know how these thugs work. No... no... there has to be another way..." He rubbed his chin and began to pace the room. "Maybe if I sign the hotel over to Loki's Legion... maybe—"

On hearing his words, I gripped my stomach as if someone had struck me. "What? No! You can't do that. Then they win and what the hell happens to you?"

He shook his head. Defeat clouded his eyes. "Eleanor, sweetheart, I'm tired. I'm too old for all this shit. I just want some peace."

I had never heard my father use curse words before. The seriousness of the situation was evidently clear and present.

I walked over to him and slipped my arms around his waist. "Please let me help, Dad. Just let me try. If it doesn't work, then you can do what you feel is necessary. But just let me see what Company of Sinners can do, okay?" I peered up at him, and he returned my gaze for a silent moment before kissing my forehead.

He let out a hopeless sigh. "We're running out of time. I'm lost. And I'm so, so sorry."

"Dad you have nothing to be sorry for. None of this is your doing. I'm going to speak to the Sinners and see what they suggest."

He nodded with an air of reluctance. "But... promise me, Eleanor. If they ask anything of you that involves... well... danger or... or prostitution of yourself don't agree to it. Don't agree with anything that could harm you. Promise me."

My mind leapt back to the way I had thrown myself at Colt and I forced a smile. "I promise."

CHAPTER SIXTEEN

Colt

No matter what I tried to do to take my mind off the redhead, nothing worked. She would force her way to the forefront of my mind until I was driven to distraction. What it came down to was that I wanted to fuck her.

No, I *needed* to fuck her.

That's the only conclusion I could draw. It was pure and simple lust. Well maybe not exactly pure.

As night fell, most of the guys were going to the Fox Hub to drink too many beers and watch half-naked women dance. Most of them hoped that they'd get lucky with one of the sweet pieces of ass. Some of them *would*. I knew that for sure. Usually I'd be tagging along in the hope of getting my rocks off too, but instead, I took a rain check for some shit or other. Thankfully the guys were too revved to care about my lame excuses and they all left at around ten.

I poured myself a whiskey and stared into the bottom of the glass, but not a drop passed my lips. For some reason, I was taken back to the moment I'd poured one for Red as she sat there, looking pale and fragile only a day ago and my dick twitched in my jeans. *Why the fuck does that keep happening?*

Deciding not to bother with my drink, I grabbed my keys and headed outside to my bike. I was deluding myself into thinking I was going for a ride to clear my head. But where did I end up? Yeah... you guessed it.

Ellie opened the door in a pair of pale blue short shorts and a tight-fitting, white tank top. Her red curls were tied in a messy knot on the top of her head and her mostly pale, freckled skin was free from any make-up. The rosy glow to her cheeks made her appear fresh and wholesome, but my dick wanted to change all that.

She scowled at me. "What the hell are *you* doing here?"

I raised an eyebrow. "As pleasant as ever, I see."

She shook her head as confusion clouded her eyes. "Sorry. It's just... I wasn't really expecting to see you." She crossed her arms over her perky tits and covered the nipples that were poking through the flimsy fabric.

I couldn't help the corner of my mouth curving up appreciatively. "So I see. You didn't dress for the occasion, huh?" I chuckled. "In fact you didn't really *dress*... period." I trailed my gaze down her body to where the shorts clung to the curve of her hips, and her belly button was exposed. My tongue came out to wet my lips as my mind began to wander and I imagined dipping my tongue into the little indentation.

"Eyes north, Biker," she growled.

When I lifted my chin and locked my gaze on hers something sparked between us. A charge in the atmosphere like electricity, and I kicked the door closed behind me with my boot.

She inhaled sharply and dropped her hands to her sides as if she was preparing to run. "W-why are you here, Colt?"

I shrugged. "Wanted to check you were okay."

"Liar."

I scrunched my brow. "I'm *not* lying."

"Well, you can see I'm okay, so maybe you can leave now." Her tone was cold, but something within it told me she didn't mean it.

I nodded and stepped toward her. "Okay... I'll leave. If you *really* want me to."

She cleared her throat and stepped back. "I... I..." Her chest began to rise and fall rapidly and a flush of pink spread from her tits all the way up to her cheeks.

I stepped closer. "So, *should* I leave?"

She licked her lips and kept her eyes firmly focused on mine. "I don't like you as a person, Colt. Not *at all*. You're annoying and arrogant. And too old for me. And I really... *really* don't like you."

The feeling was mutual. I smiled as I took another step. "Not too keen on *you* either, Red."

"So why *are* you here?" she breathed.

Another step closer and this time she didn't back away, so I lowered my mouth to hover close to her ear and I whispered, "Because for some stupid reason I want to fuck you. I want to be so deep inside of you that it's all I can think about. My dick is so fucking hard for you, Ellie and I think you want to be fucked by me, too. Like I said, I can't explain it, but maybe we should just take what we each need."

I wasn't sure whether she would slap me or tell me to get out and I waited, holding my breath. I wasn't going to force myself on her after all. But she did neither. I watched in amazement as she swiped the tank top from her body and slipped her shorts down her legs.

Once she was naked, she released her hair and shook her titian curls down her body. "Just fucking. Just a release, Colt. Nothing more. I need something to take my mind off all the

shit. So don't talk to me. Don't kiss me. Just make me come."
She turned and walked through the door that led to her
bedroom, and I followed behind watching her little round ass
and imagining what it would look like rosy red if I spanked
her there.

Once we were in her bedroom, she laid back on the bed
and spread her thighs wide. I quickly dragged all of my
clothing free from my body, discarding it where it fell and
bent to take a condom from my pants pocket before climbing
onto the bed.

I loomed over her naked curves and raked my eyes over
every sexy inch. "No talking I *can* do. But no kissing? I hope
that only includes your mouth," I told her as I lowered my
face between her thighs and licked straight up the center of
her pussy making sure to concentrate a little pressure on her
clit. She groaned and writhed but didn't stop me, and so I did
it again.

I wanted to tell her how amazing she tasted and to
describe all the things I wanted to do to her, but I'd agreed to
stay quiet. At the back of my mind, the thought niggled at me
that maybe she was fantasizing about someone else again, and
my silence was paying into that plan, so I quickly stretched
the condom over my rigid cock and teased her wet glistening
entrance with it. Her eyes were closed, and her lips were
parted.

"Hey, Red. Open your eyes and look at me," I
commanded in a gruff, strained voice.

Her eyes opened. "Why?"

"Because when you've come so hard that you can't stand
up later, I want you to remember that it was *me* who made
you feel that way. You may not like me, Red, and I can't say
I'm your number one fan, but I'm gonna make you feel so
fucking good that no other man will ever match up." And with

that, I thrust my thick length into her body making her cry out and grab at my back. She pulled me deeper until my balls slapped hard on her ass.

The way she enveloped me and tightened around my cock came as close to ecstasy as I had experienced in what felt like forever.

Thank fuck no feelings were involved.

Best of both worlds.

CHAPTER SEVENTEEN

Ellie

As I laid there beneath the delicious weight of his hard body with his rigid cock filling me to the brim, I reveled in the sensations he was creating. No man had ever taken charge of my body so masterfully or with such dominance. And I doubted any man ever would again.

He'd been right about the pleasure he'd promised, and I didn't want it to end. With every thrust, his pubic bone ground into my clit and each time his vigor pushed the air from my lungs in a loud huff.

I gazed up at him where he hovered over me and watched the muscles of his tattooed chest rippling. There wasn't much of his chest that was free from ink, and even though I had never really liked tattoos, his were beautiful. His thick biceps were rock hard as he held himself tensed above me, driving into my body with such precision that I simply stopped caring about the noises I was making.

Without warning, he pulled out of me. "On your stomach, Red," he ordered, and I happily obliged.

Before I knew what the hell was happening, I heard a loud smack and my ass stung like hell. "Ow! What the fuck?" I cried as I realized his palm had connected with my skin.

But he rammed his cock deep into me from behind, and I was lost again. *How the hell could he do that? He just fricking hit me!*

"Fuck, your ass looks fine with my hand print on it," he growled. S*o much for not speaking.*

I should have been disgusted. I should have been alarmed, but instead a wanton groan left my throat, and I lifted one of my hands to tweak my nipple, intensifying the pleasure tenfold.

"Yeah, I like to watch you touch yourself," he told me as he fucked me hard. He rubbed my ass to soothe where he had spanked me, and I closed my eyes trying to comprehend the confusing sensation of pleasure mixed with pain.

He reached around and circled my clit with his rough fingers, and I was done for. I sky-rocketed into the abyss, crying out incoherently and trying hard not to collapse face down onto the bed.

"I could fuck you all night long, you feel so good. So fucking tight and wet," Colt exclaimed as his cock rubbed at the front wall of my pussy prolonging my orgasm and making me cry out again.

His hands were then cupping my breasts as his pelvis ground into me, and I tried hard to absorb every movement. Every thrust.

All the worries I'd had taking up space in my head were nothing in that moment of sheer blissful release. And I was grateful for the fact.

In the mere blink of an eye I was on my back again and my ankles were over Colt's shoulders. The intensity in his expression was unexpected. His brow was furrowed, and glistening with his exertion, and he thrust even deeper this time.

"I can't get enough of this body," he told me as his thumb connected with my clit and once more pushed me over the edge into another earth-shattering orgasm.

"Oh God, Colt… oh God." I kept my eyes locked on his and I swore a slight smile tugged at his lips at hearing me call his name.

Without further words he slammed into me again, throwing his head back and he gasped as he came long and hard, eyes closed and thumb still at the junction of my thighs.

Oh. My. Fricking. Goodness.

Once his breathing was almost back to normal, he pushed himself off of me and walked out of the room. I was in a jellified state of just-fucked relaxation, and I laid there, arms and legs stretched. He was only gone for a few moments, but when he returned, I got a really good look at his naked, tattooed body. He really *was* huge.

In *every* way.

He laid down beside me on his back and rested his head on his folded hands, staring up at the ceiling. I rolled onto my side and watched with intrigue as his chest expanded and contracted and several indecipherable expressions washed over his features in waves.

We lay silent for a short while until he turned his face toward me. "That was… fuck… fucking *awe*some."

I giggled. "It *was* pretty good." He smiled, and I hated that I noticed the cute crinkle of his eyes.

He rolled fully onto his side. "So this no strings attached fucking thing is kinda working for us, huh?"

I cringed. "Oh God, you're so romantic."

He laughed, and the bed vibrated. "Oh yeah. I'm all about

the romance." After another pause, he scrunched his brow. "So you really *don't* like me?"

"Let's say I won't be starting up a Colt... thingamabob fan club anytime soon."

His smile widened. "Colt *thingamabob*?"

I felt my cheeks flush. "I don't actually know your full name," I informed him and in that split second, I was a little disgusted at myself for sleeping with a stranger. But I shook my head to eradicate the useless thought. "So, is your real name Colt or is it a nickname you were given because you're hung like a horse?"

He opened his mouth, and his eyes widened, but suddenly he was flat on his back belly-laughing and holding onto his stomach. He closed his eyes and covered them with one hand as he guffawed at my words.

I slapped his chest. "Come on. Enquiring minds need to know."

Once he had stopped laughing, he rolled onto his side again. "Colt *isn't* my actual name."

Okay, *now* I was intrigued. "Oh *really*?"

He nodded. "Really."

So he's not giving anything away, huh? "Are you going to explain?"

"No need. It won't make me fuck any better than I already do, baby. You can't improve on perfection." He winked, and I rolled my eyes.

Arrogant ass.

But then I watched as the smile slowly slipped from his face and a frown replaced it. "Colt is taken from my surname. My family name. It's kind of the only thing left of me that's connected to them I guess."

I presumed I was on the verge of finding out some pretty personal stuff. We were entering territory that we didn't *need* to venture into. Fuck buddies didn't need the whole, full disclosure on family background, but I actually *wanted* to find out what made this hard-hearted guy tick.

"Oh... you don't see your family?"

He shook his head no. "Let's just say I didn't fit into the Coltman mold."

So now I know his surname. What else will he divulge? "I see. That's a shame."

He shrugged. "Not really. I chose to leave. Nothing there for me anymore." As if coming out of a trance he glanced over at the clock on my nightstand. "Shit, it's after midnight. I'd better leave you to get some sleep, huh?" Before I could answer, he was off the bed and pulling on his clothes.

Once he was fully dressed again, and I had slipped into my robe, he turned to face me. "Look... probably not a great idea to let the others know what's going on with us. You know, they'll probably nag us about being a couple and all that crap. Neither of us got time for *that*, am I right?"

"Oh, yeah. No, you're *so* right. Don't worry, it's our secret." *Our dirty, sordid, illicit, amazing-sex-filled little secret.*

He nodded in agreement. "Yeah, we don't want them making out this is something it's not. I mean it's not like we're *friends* or anything crazy like that. And some people don't get that a man and woman just like to fuck each other without all the hearts and flowers bullshit."

I nodded but the more he spoke, the cheaper I felt. It dawned on me that up to *that* point *I* had been one of those people who *didn't quite get it*. So what had changed? I didn't know.

But then again, I was losing sight of who I was anyway.

CHAPTER EIGHTEEN

COLT

As I walked to the door, ready to leave Ellie's after the intense evening we'd shared, a strong urge began to bubble up inside of me. It was an urge that I *really* needed to ignore. An urge that I wasn't expecting.

The urge to kiss her goodbye.

Thankfully it was fleeting and the way she glared at me, arms folded probably helped to douse it.

She huffed, tapping her foot impatiently. "Are you going or what?"

I realized I must have been staring blankly as I disappeared into my own mind for a moment. "Jeez, okay. I'm goin'," I replied as I shook my head and opened the front door of her little apartment. "See you around."

"Yeah. Whatever." I felt her hand on my back pushing me out the fucking door. Once I was through it, she slammed it before I could wave or anything.

You'd think she'd be a bit more fucking grateful after the way I just rode her ass.

But the more I thought about it, the more it dawned on me that this was probably a new kind of situation for her to be in. After all, she was only in her twenties and her *early* twenties at that. She'd clearly not been the kind to sleep around, and I guessed that the only sex she'd had up to meeting me had been the sweet, missionary, in-a-meaningful-relationship kind. In fact, it had been a while since *I'd* had a regular sexual partner. Since losing Maria, all I'd had was a series of one night stands, rarely fucking the same woman more than once. That way—in my own twisted mind—I wasn't *actually* being unfaithful to my woman regardless of the fact she was dead.

Now if I fell in love... that would be a *whole* different story. It was a relief to know that wouldn't be happening anytime soon.

ELLIE

I couldn't wait for him to leave. I'd literally shoved him out the damn door. Once he was out of my apartment, I slumped on to the couch and closed my eyes. I wasn't sleepy. I just needed to try and make sense of what had happened between us.

The sex was mind-blowing. And my God, I lost count of the number of times I came. He certainly knew what he was doing, and he played me like he'd known me forever. All the other sexual encounters I'd had could in *no way* match up to the way he made me feel. The lightning bolts of electricity coursing through my veins as his fingers and his cock worked their magic on me. He made every single guy I'd ever slept with... all *two* of them... look like complete amateurs. The fact that he had been the only man ever to make me come just by fucking me probably had something to do with the fact. I had always had to play with my clit as the other guys had pleased themselves. But not Colt. He had put my pleasure first. In fact, he had pushed me to a limit I never imagined I would reach.

I wanted to give my body over to him and allow him to do whatever the hell he wanted. He was a master in the bedroom, and I wanted to experience more of what he had to offer. I thought back to the way he had spanked my ass, and my pussy clenched just at the memory of the vibration he had caused there with that single slap.

I chewed on my lip as my stomach knotted with guilt. I shouldn't have been letting myself experience such pleasure when my folks' business was on the line. I shouldn't have allowed Colt into my apartment. And I shouldn't have been planning the *next* time I'd let him handle my body. But then again he had given me a release for all the tension that had been building up inside of me since the whole mess with Loki's Legion began.

And I now knew there was definitely more to him than met my eyes. For starters, the way he mentioned his family spoke of some deep emotional scarring. He didn't say much on the matter, but he didn't *have* to. I could see it in his face. The way he frowned and broke eye contact. The fact that he was reluctant to go further.

So his name wasn't Colt. But what *was* his name? And why did I want to know so much? After all, we were just 'fuck buddies'. Urgh... I hated that term. And I never in a million years anticipated the fact that I would someday *become* one.

But then I allowed my mind to drift back to only a short time before when he was inside me, possessing me. Hands exploring, tongues licking, muscles tightening. Pleasure that I had never experienced before. And *he* had given that pleasure to me. My body had responded to his in a way that I never knew was possible.

My nipples brushed at the fabric of my robe, and my clit began to throb as I replayed the experience over and over in my mind. His naked form, inked, but sculpted to perfection. Almost carved like a beautiful statue. The way he stalked toward me as I lay, spread out before him, waiting, wanting.

My hand moved almost of its own volition down to my breasts, and I circled my nipples through the soft satin fabric. More memories returned of our illicit night and this time, he was looming over me, his cock thick and erect, ready to enter my body. I felt liquid heat pool between my thighs and my hand traveled down to find my pussy wet from my vivid fantasy. I teased my pantiless, bare flesh as I remembered how he filled me and pounded into me, catching my clit each time and sending shock waves of pleasure throughout my body. My fingers rubbed and mimicked those erotic sensations once more, and I rested my head back on the couch as I let my mind take over.

My flesh began to quiver, and I wished he hadn't left. I wished I hadn't *made* him go. I tweaked my nipple hard and imagined his teeth on me, his tongue soothing the stinging bud before biting down again. My fingers worked harder, faster and my breathing rate increased. I imagined his weight on me, pushing into me and his breath on my neck as he told me how tight I was. How wet I was. *Fuck, why did I send him away?* My hips began to rock in rhythm with my strokes, and I was on the verge of coming again. I increased the pressure of my fingers as I remembered the slap that connected with my ass and it sent me over the edge once more. I cried out as another intense orgasm ripped through my shaking body, and I moaned his name over and over as I came down from yet another natural high that involved the older, tattooed biker that I didn't even like.

———

Colt

I'm not entirely sure what it was that possessed me to go back and check on her. I'd reached the bike, but something inside me was unsettled. I think somewhere deep down I was worried about the fact that I had spanked her, and we hadn't talked about it afterward. My own desires were something I had never had to explain to Maria, and no-one else had seemed to mind when things got a little rough in the bedroom. The women I fucked were up for anything. But this woman. This *young* woman was like a blank canvas to me. God, the things I knew I could do for her... How I could make her scream my name and beg for more.

My cock was rigid again just thinking about it.

I climbed the stairs back up to her apartment and was about to knock when I heard moaning. How the *fuck* had she gotten some other guy in there so damn *quick*? And more to the point, *why*? What *hadn't* I done to fucking satisfy her that she needed some other dude to finish off what I thought *I* had?

I peered in through the crack in the drapes on the little sidelight window beside the front door, and the sight that greeted me had me mesmerized. Glued to the spot like I was in a kind of trance.

She was seated on the couch, legs wide with one hand on her pussy and one squeezing her breast. My cock strained at the denim cage that restricted its movement, and I had to fight a groan. I bit down on my lip, hard, hoping that the pain would distract me enough to calm me down. But of course, it didn't.

Her head was back, and her red curls cascaded over the back of the couch, all fanned out. Her mouth was open, and her chest heaved as she worked her clit hard and fast. She twisted her nipple and tugged at the taut flesh where it poked through the satin of her robe. Fuck she looked amazing, and I wished it was *me* in there doing those things to her. Or better still, *watching* her touch herself with her permission for me to do so. I found myself gripping my dick through my jeans in a bid to try and get some relief.

I watched in awe like some pervert in one of those peepshow theaters, as questions began to race through my mind. *Who is she thinking about? What's going through her mind as she works herself into an orgasmic frenzy?* My questions were soon answered as her body began to writhe and her hips bucked. Then my name fell from her lips like some kind of plea. Repeated over and over and over.

My name.

She was fantasizing about *me*.

CHAPTER NINETEEN

Colt

Is it *really* stalking if you're just looking out for someone? *Really?*

It was the night after I had witnessed Ellie masturbating and calling out my name as she came. Fuck, every time I thought about that I wanted to watch over and over again. If that makes me some voyeuristic pervert, then... well if the cap fits and all that.

It was 10:30pm, and I was waiting for Ellie's shift to end so that I could make sure she got home safe. I was waiting in the shadows of an empty property across the street from the hotel, freezing my fucking 'nads off. When had the weather gotten so damn cold? I zipped up my biker jacket and shoved my hands into my pockets.

As I stood there waiting, a couple bikes turned up at the hotel, and I recognized the Loki's Legion insignia when one of the riders clambered off his bike under the street light. The two guys and their scantily clad female companions were loud and leery. They were making a very public display which bordered on pornographic right there on the street. And it was becoming difficult to figure out which woman was with which guy.

Fuck. They're going in to get rooms and Ellie's on the damn desk.

I waited until they began to make their way up the driveway and I pulled out my cell.

"Cassidy's Family Hotel, Ellie speaking how may I help you today?" Her bright and breezy voice vibrated over the airwaves, and I could hear the forced smile even if I couldn't see it.

"Hey, Red. You got visitors. I'm on my way, but I want you to go in the back and lock the door okay?""What? Why? I can't do that, Colt," she hissed.

Gritting my teeth, I growled, "Yes you can, and you *will*. Just do as I've told you or God help me I'll spank your pretty little ass again."

She huffed and chuntered, "Fine." And for a split second, I was disappointed that she hadn't fought me on this. The thought of spanking her ass all rosy again...

After adjusting the wood in my jeans I jogged across the road and into the hotel reception.

"Oh I'm sorry folks, no rooms available this evening," I informed the two couples who were continuing their X-rated floor show inside the hotel.

One of the greasy tattooed fuckers freed his mouth from the neck of the bleached-blonde woman he had been attached to. "Who the fuck are you to say there are no rooms? You the fucking hotel police?"

The blonde snickered and the other ass-hat, a chunky bald guy I didn't recognize, stepped forward shoving his own human version of a blow-up doll aside and crossing his tree-trunk arms over his pot belly. "Hey, you one of the Sinners?" he asked as he chucked his chin in my direction.

"Yeah. What of it?"

"You do know this is our territory now? And that we got an agreement with the owner?"

I reached into my back pocket and pulled out my gun. I tapped it on my chin and narrowed my eyes. "Umm... nah... the way I see it is you *forced* an agreement on the guy who owns this place. An agreement that he doesn't want. And in my opinion, that makes your little visit here null and void. You see *I* have an agreement here too. My fiancée is the owner's daughter and so things are gonna be changing around here."

The fat, bald guy laughed. "You're gonna fucking *marry* the redhead? Jeez man. Good luck with that. She's a royal pain in the fucking ass from what I've heard. Nice tits and ass though. And I bet she has a dirty streak, too."

Before the bastard knew what had happened I whacked him with the butt of my gun, and he staggered backward, collapsing on and breaking a chair in the process.

"Now get the fuck out of here before I use this fucking thing for real! You hearin' me?" I hollered at the other three bewildered idiots as they gaped open-mouthed at me. "You really wanna stick around? Huh?" I stepped toward them, and the two women squealed and dashed out the door. The greasy haired fucker helped his 'friend' to his feet and they left too.

"This ain't over, asshole. Deak'll be coming for you," Grease-ball informed me as he stepped outside and tried to slam the door. He hadn't realized it was a soft close hinge, and I pulled my lips in, trying not to laugh at the dumb fucker.

As soon as the coast was clear, Ellie appeared from the door at the back of the reception.

"Oh. My. God. You waved a *gun* around in here? Are you fucking *crazy*?" Her voice rose an octave as she spoke.

I held up my hands with the gun still gripped in my right. "Hey, really no need to thank me, Red. It's all good."

She crossed her arms defiantly over her tits. "You sarcastic, arrogant, patronizing bastard."

Seriously? What the fuck? "Come on, stop with the overzealous, outpouring of thanks, really."

Her nostrils flared, and she glared at me, wide-eyed. "I'm going home. *Alone.*"

She grabbed her bag and opened the door out into the foyer. I stood there in shock. How the hell could she be this angry at me for saving her damned ass?

As she stomped past me, I grabbed her arm. "You could show a little fucking gratitude, Red. I got rid of those ass-hats for you. Saved you from having to deal."

She struggled to try and yank her arm free. "Yeah, well I could've *dealt* myself, thank you very much. What the hell do you think I am? Some little timid, fragile girl who needs your protection? Jeez. You really do have a high opinion of yourself don't you?"

I pulled her closer still and lowered my face toward her. I was strangely aroused by her anger and my dick wanted in on the action. The closer I got the more her scent infiltrated my brain.

"It wasn't so long ago that you were begging for my protection or have you forgotten about that little incident? And you know what, Red? Yeah, I do have a high fucking opinion of myself because let's face it, *someone* has to. Now run along home before the vultures return in force. And I suggest you lock the place up and let the guests know you're doing so."

She snarled at me. "*What* guests?"

I narrowed my eyes. "Wait... There are no guests? *None?*"

She broke eye contact and glanced at the floor. "Not a single one. They all canceled."

I freed her from my grip and ran my hands through my hair. "Aww, this is fucked up. Something's gotta give here."

"Tell me about it. Those 'ass-hats' would have been paying customers." Her disappointment-laced voice was low and quiet.

I figured she didn't realize that the Loki's Legion bastards would likely have ducked out without paying a red cent. "Okay... okay we gotta do something about this. But first, come on, I wanna make sure you get home safe."

She didn't argue, and after she had locked the place up we silently made our way across the driveway and up the stairs to her apartment. She unlocked the door and stepped inside.

I stopped her from closing the door on me. "Look, I'm sorry if I overstepped a mark tonight. I swear my intentions were good. I just... I seem to lose the ability to behave rationally in certain situations."

She raised her eyebrows. "Yeah. I've noticed you kind of think with your *other* brain often." She gestured toward my crotch.

"Oh really? And you *never* do that, do you?"

Her cheeks bloomed a stunning bright red and I reveled in her embarrassment.

She shook her head and tucked a strand of curly red hair behind her ear. "No. No, I don't. I'm a very level-headed person, actually."

I couldn't resist teasing her some more, and so I stepped over the threshold toward her. "Yeah? Is *that* why you and your hand were getting wildly acquainted last night while you fantasized about someone you profess to hate?" I smirked and watched as the redness brightened again.

She opened and closed her mouth several times before clearing her throat. "I don't... I mean... how... what... I mean..."

I stepped closer still and lowered my mouth to whisper

seductively in her ear. "Yeah, I got quite the peep show. You have no idea how turned on I was. And how much I want to watch you again."

She shivered and stepped back. "You were *here*? You... you *s-saw* that?" She swallowed hard.

I smiled and pulled back to look into her eyes. "Oh yeah, I saw. Sadly, I couldn't see enough. But it looked like you had a good time. Did you?"

I expected her to slap me and shove me out of her apartment. But instead, she shook her head. "I really... *really* hate you. You *know* that? You disgust me."

I rubbed at the hair on my chin and frowned. "Hmm... is that why your nipples are poking through your blouse and your pupils are dilated?"

Silence.

Her eyes clouded with a combination of lust and anger, and I stroked a finger down her cheek. "I could come in and help you out of those clothes if you wanted."

She'll definitely slap me now.

Without warning she grabbed my hand and yanked me inside, slamming the door behind us. She leapt into my arms and crushed her mouth into mine.

What the fuck?

I staggered back a little, but once I found my footing I slipped one hand under her ass and one into her hair and kissed her back roughly, desperately, forcing my tongue into her mouth. I carried her over to the couch and laid her down so that I was on top of her.

I pulled away for some much needed air. "You're full of surprises, you know that?"

"Yeah. Well, this changes *nothing*. I still hate you. But you happen to be a great distraction, and I need to release some pent up tension."

I raised my eyebrows as I stared down at her feigning hurt. "Oh, so I'm nothing more than a *distraction* to you? You're basically using me to get off?"

She pulled her lip between her teeth and nodded as a look of shame descended over her features.

I gripped the two halves of the front of her blouse and shrugged. "Yeah sure, I can handle that." And with that, I ripped the blouse apart sending buttons flying across the room and pinging off the table.

CHAPTER TWENTY

COLT

She gasped as I pulled the cups of her bra down to expose her tits and rolled my thumbs over the tight buds. I squeezed one and lowered my mouth to the other, sucking a rosy nipple into my mouth and eliciting a sexy moan from her throat.

I reached down between her thighs where her short skirt had ridden up and slipped my fingers into her panties finding her already wet. "I want you to do it for me," I told her. "And I wanna watch."

"Do *what*?" she breathed, eyes closed.

"Make yourself come."

Her eyes sprang open. "Oh no... no I can't... I..."

I locked my gaze on hers in determination. "You *can*. I want to see you. *All* of you."

I pulled back and hooked my thumbs in her panties, dragging them down her thighs. "You really are fucking beautiful, you know. You drive me crazy, but you're so... *annoyingly* beautiful," I told her as I pushed her thighs apart and raked my gaze over her glistening wet pussy. "Touch yourself."

I stood and walked over to sit opposite her. She just stared at me. Her cheeks were tinged that gorgeous shade of pink that turned me on so much. I could see from the crumpled brow and the lip chewing that she was suddenly shy.

The fiery, stubborn redhead was fucking *shy*.

I turned my mouth up at one side, surprised at this turn of events. "Hey, don't be embarrassed." Then I had a light-bulb moment. "I could... *join* you. We could watch *each other*. It'd be a great distraction. And a fucking huge turn on. Don't you think?"

A smile tugged at her lips, and she nodded, a mischievous glint just visible in her eyes. "But I'm... I'm keeping my skirt on." Her cheeks flushed every time she spoke, and it was so damn cute I had to stop myself from grinning like an idiot.

I nodded. "Okay. Just pull it farther up your thighs. I want to see *every*thing." She did as I had asked and I had to mentally restrain myself from diving on her. "Spread your legs wider." My voice came out all husky, and I watched as her thighs widened. I licked my lips, and my dick strained at my jeans, so I gripped the hard ridge and squeezed.

"Take your jacket and shirt off." Her voice caught me off guard.

Okay, so she's giving instructions now... so fucking hot.

As requested I stood, slipped off my leather jacket and flung it to the floor. Next, it was my black T-shirt that was swiped from my body and discarded. I unfastened my belt and unbuttoned my fly shoving my jeans and boxers down so that my cock sprang free.

"Okay, my turn," I told her with my gaze firmly locked on hers. "I want you to tweak your nipples... *hard*."

She never ceased to amaze me and her hand slipped down to her breast where she gripped a nipple and squeezed it as I'd asked. Fuck, it was such a turn on. I was having a *hard* time staying on my feet—pardon the pun.

As if she read my mind she gave her next instruction. "Grip your cock."

"Only too happy to oblige, Red." I took hold of my rock-hard erection in my hand. "Now you... I want you to rub your clit... nice and slow. Tease yourself."

With one hand still playing with her nipple, she slipped the other down her body, between her legs and found the little swollen nub. She gasped, and her eyes widened as she began to make slow, circular motions.

Needing no further instructions, I began to slip my hand up and down my shaft in time with her movements and my heart began to race, pounding at my ribs as I watched her begin to writhe in pleasure.

"Oh God... Oh, Colt..." Her eyes drifted closed.

"Hey, eyes on me Red, I'm not in this alone." Her eyes sprang open and locked on mine. "That's it baby... we're going to come together... *hard*."

———

ELLIE

I know it was always one of the first things on my mind—his age—but my goodness for a man of thirty-eight or whatever, he was so *ripped*. He had a better body than most men my own age and I was transfixed as I watched his hand slip up and down his thick cock with such self-assurance. His hooded gaze trailed my body as he licked his lips and smiled almost lasciviously. My muscles clenched and my pussy ached for him. I needed him inside of me, filling me. But watching him

—and having him watch me—was so much more arousing than I ever could've imagined.

I circled the sensitive flesh of my clit a little faster and began to breathe heavily as pleasure, like heat, spread throughout my body. I should've been embarrassed, *ashamed* even. But like he said, we were doing this *together*. Both exposed. Both vulnerable in a way.

The taut muscles of his abdomen contracted and he groaned. A deep, throaty, gravel-filled sound emanating from his body and my hand quickened.

"Two fingers, Red. Two fingers inside. *Now.*" He barked his desperate order through clenched teeth, and I obeyed.

"Unh... Oh God, Colt, I want to come."

"Na-uh. Not yet, baby." He stood and walked toward me with his cock gripped firmly in his white knuckled hand.

"But I need... I really need..." I was losing the ability to form cognitive thought, and I knew I had *never* been so turned on. My head buzzed, and my body was on sensation overload as he loomed over me, dominating me with his stance. The epitome of masculinity as his hand moved faster and he grimaced as if on the verge of losing it.

"I know what you fucking need. God, you look so fucking hot right now. You make me so hard. How does your pussy feel around your fingers, huh?"

I gasped as his dirty words rattled around my mind. "Tight, Colt... So tight."

"Yeah, I like it when your pussy tightens around my cock. I like making you come. And I want you to come now, Ellie. Come for me, *now.*"

At his command and the fact that he called me by my *actual* name, I cried out, and my body was sent into a crescendo of immense ecstasy. Muscles spasming, pelvis thrusting rhythmically, and his name falling from my lips over and over while my heart beat so fast I feared I may combust.

I opened my eyes and watched as he came all over my breasts. Warm liquid spurting onto my flushed skin, his head back and his mouth open as he groaned his release.

His pulsing rhythm began to slow and he dropped his head forward and locked his gaze on mine once more. The look of possession in his eyes almost sent me into another mind-melting orgasm, but he dropped to his knees and gripped both my hands. With his eyes fixed on me, he sucked my fingers into his hot mouth, first my right hand then my left.

"Fuck me, you taste good too." He slipped a hand into my hair and pulled me forward, crushing his mouth into mine and sweeping his tongue in a tangle with my own. Once I was thoroughly kissed, he pulled away and rested his forehead on mine. "That. Was. Amazing."

I turned my face away not wanting to meet his gaze. "I... I should go clean up."

Without answering, he stood, pulled up his boxers and jeans and then disappeared to the bathroom, returning moments later with a damp wash cloth. He leaned down and wiped my sensitive breasts clean before watching as I pulled my bra back into place and tugged my skirt down my thighs. I still couldn't make eye contact and so instead I concentrated on adjusting what little clothing I was wearing, making a bigger deal of it than necessary.

"Why do you always do that?" I noted a hint of annoyance in his tone.

Finally turning to face him I shook my head. "Do *what*?"

"Every time we fuck, you get all... I don't know... ashamed, after."

I sighed and wrapped my ruined blouse around myself

suddenly very much aware of my partial nakedness. "Maybe because I *am*."

He stepped toward me and tilted my chin up, forcing me to look at him directly. "Why? Because you're fucking someone you *despise*? Or is there some other reason?" Annoyance had been replaced by bitterness and for some reason, a twinge of regret tugged at my insides.

I closed my eyes and let my head tilt back. "Partly I guess. But..."

"But *what*?"

"You... you bring out something in me that... You *do* things that..." I couldn't get the words out. I couldn't explain. Partly through embarrassment and partly through shame.

In a surprise move, he pulled me up to a standing position and into his arms. He stroked his hand down my hair. "I think what you're trying to say is that I'm introducing you to desires you didn't know you had. Am I right?"

I nodded into his chest, and the heat from his skin seeped into my cheek, relaxing me. I rested my head on the hard, tattooed plains.

The fact that I was comfortable there niggled at me. "Maybe. You... you spanked me and... I wanted you to do it again. That just makes me feel... *weird*... like there's something wrong with me. And having you watch me while I touched myself. It felt *wrong* but... I really enjoyed it. But now... Now I feel like some kind of *pervert*."

He tilted my chin again. "Hey, chill okay? We're two adults exploring each other. It's consensual. It's private. It's *just us*. It's *just sex*. And you have nothing to worry about. I've known people who like stuff a helluva lot weirder, believe me. What we're doing doesn't even *register* on the kinky scale." He smiled, and his eyes twinkled. For a split second, I was transfixed.

Realizing I was on the verge of *liking* the ass-hat I pulled myself away, suddenly feeling awkward. "I'm gonna go clean up properly." I turned and walked away through the door that led to the bathroom.

Once I was washed up and had dressed in sweats and a T-shirt, I returned to the living room expecting him to have left. But instead, I found him sitting on my couch, still shirtless. He'd obviously found my iPod as "Fall to Pieces" by Velvet Revolver played in the background. As I got closer I realized his head was resting on the back of the couch, and his eyes were closed.

Shit, is he sleeping? I cleared my throat, and he lifted his head. A wide smile spread across his rugged features, and I found myself smiling in return.

"I was beginning to think you'd gone to bed and abandoned me here."

"Oh… no. Just… freshening up. You know." I shrugged suddenly feeling embarrassed at *why* I'd been cleaning up. "So… I suppose you should go, huh?"

He frowned. "Tryin' to get rid of me are you, Red?"

I slumped onto the chair opposite. "Well, it's not like we're… you know… *lovers*. We don't *have* to sit around and make nice. It feels… it's weird."

A fleeting look of disappointment flashed across his face, but he stood and grabbed his T-shirt. "Yeah, sure. You're right. I got shit to do anyway. But make sure you lock your door, okay?"

God, he almost sounds like he cares. "I always do."

He pulled on his shirt and jacket and walked toward the door, and I wrapped my arms around myself. "So… you really do have a Colt .45 revolver huh?" *What the hell? Why mention that now? You stupid woman.*

He turned just enough so he could hit me with a

megawatt grin. "As if I'd have anything else." He winked and
walked out the door.

CHAPTER TWENTY-ONE

Ellie

I awoke feeling tender and sore from the over use of muscles I didn't even know were involved in masturbation, and I felt my face heat at the memory of what Colt and I had done the night before. Once again he had pushed my boundaries, and I had let him. Ever the eager student of the older, more experienced man.

The scary part was that I was beginning to like the guy. I didn't *want* to, but I couldn't frickin' help it. *Damn* him. Each time I encountered him, and he did something to completely blow my opinions of him out of the water, I got pissy and angry. I really, *really* didn't want to feel that way. I just wanted to have sex with him. Uncomplicated, passionate, panties-melting sex. I'd never done the 'just sex' thing before, and I wanted it for once. I wanted to be the unpredictable bad girl for a change.

Yeah, I was pretty sure that's what I wanted.

I hated to admit it to myself, but he excited me. Maybe it was the tough, tattooed exterior. Or maybe it was the rock hard body and the rod of steel he kept in his pants. Or maybe it was the way he always seemed to be *there* at the right time, looking out for me, like some pseudo superhero. Whatever it was I was going to have to seriously rethink things. Sex was great with him so far... really, *really* great. But while I was with him I was closing myself off from a real relationship.

And *love*.

Love like my parents had.

Back in the light of day, my situation once again began to drag me down. I had to stop using sex as a distraction technique. As much as I enjoyed the things Colt did to my body I needed to figure a way out of the deep, dark hole I was sinking into.

I picked up my cell and fired a text over to Chloe.

Hey, Chloe. I need to talk to you. I have to come up with a way to sort this whole mess out, and I need CoSMiC's help. If you think they will still help after my bitchy outburst.

E x

I dropped my phone back onto the pillow beside me and went to take a shower. Enveloped in a cocoon of steam, the hot cascade went a small way to relaxing the aching in my arms, legs and neck, but the one in my heart remained.

My family meant everything to me and seeing them hurting was unbearable. I had always been a daddy's girl but in all my years I had *never* seen nor heard him acting the way he had done the day before. Knowing he was already stressed compounded my worry and I wanted to do everything I could to make it stop.

Why had Loki's Legion chosen *now* to interfere with the hotel? What was it that they hoped to gain from causing such awful problems for honest, hard-working people? Perhaps they just got a kick out of hurting others. Knowing what I had seen Chloe go through at the hands of the bastards, that would make sense.

Once I was dried and dressed in my work clothes, I made my way over to the hotel. My dad was sitting at the reception desk when I walked in.

"Hey, Dad. How's it going?"

He shook his head and rubbed both hands over his now stubbled face. "Not good, sweetheart. More cancellations. More money lost. Ever since that asshole printed his story, the news of our apparent brothel activity has spread like wildfire. I can't blame people. Why would anyone want to have a romantic weekend or a family vacation in a place where people are using prostitutes?"

"We *will* deal with all of this, Dad. I promise you that," I informed him with determination, but in the back of my mind I wondered what the hell could be done to change things.

My cell pinged in my pocket, and I lifted it out to see a reply from Chloe.

Hey C. Have spoken to Colt and Six. They are meeting to discuss the situation. Hold tight. We will get through this together. All of us <3

CD x

Colt. There was his name again.

In spite of the strange tightening in my stomach at my memories of his eyes, I smiled at the way Chloe had signed off the message. CD was a sweet nickname Six had given her when they first met properly. The song "Chloe Dancer" by Mother Love Bone was one that he said reminded him of her, and so the name got shortened to CD. My heart skipped when I remembered the fact that I too had my own nickname, thanks to Colt.

Although *Red* was more of an observation, really.

The working day was so quiet. No new bookings but plenty of cancellations. I even resorted to explaining to customers that the newspaper article was *wrong,* but all that seemed to do was cause people to hang up on me. Not a single person was prepared to listen.

Just after lunchtime I heard a ruckus outside, and my dad burst into the reception area all pale faced and fast breathing.

"Call the cops, Ellie. Do it *now*. This is getting out of hand. Out of *goddamn hand!*"

I stood and reached out to him. "What the hell, Dad? What's going on out there?"

"Protesters. People from the town with placards. They want us *closed down*, Ellie. They hurled abuse at me calling me a *pimp*. They're saying I'm *letting* things happen here. They're saying…" He clutched his chest and sunk to his knees.

"Daddy! Daddy, what's wrong?" I screamed and covered my mouth as his face colored bright red and he struggled to breathe.

"9…1…1… please." He collapsed unconscious, and I scrambled for the phone.

Tears sprang from my eyes. "Hang on Daddy, *please* hang on… oh God… no don't let this happen, *please*." With shaking hands, I dialed 911 and when the call was answered I barked the hotel address down the line at the poor woman at the other end. "Please, *please* come quick." I hung up and dropped to my knees beside my father to carry out the instructions given to me by the paramedic control center.

"Oh my God, no!" I glanced up, and my mom stood there wide eyed and holding the wall to keep herself upright. All the color had drained from her face.

"Mom, the ambulance is on its way. Please stay with him so I can go out and meet the paramedics, okay? He'll be fine," I lied as more tears escaped down my cheeks. "He *has* to be fine." I squeezed her shoulder and pushed out through the door.

People with placards chanting, "No hookers here" and "Get the hookers out" over and over again stomped in a circle around the entrance way to the hotel. My blood began to boil. Some of these people had known my father his whole life. He had been born and had grown up right *here,* yet they were quick to judge and assume. It made me feel sick to my stomach to think that people had come to their own conclusions without hearing *his* side.

Then it hit me.

I was just as bad.

I had made assumptions about Colt and the Company of Sinners over and over again when all they had done was protect Chloe and try to help me. I suddenly had the urge to call Colt and apologize, but what good would it do. I had virtually pushed him out the door after we'd had sex like I couldn't wait to get rid of him.

As the distant high-pitched call of the ambulance siren could be heard a little way off I screamed at the gathered crowd. "SHUT UP!" They finally fell into a shocked silence, and they stood there eyes wide and mouths open. "You people make me *sick*! My dad has *nothing* to do with the shit going on here. But instead of letting him figure it out and maybe *explain* to you that he's been threatened with violence, you go ahead and believe a dumb article by a fucking wannabe journalist who professed to be my *friend*, in a news-paper that will line tomorrow's trash cans. Have you ever once stopped to think what this might be doing to him? Well, *have* you?"

The ambulance blipped its siren to part the throng of people, and some of them gasped and covered their mouths when they apparently put two and two together at seeing the paramedics arrive.

"I hope you're all satisfied now. And I'll tell you what, if he makes it through this you *all* owe him. Every. Single. One of you." I waved my pointed index finger around the stunned people before turning around to follow the ambulance up the driveway to the hotel.

CHAPTER TWENTY-TWO

ELLIE

My dad lay there attached to all manner of bleeping, flashing machines that were keeping him alive. I sat beside him holding onto his arm just above the bandage that covered the cannula. I felt completely useless. My mom sat at the other side gripping his hand and rocking back and forth as tears left damp trails down her cheeks. She'd given up wiping them away. In all honesty, I didn't know how my mom would cope if my dad didn't make it. She relied on him so much that I worried she would have a breakdown if he passed away. It was a horrible thought and one I was unhappy to have rattling around my head.

But thoughts were all I had just then. My own stupid, mixed-up thoughts. It struck me that I hadn't contacted anyone to let them know. I hadn't even told Chloe. But then again after what she had been through it didn't seem right to bother her. The sad fact was that she was *it* as far as my friends went.

I squeezed my dad's arm and stood. I had to get out of the

room if only for a little while. The walls were closing in on me, and it seemed the longer I stayed there, the worse my train of thought was becoming.

"Mom, I'm going to grab a coffee. Want one?" The dryness of my throat was evident as I croaked my words.

She didn't take her eyes off my dad. "No, sweetie. Thank you though."

I silently walked out of the private room and into the bright, clinical corridor. I slipped my hand into my pocket and gripped my cell. *Should* I call Chloe? She'd want to know. She might even be pissed at me for *not* calling her.

I made my way along the corridor and down the stairs to the exit. The sun's heat caressed my skin, but I couldn't take pleasure in the warmth. Not when my heart was breaking. Pulling my phone out of my pocket, I lifted it and hit dial.

As the ringing tone kicked in, I closed my eyes and tried to compose myself. The composure lasted mere moments, and I was pacing up and down outside with one hand in my hair and my heart hammering at my ribs.

After only a couple of rings, a gruff voice answered. "Go for Colt."

"H-hi. I... I... don't know why I chose to call *you* but... I didn't really have many other options."

"*Red*? Umm... I mean Ellie? Is that *you*?" I could hear the concern in his voice, and it lifted me slightly.

I cleared my throat. "Yeah... yeah, it's me." I sniffed and inwardly cursed my voice for cracking.

"Ellie, what's wrong? You sound... Are you crying?"

I nodded as I tried to muster up the courage to speak. "My... my dad. He... I'm at the hospital. I don't know if he'll make it." The latter half of my mumbled sentence came out in a sob.

"Aww fuck. I'll be right there." The line went dead, and I

crumpled onto the bench behind me which had just been vacated by an elderly lady and the cloud of cigarette smoke she was creating. I leaned forward and stared down at the asphalt, watching my tears splash down creating little glistening patterns with the shadows of people's feet as they passed me by, oblivious to my pain.

Minutes ticked by and the realization of what I'd just done began to sink in. *Shit. Why him? What the hell can he do? You dumb, stupid bitch. You should've just called Chloe like you set out to.*

I was on the verge of calling him back to apologize when a familiar pair of black biker boots appeared in my line of sight. Slowly I raised my head and shielded my blurry eyes from the sun's rays.

He rested his hands low on his hips in a stance that told me he meant business. "What the hell did Loki's bastards do to your dad? I swear to God I'll make them pay." The worry and concern that clouded his eyes and crumpled his brow both surprised and touched me.

I shook my head and wiped the moisture from my cheeks. "N-no. It wasn't them. Well... not directly anyway. He had a heart attack." My lip trembled and I inwardly cursed myself for not being stronger.

He huffed a heavy sigh and tilted his head skyward for a moment before holding out his hand toward me. "Come on. I'll buy you a coffee, and you can tell me what the hell happened."

Fighting back the tears brought on by the sense of relief that his presence had somehow delivered, I slipped my hand into his, and he gripped mine in return, helping me to stand. When I stood before him, he tilted my chin up so that I faced him.

"Do you maybe need something stronger than coffee?" I

shook my head no, and he smiled as he smoothed his thumb over the apple of my cheek—an overly affectionate gesture but appreciated in the circumstances. "Okay then Red, let's go grab us a cup of joe."

My heels clicked on the tile floor as we walked toward the hospital's cafeteria. People stepped aside when they saw us coming, and for once in my life it pissed me off that they were assuming the worst about the tattooed biker who had come to my aid when I'd had no-one else to call. I began to throw harsh looks at the ignorant folk who either sneered at Colt or turned away, nervously fidgeting so they wouldn't have to make eye contact.

"It's not a problem, Red. Don't sweat it," came a husky voice from beside me. I glanced up to find him watching me with a wry smile as we walked.

Scrunching my brow, I shook my head. "What do you mean by that?"

He pulled his bottom lip between his teeth and grinned. "I saw the way you were shooting daggers at people. It's sweet that you feel that way but... well, I'm used to the way I'm perceived is all. You don't need to stick up for me. I'm a big boy." His playful grin and arched brow told me he wasn't just talking about his physical presence.

I slapped his arm. "*Seriously*, Colt? Jeez." I shook my head. He was being completely inappropriate, but I couldn't help smiling. Why was that? Hysteria? Over-tiredness? Or did I actually out and out *like* the damned guy? I shuddered and hugged my arms around myself at the thought.

"Hey, you're shiverin'," he pointed out as he slipped off his leather jacket and placed it around my shoulders.

Yeah, I am. But not for the reasons you think.

I pulled the heavy jacket around my shoulders and inhaled the masculine scent of him that clung to it, momentarily closing my eyes and feeling some of the tension leave my body.

Colt ordered us coffee while I found a table in the corner of the restaurant far away from prying stares and disapproving glances. After a few minutes, he placed a steaming mug before me and sat in the seat opposite.

"Okay Red, spill it."

I recounted the whole situation that had occurred. From the angry mob to my father's collapse, to the paramedic trying several times—in vain initially—to resuscitate him. I couldn't help the wavering of my voice as images of my dad's pallid skin tone and limp body replayed in my mind. It had been one of the scariest situations I had *ever* experienced, and I wanted desperately to erase it from my memory.

Colt listened intently with a concerned frown and every so often he would reach over and squeeze my wrist when my emotions began to get the better of me. Something about him being there felt right and after a while it entered my mind that perhaps calling him had been the most natural thing to do. After all, we all need someone to hold us up and be our strength when we're running on empty... *right?*

"Look... you're probably not going to like what I have to say... but I have an idea of how to help you and your family out of this shitty situation. Are you prepared to hear me out?"

The furrow of his brow told me that I was going to somehow disagree wholeheartedly with his suggestion. But I had to listen. I had no other choice. Living in constant fear and under the beady eyes of judgmental assholes was no way to carry on.

I shrugged. "Sure. What do I have to lose?"

CHAPTER TWENTY-THREE

COLT

Her response shocked me. I had forewarned her that she wasn't going to like my suggestion, but she agreed to listen anyway. *Shit, she must be fucking desperate.* As I sat opposite her in the hospital cafeteria with its fake plastic flower displays and a faint hint of disinfectant hanging in the air, I saw a very different girl than the feisty, stubborn-ass redhead I'd grown to... to *what*? *Like*?

Fuck.

Trying to stay calm I told her, "Okay. But you may *actually* need something stronger than java to drink when I put my proposal to you."

Her nostrils flared and for a split second the feisty bitch returned. "Just cut to the chase, Colt. Don't tease me with some kind of half-assed build up. Ain't nobody got time for that."

I fought back a chuckle at her choice of words, and rubbed my chin. "Okay, okay retract the fangs, Twilight."

A ghost of a smile appeared on her face, and she blushed. "Sorry. Go ahead."

I nodded and took a deep breath. "Okay. So... Loki's Legion have decided that your family business is a nice little road into the prostitution and brothel business. And as you *know* they're not exactly open to negotiation on that while Eamon still owns the hotel."

She held her hands up to halt me. "Whoa, wait a minute. Before you suggest that he *sells* the business don't bother. There's no-one who'd buy it anyway after that damned article in the paper."

I paused, bracing myself for her reaction to my next words. "But you didn't consider him selling it to *me*."

———

The color drained from her face, and she swallowed. "What?" Her voice came out all mousy and weak, but I sensed this was definitely the calm before the raging storm. "That's what this all is about? Your offer of help is to get *your* hands on my dad's business?" She pushed herself up from the table and glared down at me where I sat. "You *bastard*. I actually was dumb enough to think you *really* wanted to help me. But instead you just want to take over what Loki's Legion have already set in motion. Build your own little *'biker empire'*." Making air-quotes around biker empire, she snorted with a huge amount of derision. "I should have known. How fucking *stupid* of me."

She began to storm away, but I grabbed her arm. "Hey. *Now* who's being judgmental? Huh?" I made sure to keep my voice calm despite the tumult that had begun to rage beneath my skin. How the hell *dare* she compare me to those cock-suckers?

Her responding smile was one of disdain. "Yeah, well I guess that's just the kind of response dickheads like you elicit. Now let the fuck *go* of my arm. I'm leaving."

Realizing she was in no state of mind to be negotiated with, I released her and turned away as she left in a hurry. Heaving a deep frustrated sigh, it dawned on me that no matter *what* I did she always saw the bad in me, and it hurt like a bastard. Not because it was *her*. Not really. It was due to the fact that my intentions *had* been honest. There was so much more to my plan, but I hadn't been given an opportunity to speak. I figured I'd let it go and maybe speak to Eamon when he was up to it.

If that ever happened. I just hoped it wasn't too late.

———

Sleep eluded me.

Nothing at all that I did even remotely relaxed me. I couldn't even jack off to images of the redhead after the way she had reacted to my partial offer of help. Even the *best* memories—ones of her orgasmic cries and the way her cheeks flushed and how she moaned when she was going to come—didn't do the trick. Don't get me wrong I've *never* had a limp dick, and that really wasn't the issue. It was simply that thinking about her made me *angry* rather than horny.

Why the fuck did it bother me so damn much? I'd spent most of my adult life being judged by narrow-minded people and okay some of the time it was deserved. But *this* time it wasn't, and I was so damn pissed.

After tossing and turning all night, I finally gave in and got up around seven to shower. Part of me—and no, for once I don't mean *that* part—wanted to go to Red's apartment and set her the hell straight about her presumptions. But another part of me—a more dominant part as it turned out—knew that I had to go about things differently. And that meant going behind her back; something that really didn't lay easy on me.

Once I was dried off and dressed, I went down to the bar area hoping to grab a cup of coffee. However, for once the area was quiet which meant no-one had put the machine on. *Just my fucking luck.* The fact just added to my pissed off mood, and I decided I'd grab a coffee at the hospital. I heaved a disgruntled sigh and left the clubhouse to go out to my bike.

The chilled morning air smelled fresh with the scent of pine trees and that sweet fragrance you get when it's been raining. The sun was almost up, and the sky was a mixture of golden orange and pink. Even a tough guy like me can appreciate the beauty of nature. Bet ya didn't expect that, *huh*? After I had filled my lungs with some deep breaths, I straddled the bike. The cold of the metal and leather seeped through my jeans and I almost considered taking the car. But I knew there was nothing like a cold blast of air on the bike to wake me up—except coffee... coffee would've been good.

Once I was on the road, I began to try and formulate a plan. What would I do if Ellie's mom was there at Eamon's bedside? It was early, but I guessed she wouldn't have wanted to leave him. And then a worse thought landed in my head. What if *Ellie* was there? *Fuck.* It was a risk I'd have to take. Time was of the essence if my plan was going to work but as I drove through the waking town, I laughed at myself for being such a jackass. Ellie had made it perfectly clear that she wasn't prepared to listen despite her initial agreement to do so. So why the hell was I insisting on trying to get through to her father? How the fuck was I going to benefit from putting myself and my club on the line like this?

I pulled into the parking lot at the hospital and turned off the ignition. Glancing around I could see only a couple other cars there and guessed they were more likely to be staff, and so I made my way into the building and up to Eamon's room.

Through the glass panel beside the door, I could see the man lying in bed with his head tilted toward the window. After I had glanced around to ensure that no-one from the nursing staff was watching, I pushed down the handle and walked into the room.

Eamon turned to face me, and his brow scrunched. "Colt? What are you doing here?"

I smiled and stepped toward the bed raising my hand in a greeting. "Hey, Mr. Cassidy. Good to see you awake. Is your wife here?"

He shook his head slowly. "No... no I insisted she went home to get some rest. And Ellie too. Why do you ask? And you didn't answer my first question. What *are* you doing here?"

The fact that he didn't look too pleased to see me didn't go unnoticed, but I straightened my spine and hoped that he could see the seriousness in my expression. "I came to offer you some help."

The creases in his brow deepened. "Help? With what?" His tone was icy, and so I didn't sit down for fear of stressing him out further.

Choosing my words carefully I began to speak. "Look, Eamon... may I call you Eamon?" He nodded and waved his hand limply for me to continue. "I know what's going on over at your business with Loki's Legion. What they're doing is unacceptable, but I think I have a solution."

"Oh you *do*, do you? And what would *that* involve? Me paying you protection money?"

In spite of his sneer I chuckled as I figured where Ellie had gotten her attitude from. "Not at all. It's not like that Eamon. I really do want to help you."

He narrowed his eyes suspiciously. "And why would *you* want to do that?"

"You were always good to me when that fiery Italian-blooded wife of mine kicked me out of the house after a fight. Now I know it didn't happen often but... you always took the time to listen to me. And to advise me on the ways of handling a... how can I put it? Umm... *passionate* woman."

His features softened. "Ah yes. Beautiful Maria. I was so sorry to hear about her death, Colt. So very sorry."

Hearing him say her name with such sorrow caused a lump of emotion to catch in my throat, forcing me to cough in a bid to clear it. "Yeah... yeah thank you. It was tough there for a while."

"I can imagine. Look why don't you take a seat and tell me about this plan before the nursing staff realize you're here and throw you out."

I began to relax as Eamon's demeanor eased up and I took a seat beside his bed so that I could begin to fill him on my proposal.

CHAPTER TWENTY-FOUR

ELLIE

My stomach churned and I wretched over the toilet. The stress was getting to me, and I hated that. I was usually a together woman of the new millennium, but this whole shit storm was fucking me up. I'd begun to resort to both foul language, *and* excessive alcohol consumption, and neither were befitting of me.

The one thing that got to me more than anything was the fact that the person I had turned to for help—the *biker*—had seen a chink in my armor and had been hell-bent on driving his sword right on through there. I hated myself for approaching him. And I hated myself for thinking for one *second* that he would be able to help. I should've known that once a bad-ass-manipulative-piece-of-shit always a bad-ass-manipulative-piece-of-shit.

After unhappily emptying out the contents of my stomach, I showered and dried myself off feeling a tiny amount of relief for the freshen up. After applying a thick layer of concealer under my dark-rimmed eyes, I grabbed some clean clothes, dressed, and tied my hair in a low ponytail. I really couldn't be bothered to do much more. And I had to go see my dad. The fact that he had woken the night before and insisted my mom and I go home to rest was wonderful, but frustrating at the same time. I hadn't wanted to leave. I was worried that Colt might show up and make a scene, and Dad *really* didn't need that shit.

I arrived at the hospital at around ten, and as I approached my father's room door, I could hear the distinct sound of deep, male voices. Initially, I presumed it was a doctor who was visiting with my dad but as soon as I opened the door a familiar husky tone sent a knot of anger coiling in my stomach.

I stormed through the door. "My God, you just couldn't *wait* could you?" I yelled at the bearded biker sitting beside my father's bed.

My dad held up his hand. "Whoa, hey princess it's—"

"No Dad! Before you tell me it's *fine* for him to be here, I want you to know what he's going to try and do with your business. He's—"

In a split second Colt was standing before me gripping my arms and peering into my eyes as a deep furrow creased his brow. "Calm the fuck down, Red. It's all good. Your dad doesn't need this."

I glared up at him as my chest heaved and my heart tried to escape through my chest. "You have no *right* to presume you know what my dad needs, Colt. And what you're really saying is that he doesn't need to know the truth, right? He doesn't need to know what you're trying to pull!" He clenched his jaw, and I watched the muscles in his face tensing further.

It dawned on me that a discussion had already taken place and I gasped. "What the hell have you told him? What have you done? Don't you have a decent bone in your goddamn body?" I growled through gritted teeth.

He squeezed harder on my biceps, and I winced but he shook me slightly. "Eleanor, I said calm. The fuck. Down. Your dad and I have come to an agreement on things so just quit with the melodrama, okay?" He was growling now too, and a shiver of something I didn't want to acknowledge traveled the length of my spine.

I stared in disbelief, but my father chimed in too. "He's right Ellie. We have a way to deal with all the bad things that are happening because of Loki's Legion. Let Colt explain honey, okay?"

My gaze flitted between the two men—one who meant everything to me and the other who meant nothing. Well, at least that's what I was telling myself—and my lip began to tremble. I was beginning to think I was losing my mind. Either that or my *dad* was.

Colt still had his hands on me, but his grip had eased. His thumbs began to graze soothingly over my skin where it was bare beneath my shirt sleeves.

I focused my attention on him. "This had better be good, Colt. I want a proper explanation, and I need to know that you aren't trying to take what's not yours." The anger I was feeling inside was evident in the way my voice wavered.

Gazing deeply into my eyes, Colt smiled. "I swear to you that I'm only trying to help. Now can I take you for coffee somewhere to discuss this?"

I sighed and momentarily closed my eyes before fixing him with a determined stare. "You'd better come to my place. I don't want to discuss our *problems* in a public place. Nowhere feels safe anymore."

He released me and nodded. "I'm on the bike. Should I meet you there?"

"I'll need to hail a cab. I felt too tired to drive so I don't have my car here."

He rubbed his chin and looked thoughtful for a moment. "It seems dumb you going home in a cab when I can give you a ride on the bike. That's if you're feeling *brave*." He winked, and I felt my cheeks heat.

In a bid to hide my embarrassment, I rolled my eyes and huffed like an errant teenager. "Whatever, Colt." I shoved past him and walked over to my dad. "I'll be back later. Don't go agreeing to anything *else* until you've spoken to mom and me, okay? I'm not sure you should be making decisions at the moment."

It was my dad's turn to roll his eyes now. "Eleanor, I'm a big boy. Please don't patronize me. I had a heart attack, not a brain injury, and I still know my own mind so let me use it."

I leaned in to kiss his head and smiled as I pulled away. "I'm sorry. I love you, Daddy."

"Love you, too. Now scoot. It's time they brought me some food."

As Colt and I left the hospital in silence, a sense of relief washed over me. Whatever it was that Colt had suggested to my dad, it had clearly set his mind at ease, and therefore I decided I should at least *listen* to what he had to say.

Once we reached the bike, Colt slipped off his leather jacket leaving just his cut and T-shirt on his top half while the jeans he wore sculpted perfectly to his thick, muscular thighs. He handed the jacket to me, and I scowled at him.

"Just put it on, Red. I'd never forgive myself if we got in an accident and your beautiful skin got damaged."

His softly spoken words disarmed me, and without further argument, I slipped my arms into the huge sleeves. Once the jacket was zipped up, I looked down at my body and giggled. My slender frame was swamped by the heavy black coat, and I looked utterly ridiculous.

A deep rumble of a chuckle emanated from his chest. "Looks good on you." No sooner had the words fallen from his lips than he stepped toward me with a serious expression in place. He cupped my chin and tilted my face up. "You're gonna need to hold on real tight. I don't have a helmet with me, and I don't want anything happening to you. So you grip my waist *real* hard. You got me?"

Suddenly mesmerized by his request and the determination in his eyes, I nodded and my stomach flipped. "You... you don't wear a helmet?"

He shrugged but dropped his attention to my mouth and licked his lips. "Not always. It's not a legal requirement for a guy my age in Utah. And my journey today wasn't long."

I began to speak but no sound came, so I cleared my throat as I squirmed under his scrutiny. "Even so, y-you never know what could happen. You... you *should* wear one... always." My voice came out as a whisper and I swallowed as annoyance at myself began to bubble up inside of me.

A knowing smile spread across his face, and his eyes seemed to light up as they met mine. "I had no idea you cared. Your request is duly noted, Miss Cassidy." He saluted me and then paused for a moment, letting the air crackle with sexual tension between us. My heart skipped a beat as he lowered his face toward me but stopped and clenched his jaw. I released a silent sigh of relief and stepped back. After what had gone on between us in the very recent past I wasn't ready to kiss him, regardless of the fact that my head and more intimate parts of my body were screaming otherwise.

He stepped away and swung his leg over the hunk of metal and a twinge of desire tugged below my waist at seeing him straddling such a powerful machine. After mentally pulling myself together, I clambered clumsily onto the back of his bike and slipped my arms around his huge body. He reached behind me and roughly cupped my behind before yanking me closer and causing my clit to collide with the ridge in my jeans and rub against his ass. I didn't quite manage to stifle a squeak, and I felt a rumble of laughter vibrate through his back. The bastard *knew* what he was doing.

"Just making sure you're nice and *tight*. Don't want to be losing you now, do I?" he informed me over his shoulder. I tried to ignore the double-entendres that laced his words as he revved the engine.

He pulled out of the parking lot at high speed, and my stomach was almost left behind. As exhilarating as it was to be on the back of his bike, I was willing the journey to be over and for me to get out of it in one piece... or at least *alive*.

The wind whipped my ponytail around my face, and I scrunched my eyes closed both out of fear and the need to shield them from grit and bugs. From the whooshing in my ears, I would have guessed we were going at around 150mph, but I hoped to *God* I was wrong. No doubt Colt was trying to either impress me or scare the living shit out of me. My guess was the arrogant ass was going for the latter.

It was working.

Well, there's absolutely no way in hell I'm letting him fuck me again. Not after this. No way. No sir.

Nu-uh.

In that split second, I vouched that I was completely and utterly insane. I *had* to be. Only an insane person would think about *fucking* when they were facing certain death on the back of a bike, and at the hands of a six-foot-four, muscled, brick outhouse of a biker.

Yup.

Crazy as a damned box of toads.

CHAPTER TWENTY-FIVE

Colt

I pulled the bike into the driveway of the hotel just in front of Red's apartment over the garage. I felt sure that when I looked down, her fingers would be embedded in my damned flesh. It was my own fault for telling her to hold on tight but jeez, I didn't expect to have to surgically remove her from my body.

She swung her leg over to get off the bike and somehow landed in a heap on her cute little ass. I tried hard not to laugh... well actually I didn't try *that* hard.

It was funny. What can I say?

She clambered to her feet and scowled at me before turning to stomp away up to the apartment. Like a good little puppy dog, I followed close behind.

Once we were inside, she dragged my jacket from her body and thrust it into my arms catching me completely off guard.

I staggered back. "Hey, Red, careful. *Jeez.*"

She stood there, glaring at me, arms folded across her chest which only served to draw my attention to her rack.

She hollered at me, "Yeah, well you tried to *kill* me you asshole."

I couldn't help laughing at her melodrama. "Believe me, if I'd *tried* to kill you, you'd be dead already. Now are we gonna sit and talk like adults?"

She huffed and flopped onto her couch. "Huh, well *I* am, but I don't know about *you*."

Shaking my head, I chuckled at her petulant behavior. "You *do* know how immature you sound right now, don't you?"

"Fuck you."

I nodded. "Yep, *so* much more mature. I should take you over my knee and spank that ass." My dick twitched at the thought of her ass all pink.

She rolled her eyes but her cheeks flushed. "Look, Colt, just tell me what the hell you're planning for my dad's business and then you can get the hell out of my home."

I was a little taken back by her hostility and held up my hands in defense. "Whoa, hey, sugar, why are you being so damned pissy about this? I told you I was *helping* and your dad has accepted my offer, so I don't get the attitude."

Her nostrils flared, and I could tell I was in for a tongue lashing. And *not* the kind I actually enjoyed.

"Don't call me sugar, Colt. You went behind my back. You offered my dad your *own* version of help when he was too vulnerable to see straight, and you took advantage. *That's* why I'm pissy. Now just talk."

So she was back to being the judgmental little bitch who was unwilling to believe I was being genuine. Great. I leaned forward and rested my elbows on my thighs, already aware I was fighting a losing battle. I locked my eyes on hers in the vain hope that she would realize this was *not* about me.

"Okay, Red. The plan is that I buy the hotel from your dad—"

"I knew it!" She stood and stomped across the room to me, and I felt sure she was going to slap me. I straightened up and braced myself, unsure as to how I would react if she did. When she simply stood there, chest heaving, hands on hips, I stood to even the playing field.

Now *I* was getting pissed. I clenched my jaw and pointed a finger down at her. "You know *nothing* yet, bitch. So quit getting all high and fucking mighty with me. When I've *told* you the plan you'll fucking *know* it. Okay?"

She clamped her mouth shut as if realizing who she was messing with and backed away until her legs caught the couch and she sat. "Okay. G-go ahead."

I sat too, my stomach knotting at her reaction. There was fear in her eyes, and I felt like a bastard for putting it there.

"So... I buy the hotel on a *temporary* basis. Me and the club own the place and run it properly, but with your staff working for us. We're just on the paperwork to make it clear to Loki's Legion that it's our turf, and they aren't welcome. We make sure the bastards leave and don't come back. Once they get the message, and we eradicate the... erm... *problem* from the town, your dad gets the place back, and we stick around in a protective capacity to make sure he has no more issues with them. That's it. Your dad's staff will carry on doing their jobs and your dad deals with the day to day bullshit, but we make it known that the place is ours."

Confusion and worry clouded her eyes. "But... why do you have to actually *buy* the place? Why can't you just *say* you own it?"

"Because, believe it or not, those idiots have friends in high places—there's no accounting for taste—and they would see straight through it all once one of their cronies looked into

things. But if it's done *officially* they'll know we mean business. They'll only try to step on our toes for so long until they
get bored and fuck off somewhere else. Hopefully a whole
other town."

"But... how can we trust you? How do we know *you* won't
just do what *they* were planning?" Her voice was small and
weak and her gaze lowered to the floor.

I crossed the room and crouched before her, tilting her
chin up so she faced me. "Red, if you *don't know* you can trust
me... If you *don't know* that I only want to help a man who has
helped me in the past... Then maybe we should just forget it."
My heart sank as I said the words, but I wasn't willing to go
through this shit if she was unhappy. For some dumb-ass
reason, her opinion and feelings mattered to me.

Her eyes were glassy, and I could see the hopelessness
there. But she shook her head in spite of what I was expecting.
"No... no. My dad has agreed, and if he's happy then I'm..."
She shrugged. "Well, who am I to argue?"

The fact that she didn't say "then I'm happy" troubled me,
and the fact that she saw my help as some kind of last chance
saloon hurt more than I wanted to admit to myself.

I reached up and tucked her hair behind her ear. "I wish
you'd trust me," I whispered.

Her threatening tears spilled over and trailed down her
cheeks. "Me too."

Pulling myself up to my knees, I leaned toward her and
placed a chaste kiss on her forehead before standing and
heading for the door.

"Colt."

Her voice stopped me in my tracks, and I turned my face
so I could see her over my shoulder. "Yeah?"

"I'm sorry. I do appreciate the fact that you're helping.
Honestly, I do. It's just... I'm trading one set of bikers for

another and what should *feel* like a 'lesser of two evils' situation still feels wrong. I wish... I wish you *weren't* a biker. And I wish I knew more about you. That way I might feel more inclined to trust you."

I shook my head, knowing full well that if she knew more about me it would have the exact opposite of the effect she desired.

"My twin brother, Jared and I were born and raised in Florida. And my real name is Jacob. Let's just leave it at that for now, huh?" And with that, I opened the door and left.

CHAPTER TWENTY-SIX

Ellie

Well, I finally knew his name.

Jacob Coltman.

Trouble was it didn't do *anything* to alleviate my worries. All it did, in fact, was intrigue me more. Jacob was quite a sexy name, and it somehow suited him more than the name he went by. Although I wouldn't be brave enough to actually *use* it in his presence, just in case he took offense. After all, he had been known as Colt for many years, from what I could gather, and considering what he had hinted at about his family it was clear to me that he had put them *and* his name behind him.

I couldn't help wondering why.

And the cryptic way he disclosed his name to me preyed on my mind. I had said that I wanted to know more about him, and all he had felt able to reveal was his given name. Alarm bells rang in my mind, and I wondered if I should advise my dad against accepting the club's help. But the more I thought about it, the more I realized that we had no other options available to us, except for the cops, and from what I had seen of them it appeared they were either hell bent on keeping out of biker business or they were in the pockets of the criminals already. If the Sinners didn't help us, then Loki's Legion would continue to try and use the hotel as a damned brothel, and we'd lose *credibility* as well as all our loyal customers. Many of whom were lost already.

So basically no matter what we did, we were pretty much screwed.

Great.

―――――

It was so good to have my dad home from the hospital. He had been ordered to make changes to his diet and to cut down on caffeine as well as removing any stress from his life. Like that was going to be easy. He had met with Colt the day after his release and with the help of one of the MC, a guy named Weasel—who I was shocked to discover was a law graduate—a contract had been drawn up and signed by both parties and witnesses.

Our family business and home were now in the hands of the Company of Sinners.

I was still struggling to come to terms with the idea that Colt was now—for all intents and purposes—my boss. The good thing was that for the first day or so he wasn't around, and we were able to get in and carry out some cleaning work on the rooms that had been trashed by Loki's Legion. Those bastards had no respect for anything, and they had helped themselves to artwork from the walls and pretty much anything else they had taken a liking to.

My first night shift was looming, and even though there was the added protection of the Sinners, I was nervous as hell and wondering what I was going to come up against. I showered and dressed in my usual smart attire, settling on an understated pair of black pants and a high neck cream blouse. I was trying not to stand out in any way. Dumb, considering Loki's Legion were fully aware of who I was.

I walked into the reception area as Candace was getting ready to leave. She looked pale, and something niggled at me that things weren't quite right.

"Hey, Candy. You okay?" I asked as I placed my bag in the office locker.

"Umm... sure. Everything's fine. Why? Don't I look fine? Is there a reason you asked?"

Her behavior was strange. She was a tough woman and not one to be easily spooked, but something about her demeanor was off.

I stepped toward her and reached to put my hand on her arm, and she almost jumped out of her skin. I held my hand up. "Whoa, hey Candace what's wrong? You're not yourself tonight."

Her lip began to tremble, and she stepped away from me and toward the door. "I'm so sorry, Ellie, but I won't be coming back to work here anymore. I just... I can't."

Before I could ask any further questions, she opened the office door and dashed out of the hotel without looking back.

Oh great. Not only have we lost guests but the staff is jumping ship too.

I was totally confused. As far as I was aware Loki's crew hadn't been around for a couple of days and so I had no idea what had caused such a strong reaction in Candace, but I vowed to contact her and find out.

Sitting there at the reception desk, I stared at the phone willing it to ring with bookings. Surely not *everyone* had been put off staying? But as the night wore on I realized that I was wasting my time sitting there. At half past midnight, I was on the verge of calling my folks and telling them I was going home when I heard loud crashing noises coming from outside. I rushed to the door in fear of what or *who* was causing the ruckus, and as I gripped the handle, the door flung open and I was knocked backward.

I screamed as two huge tattooed guys grabbed my arms and feet and carried me out toward my apartment. I struggled and managed a half yell, but a large shovel-like hand that smelled of tobacco covered my mouth.

"I think you know that screaming is a big mistake, sugar lips. We're gonna take you home and have ourselves a little fun, just like we promised that other woman who works here. She was sensible and left. But knowing your dear old dad owns the place, we guessed you wouldn't go quietly. But just know, if you *do* scream, we'll be back for your folks too."

My heart hammered in my chest, and fear caused my eyes to relinquish the tears that had welled up. What the hell were they planning? And was I going to come out of it alive? In my head I pictured my mom and dad coming to look for me and finding me gone, kidnapped or worse, and more tears came.

They carried me up the stairs to my apartment and when we were inside, the front door was slammed, and another of the crew was waiting there.

"Oooh, you found the pretty redhead. This is gonna be fun with a capital *fuck*." The ugly, bald man said. I recognized him from his unwelcome visits to the hotel and my stomach roiled. I wretched into the hand of the biker who was keeping me silent and my vomit seeped through his fingers.

"Aw fuck, man! Now look what she did." He released my mouth and the men dropped me onto the couch. The guy with puke on his hands disappeared to the kitchen swearing and cussing to himself and anyone else who would listen.

The other guy who had helped carry me in yanked me

back and pinned my arms across the back of the couch, and the bald ugly guy bent toward me and tugged at the buttons on my blouse until he ripped several off exposing my bra. I yelped.

He slapped me across the face sending my head careening to one side. "I suggest you shut the fuck up, bitch, and let us have our fun. No-one likes a whiner."

I sneered up at him and started to laugh maniacally. He scrunched his face and slapped me again, this time bursting my lip. But I continued to laugh.

He grabbed my throat and lowered his face to mine until his rancid breath almost singed my nostril hairs, and he spoke through gritted teeth. "What's so fucking funny?"

Forcing a smile through the paralyzing fear of what was to come I said, "Oh nothing much. I just think you're fucking ugly and could do to lose a few pounds, but you clearly have a high opinion of yourself if you think you're getting anything out of me. I'm one tough lady."

I had no clue where the bravado was coming from but for a moment he was clearly shocked at my words and he released my throat before standing up straight and unbuckling the belt that must have been hidden under his huge belly.

In a mocking voice, I continued, "Ooh yeah baby, show me what you got... If you can even *find* it under the blubber." I burst out laughing again, and the other guys sniggered a little too.

"You do realize you just signed your own *death* warrant don't you, bitch?" The bald, fugly guy informed me with a sick grin.

"Oh, I wouldn't move another inch if I were you. But that's just my advice. I suppose the question is; do you actually need your dick for anything other than pissing through?"

All eyes in the room darted to the doorway where Colt

stood. He held a gun in each hand. One aimed at the bald guy's junk and the other aimed at the head of the man who held me trapped.

"Don't just stand there, someone fucking shoot him!" ugly, bald guy hollered, but the guy who was holding me seemed frozen to the spot.

Just then pukey hands guy returned from the kitchen and stopped dead in his tracks. "Aw fuck. I told you guys this was a bad idea."

Colt chuckled a deep dark noise that vibrated from his chest, and the menace in his eyes sent shivers down my spine. "So which one of you bastards do I shoot first? Eeny... meeny..."

"Whoa! Stop, Colt. We're leaving." The guy behind me released his grip on my shoulders and stepped back.

"Damn right you are." He fired a shot, and the guy screamed.

He gripped his shoulder and dropped to his knees beside my couch. "You fucking shot me. You shot me."

Bald, ugly guy scowled at his friend. "It's only a fucking scratch, asshole, get the fuck up and get your gun."

Colt stepped toward him, gun still poised in the direction of the fat guy's crotch. "Go ahead. See how far you get. I heard that they can operate these days so you can piss through a kind of straw. But I could be wrong." He shrugged and kept his eyes trained on the guy who stared right back at him. Pukey hands guy suddenly made a dash for the door and ran down the stairs. His footsteps sending vibrations through the apartment as he tried to get away as fast as possible.

"Hey, you." Colt nodded toward the guy on the floor. "Get the fuck out of here. And tell Deak if any of you come around here again I will shoot to kill. You hearing me?"

The guy dragged himself up from the floor, still holding

his arm. Blood seeping through his leather jacket, although the injury didn't look life threatening to me. He glanced at ugly, fat guy and opened his mouth to speak, but closed it again and ran out the door.

As Colt stood there with the gun still cocked, he spoke to me. "Hey, there anything you wanna say to this piece of shit, Ellie?"

Without even trying to find the words, I lifted my foot in a swift jabbing motion and kicked my assailant in the balls. He crumpled to the floor holding his crotch while coughing and crying at the same time.

Colt turned his attention on me. "Nice work, Red. Remind me to stay on your good side." He winked, and I managed a small smile. "Come on, you dumb fucker, let's send you on your way." He grabbed the crumpled heap of a man from the floor and dragged him toward the door, shoving him out so that he stumbled and tripped on his way down the stairs. Colt slammed the door and tried to bolt it, but the lock had been broken.

It was then that I glanced around my little home to see that they had completely trashed it. It hadn't registered before that moment and as I stood there the horrible events of the past thirty minutes hit me like a ton of bricks and I collapsed to the floor in a sobbing heap.

CHAPTER TWENTY-SEVEN

Colt

Watching her collapse to the floor like that almost broke me. The hell she must have gone through at the hands of those bastards terrified me. What had they done to her? There was blood on her face, and I swore that I would deal with Loki's Legion once and for all. I fired a quick text to Dee at the clubhouse and told her to send some guys down to the hotel to stand guard over Ellie's folks, and she fired one straight back assuring me that they were on their way.

I wrapped Ellie in my hooded jacket and scooped her up into my arms to carry her out the door without bothering to close it. There was no point, with the lock being busted. Carefully, watching every step, I carried her down the stairs to my waiting car, thankful that the bike was in pieces back at the clubhouse, and that I'd chosen that week to strip the engine, meaning I'd had no choice on what vehicle to bring.

Once she was secured in the passenger seat, I slammed the door and went around to the driver's side. After buckling my seatbelt, I turned to face her where she sat head down and shoulders shuddering as she sobbed.

"Hey. Are you okay? What did they... what did they do to you?" My voice cracked as I asked the *one* question I wasn't sure I wanted an answer to.

"Nothing. They hurt me physically a little, but you got there before any real damage was done." She tilted her face toward me. "Thank you. Thank you so much." Her lip trembled again, and I leaned forward to envelop her in my arms as best as I could in the confined space, pulling her head toward my chest as I stroked her hair.

"Shh... I'm so fucking sorry I didn't get there sooner, baby. I'm so sorry." I spoke through clenched teeth as I fought the anger at myself and the sadness over what they had subjected her to that warred inside of me.

She pulled away and stared up at me. "Are you kidding me? You got here just at the right time you big oaf." She smiled and my aching heart nearly fucking melted. She still had a sense of humor after all that she had been through.

A stupid grin spread across my face, and I shook my head. "You're quite something. You know that?"

She frowned. "Is that a compliment?"

"Hell yeah, it's a compliment. After what you've been through tonight... You remind me of..." Realizing what I was about to say out loud, I stopped myself and turned to face front.

Dumb-ass.

"I remind you of...?"

I sighed a long deep exhale and kept my eyes front. "Maria was being abused by her boyfriend when I met her. I actually watched him slap her in the restaurant she worked at. No regard for who was around. So damned arrogant that he didn't care who saw. I flipped. Although looking back, I was pretty restrained. I didn't kill the guy even though I wanted to. I have a major fucking issue with anyone who hits women. And before you jump down my throat and call me a chauvinist or something I should tell you it's me, it's how I feel, and I don't really care if people don't agree with it. As a man, you should never, and I mean *never*, hit a woman." I glanced sideways at Ellie to try and judge her reaction to my words and fully expecting a pursed-lipped *I'm-just-as-capable-of-looking-after-myself-as-any-man* kind of retort from her but instead she sat there with a sweet smile on her lips. "What? You're not gonna berate me for my opinion?" Maybe I was a little more defensive than I intended, but I was shocked at her response… or lack of.

She shook her head. "Believe it or not, I'm actually glad you feel that way." Her voice was a whisper. "I was so scared, Colt. I thought they were going to rape and kill me. But you saved me. I'll never be angry at you for that. Ever."

My next move was probably a stupid one, but I couldn't help myself. I leaned toward her, and slipped my hand into her hair, crushing my mouth to hers until she winced and I pulled back.

"Fuck, I'm such an idiot." I slammed my hand into the steering wheel, and she flinched again.

"No, no not at all. It's just… my lip hurts like a bitch."

Oh! "Shit. I'm so sorry, Red. I totally forgot for a second why we're here. Come on. I'm taking you home."

I turned the key in the ignition, and she scrunched her brow. "But… I am home, Colt."

Shaking my head, I put the car in gear and set off. "I'm taking you to *my* home."

———

Ellie

As we headed toward the edge of town to an area I didn't know too well, I pondered on the new territory we were stepping into. He was taking me to *his* house. Not the clubhouse, but his own abode. A myriad of butterflies set to flitting about my stomach and I momentarily forgot why this was happening, just as Colt had when he had kissed me only moments before.

He eventually pulled the car into a sloping driveway beside a quaint, two-story house built of slatted wood. In the dim street lighting the house looked orange but I guessed it was probably white. Once we were parked, he came around, opened my door and bent to lift me out.

Of course, I protested. "Whoa, I know I agreed about the whole not smacking women around thing, but believe me I am capable of using my legs."

He stood quickly and nodded but didn't argue. "I should've guessed that, huh?" A ghost of a smile appeared on his lips.

"I guess you should have."

He held out his hand and helped me out of the vehicle before slamming the door and locking it. I followed him up to the door and then it hit me. "Shit, Colt, my mom and dad. I should go and check... what the hell was I thinking?" I turned to walk away although God only knows where I thought I was going on foot.

He reached out and grabbed my arm. "It's dealt with. Some of CoSMiC are already there to watch out for your folks. You have nothing to worry about, okay?"

Oh shit, that's so thoughtful. He had thought about my parents before I had and I was niggled by guilt.

As if reading my mind, he tugged on my arm until I was

beside him again. "And before you go getting all down on yourself, remember what the hell you've been through tonight, okay?"

He was right.

Again.

It was becoming a habit.

I followed him inside, and he locked the door behind me. No escaping now. He threw his keys onto a table in the hallway and pushed open a door to the right. Once he flicked on the light, I took in my surroundings. The living room was quite large and decorated in creams and blues. Not at all what I would have expected. But then I remembered this was his *marital* home.

"Want a drink? I have some JD." He gestured behind him to what I presumed must have been the kitchen.

"That would be great, thank you. I think I could use a drink right now."

"Have a seat. Oh, and if you want to watch TV or maybe listen to some music…"

I sat on the cream colored couch and sank into the cushions. "I'm good. Thanks, though." I suddenly felt very shy and awkward. Like I was meeting a boyfriend's parents for the first time. Dumb I know, but my stomach was still suffering an attack of the crazed butterflies, and I wasn't sure what was causing it. Was it the sheer excitement of being here in Colt's actual home? Or was it simply the adrenaline from being attacked?

He returned a few moments later without his jacket but carrying two glasses with amber liquid and ice clinking in the bottom. He handed one to me and sat beside me on the couch.

"You doing okay?"

I nodded and took a sip of my drink, closing my eyes briefly as it warmed a path to my stomach. "Yeah. Calmer now. I just don't get why Loki's Legion are so hell bent on ruining this town."

He shrugged. "You got me. I think they just enjoy the pain they inflict. It's like they want to own everyone and everything."

"But your crew doesn't?" It seemed like a fair question when still in my head but as I spoke the words I realized it probably came out wrong.

He smiled. "In all honesty, Red, I just want a peaceful life in a peaceful place where everyone gets along."

His reply surprised me. I had felt sure that bikers were all out to get what they could from people; to make their lives more pleasurable, but it seemed I was wrong. Again. And yes, that was becoming a habit too.

CHAPTER TWENTY-EIGHT

Colt

Having Red in my house was strange but somehow comforting. There hadn't been a woman there since Maria had passed, and I guess that's the main reason I spent so much time over at the clubhouse.

Being home was lonely.

And regardless of the fact the guys grated on my last nerve most of the time, the noise was a great distraction for me. There was always something going on, whether it was a fist fight, an argument or a rowdy-ass party.

But there we were. Me and my out-of-the-blue guest.

I turned to face her, and rested my elbow on the back of the couch, my head on my hand. "Is that why you were so hostile toward me and my crew to begin with? You presumed we were out to take what we could from you and everyone else?"

She cringed and nodded slowly. "I guess so. And instead of looking at what you did for Chloe, I guess I blamed you for her being in that awful situation to begin with."

"And now? What do you think now?" As soon as the question fell from my lips, I realized I wasn't exactly prepared for her answer.

She shrugged and lowered her gaze briefly. "Now... I *know* that you saved my life, and I'm very grateful. Because I would no doubt have gotten into that situation this evening regardless of you being around and so..." She lifted her chin and locked me with those verdant eyes of hers. "I'm kind of glad you were around. I'm glad you rescued me."

A beautiful smile tugged at her lips and the urge to kiss her again washed over me, but it was a compulsion I had to fight. The last thing she needed tonight—or *ever* for that matter—was me mauling her again.

She covered her mouth as she yawned and then rubbed her eyes.

"Hey, you're tired, and there's no real wonder why after the night you've had. Come on. I'll show you to your room." I reached to place my glass down on the coffee table, and she followed suit.

Nervously twisting her hands in her lap, she said, "Are you sure you don't mind me being here, Colt? I mean... I would totally understand if—"

I stood and gestured dismissively. "Hey no. It's fine. I have a guest room. It may be a little dusty. No-one's stayed here in a while. Not even me. But you'll be safe. And tomorrow we'll figure this shit out. Get your locks changed. Fit some better security, you know?" I was aware I was rambling and hoped she was too tired to notice that I was *anything* but my usual assured self.

She nodded and stood to join me. "Well thank you. I really appreciate everything you've done for me tonight. And... and with my dad and the hotel too. You didn't have to do any of that and—" Her swollen lip began to tremble again.

I stepped forward to pull her into my arms and just held her there. My bulky embrace enveloped her slender frame. "Come on, don't cry, sweetheart. And stop thanking me. Any decent guy would've done the same."

She half pulled away and gazed up at me. Green eyes glistening with unshed tears. "No, I don't think they would've. Just *you*."

We stood there, gazes locked for a few moments and my attention drifted to her mouth again. The cut on her lip had stopped bleeding but looked damned sore.

Realizing I was staring, I cleared my throat. "Come on, let's go get some rest, huh? Oh, and can I get you something for your lip? Some ointment maybe?"

She shook her head and fought another yawn. "No, honestly it's fine, thank you."

I pulled away and led the way upstairs. Pushing open the first door I gestured for her to go in. "Here you go, this is you. There's a bathroom across the hall, and there are clean towels in the drawer at the side of the bed if you want to take a shower. I'm just next door, so shout if you need anything, okay?"

Nodding, her eyes filled with sadness and her shoulders slumped like the weight of the world was pushing her down. With what I hoped to be a warm smile I turned and closed the door and left her to go to my own bedroom.

Deciding I was much too tired to shower, I stripped the clothes from my body leaving just my boxers on and crawled under the sheets. I heard the shower start up and closed my eyes...

I was awoken by a faint knocking on my bedroom door.

"Colt?" Her voice was a strained whisper.

I sat up and glanced at the clock which told me I'd only

been asleep around a half hour. "Yeah? What's up, Red?" I called out into the darkness of my room.

The door creaked open a fraction, and she poked her head around. "I'm sorry to bother you but... could I maybe borrow a T-shirt to sleep in?"

Shit, dumb-ass, didn't think of that, did you? "Oh fuck, yeah. I forgot your blouse was... erm... yeah, hang on." I flicked on my bedside lamp and climbed out to grab her a Tshirt from one of my drawers. A faded Soundgarden shirt was the first one I laid my hand on, and I passed it to her where she stood just inside my doorway in only a bath towel, highlighted by the hallway light.

She thanked me and closed the door behind her, and I climbed back into bed flicking off my lamp. I laid awake staring into the blackness wondering if she was okay by herself and began to drift off again. But no sooner had I rolled over to get comfortable, than there was another knock.

"Yeah?" I called.

The door opened again, and I heard her step inside. "I'm... I'm sorry to bother you again." Her voice wavered, and she sniffed.

I sat and flicked on my lamp again to find her standing there, my huge old T-shirt skimming her thighs and falling off one shoulder. Her eyes were puffy and red, and her hair was tucked behind her ears. For the first time since I had met her, she looked frail.

"You okay?" It was a dumb question, but I couldn't think of anything else through the tiredness fogging my thoughts.

She shook her head. "No. I'm actually *not* okay. I'm so sorry, and I hate to admit this but I'm..." She dropped her gaze to the floor and fiddled with the hem of the shirt. "I'm afraid to be alone right now."

My heart ached for her; for what she had been through.

But I glanced to my night-stand and Maria was smiling back at me from the photo frame. I just couldn't let another woman in my bed. No matter how platonic the action would be tonight.

I just couldn't do it.

I climbed out of bed and walked across the room toward her, flicking the lamp off as I passed. "Come on. We'll sleep in your room."

I followed her into the guest room, and she paused beside the bed as if she was going to speak. Instead, she climbed into the bed and rolled onto her side to face the window.

I carefully climbed in behind her and wrapped one arm over her body, pulling her back close to me and kissing her hair. "You're safe now, Ellie. Go to sleep, sweetheart."

She gripped my hand where it rested just in front of her and squeezed it tight. "Thank you, Jacob."

Hearing her call me Jacob was not something I had expected but I guessed for that *one night* she wanted to think of me as anything but a biker, and I couldn't really blame her.

CHAPTER TWENTY-NINE

Ellie

My eyelids fluttered open, and I rolled over to find Colt fast asleep on his back beside me. One arm was under the back of his head and one lay flat on his stomach which was rhythmically rising and falling as he breathed. His lips were slightly parted, and in his slumber he looked much younger and so much more relaxed.

Incredibly handsome.

As the thought entered my head, my heart tripped over itself, and I trailed my gaze down his tattooed body to the V shape that disappeared under the sheets at his waistline.

He was one well-defined, strong mass of sculpted muscle, and physically he was absolutely, unequivocally, sex personified. Regardless of the age gap between us, there was definitely a pull. Something that drew me to him. Maybe it was that he exuded danger. Or maybe it was that protective streak I seemed to elicit from him. But whatever it was, as I lay there watching him sleep I finally had to admit that I liked him.

And not just his body and what he could do with it. But the man under the tattooed skin.

As he slept, I played over the night before in my mind from the point when we had reached his house. The way he took care of me, and the way he held me when I had gotten upset. But then the realization that he had ushered me away from his marital bed dawned on me. He was clearly still very much in love with his wife, and hadn't wanted to betray her memory by having me in his bed. Not that sex had been on the cards *at all*. Not after the hellish experience I'd had. And I knew that jealousy was a stupid emotion to be feeling, but it tugged at my insides, regardless, and for a few moments I envied the woman that had captured his heart so much that even after death it was still hers.

He awoke with a start and made me jump. His brow scrunched, and he seemed a little bewildered for a moment until he turned his head toward me.

"Oh... hey, Ellie. H-how are you doing this morning? Sleep okay?"

I smiled in response as something deep inside me that I didn't want to acknowledge stirred to life. "I did, thank you again. I should go home. I must have outstayed my welcome."

He rolled to face me and propped his head on his hand. "You don't have to go. Stay. For as long as you need."

He seemed to be genuine, but I couldn't help feeling uneasy and that I really shouldn't be in Maria's house.

"No. It's okay. I'll shower, and if it's okay, I'll borrow a shirt to wear home."

He silently stared at me, a crease formed between his eyebrows. "Do you really want to go?"

No. I really don't want to go. But I shouldn't stay. "I think it's for the best."

He reached out and stroked my cheek with his thumb. "You do?" he whispered.

Further words caught in my throat as his penetrating gaze remained locked on me. I was frozen. Mesmerized by the intensity in his eyes. I wanted him. I wanted to feel his weight on top of me. It was irrational, and I knew it. After the previous night's events, sex should've been the last thing on my mind, but in the darkest recesses, I figured maybe he could erase the memory of the animals who trapped me in my own home.

I reached out and gently grazed my nails from his jawline down to his pecs, and he closed his eyes. The next thing I knew his mouth was on mine and he had pulled me on top of him, one hand squeezing my ass and the other in my hair holding me to him.

I reached down between us and gripped his straining cock through his skin tight boxers and a deep appreciative rumble vibrated up through his chest.

"I want you, Ellie. I want you right now. And I want you in control. You on top. You make the demands."

I guessed he was relinquishing control for the same reasons I had felt guilty about wanting him. The timing was awful. He feared he would scare or hurt me. But I just wanted to feel *good*. To experience that natural, emotional high that he delivered with his body.

I pulled myself up and straddled his waist, and he reached up to cup my breasts, toying with my nipples through the fabric. Gripping the hem of the borrowed T-shirt, I swept it from my body and dropped it beside the bed.

His hands continued to roam. "Is this okay? Are you okay?" His concern for me warmed my heart and spurred me on simultaneously.

"Yes. Please, Colt, make me feel good." I almost begged as

I ground my clit into his rigid cock through the two layers of cotton that were acting as an unwelcome barrier.

"Look, I know I said you could make the demands, but I want you to stand up and take these off." He tugged at my panties, and I obliged. I stood on the bed, a foot either side of his ribcage and slipped the panties from my body, allowing them to fall and join my T-shirt.

"C'mere, I wanna taste you."

Throwing all caution to the wind, I shuffled myself so that I was kneeling over him. His mouth poised at the junction of my thighs and I leaned on the headboard of the bed as he pulled himself up to taste my core, dragging his tongue up my center, and flicking the swollen nub of my clit with quick strokes. I cried out, almost ready to explode and I pulled away.

He gripped my ass and asked playfully, "Where do you think you're going?"

"I... I don't want to come that way. I want you inside of me," I panted.

"Well, maybe you come *this* way, and *then* with me inside of you, and then any other way we damn well please. We're in no rush to go places, and I want to feast on you."

He pulled me forward once more, but this time, he reached between my thighs and slipped two fingers into my entrance, curling them to rub at that sweet spot deep inside. *Oh. My. Goodness.* He flicked my clit again with his skilled tongue while stroking me internally and I gripped the headboard harder as intense sensations of pleasure fired throughout my body, causing me to circle my pelvis rhythmically with his strokes.

"Yeah, that's good, baby, keep going. Take what you need." His words were such a turn on. I would have done *anything* for him in that moment. *Anything.* Reaching up, I tweaked my nipples as he continued with his delicious torture. "Come on, Red, don't hold it back. You know you wanna come."

And I did. I exploded into a wanton mass of gyrations and thrusts as an intense orgasm ripped through me, and I cried out his name.

His *real* name.

"Jacob... oh God, Jacob."

Suddenly I was flipped onto my front, and he was on my back, grinding his cock into my lower back. The weight of his full body pressed me into the mattress, and his mouth was by my ear.

"*Why* do you insist on calling me that?" he growled angrily, and I flinched. The atmosphere in the bedroom had changed rapidly, and I was uneasy.

"Because... because it's your name," I breathed.

"Not anymore, Red. *He* was gone a long fucking time ago. I'm Colt and *you* need to remember that." He clambered off me and left the room, slamming the door behind him, and leaving me in a jellified but confused stupor on his guest bed.

CHAPTER THIRTY

COLT

Her insistence at calling me by my given name was getting under my skin. But not for the reasons you would expect.

I hated that I *liked* the way it sounded falling from her lips when she came undone like that. But I couldn't let that happen. I couldn't start acknowledging feelings for another woman. I wouldn't allow it. I'd had my one true love, and she had fucking died, taking the shattered pieces of my heart to the grave with her. And okay, four years is a long time, and maybe others would be okay about moving on, but not me.

Not *Colt*.

And it had been *Colt* that Maria had loved, so it was *Colt* who I wanted to be. No woman had ever loved Jacob, and I wasn't about to start allowing that to happen now after all these years. He was long gone, and I was glad of the fact. He was the guy who let his heart rule his head. He made bad decisions and allowed himself to get hurt which resulted in him hurting others.

But Colt was one tough fucker. And that was the way it needed to stay.

I had gotten dressed and gone downstairs to make coffee. I didn't really want any, but I had to get out of that room before... Well, let's just say I didn't like the way I was feeling when I was in that bedroom with Ellie. And it wasn't like I was unfamiliar with blue balls, so dealing with it again was no biggie.

I was lost in my own head, staring out the window into the overgrown yard, when the redhead pulled me back to reality.

———

"Colt? I want to apologize. I... I *like* your name, and I like how it fits you but... You don't, and I should respect that. I'm sorry for spoiling this morning. It won't happen again."

"Damn right it won't, Ellie." I turned to face her where she stood in the kitchen doorway. She wore my grey hooded jacket with the zipper pulled all the way up. Her hair fell in loose curls about her shoulders, and there was a bruise on her face below the cut on her lip. Her vivid green eyes were filled with sadness and her hands knotted in front of her. I took a deep breath and tried to stop noticing *every fucking detail* about her. "Look, Red, whatever this is... *was*... I'm done. It's over, okay? I'll help with the hotel and keeping you and your folks safe, but that's it. I have no time for anything else right now."

Her lip trembled, and she glared at me. "Because I called you *Jacob*?" The incredulity in her voice wasn't lost on me.

"No, Ellie. Because I'm just *done*, okay? You're out of my system. That's it." I shrugged and held my hands out as if to gesture how free of her I was feeling. But it was an out and out lie.

She laughed without humor and shook her head. "You really are a piece of shit, just as I first thought, huh?"

I chucked my chin. "I guess so."

———

Ellie

Colt and I traveled in complete silence back to the hotel. I had nothing to say to him. Well, nothing that would have been calm and pleasant anyway. After the shit of the events that had taken place at my house, I expected a little more from him than finding out he was getting me 'out of his system'. At least he had found a shred of human decency and taken me home. I could credit him with *that* much.

He pulled up outside my apartment and turned off the engine. I immediately opened the car door and climbed out.

I bent to glare at him through the open space. "Thanks *so* much for the ride..." I gave a bitter laugh. "For *all* of the rides, in fact. It was a *real* pleasure knowing you, *Colt*." My voice dripped with every bit of disdain and sarcasm I could muster, and I slammed the door before turning to walk toward the hotel and trying hard not to cry from the shame churning in my stomach.

I heard the car door slam and turned around to find him following me, and I stopped walking as anger gripped my insides. "Where are you going?"

He sneered. "To check on *my* business. Is that okay with you?"

Baring my teeth, I clenched my jaw, and all feelings of shame and sadness were gone and replaced by fury. He was an asshole. Speaking in as controlled a tone as I could manage, I informed him, "Just remember this is a *temporary* arrangement. And the sooner you get the hell out of the place the better."

He laughed darkly. "Do you think you should be speaking that way to your *boss*?"

"Go fuck yourself, Colt." I turned and stormed away from him as fast as I could.

"By the way, Red, I had Dee bring your personal belongings down to the hotel so the locksmith and security guys could work in peace. You can use one of the rooms there for a while."

Without facing him, I called over my shoulder. "Don't do me any favors, ass-hat. I'll stay with my parents in their living quarters."

"Suit yourself, Ellie."

"Don't worry, I will."

———

COLT

After checking in on Eamon and his wife and discussing with them their details of the changes I had arranged to the security, I left to go back to the clubhouse. Thanks to Loki's Legion fucking shit up again, I had stuff to deal with. I parked the car in the lot and made my way inside. Dee was standing behind the bar grinning like an idiot and as I walked toward the bar music began to play over the sound system forcing me to a halt.

The intro to "Folding Stars" by Biffy Clyro began to play, and I clenched my jaw, knowing full well why it had been chosen. The chorus kicked in, and *her* name rang out into the room causing my stomach to knot. I had expected something like this to happen if I had let things continue with me and Ellie, but it seemed I had put a stop to things too late. They already thought I was hooked. But they were wrong.

So. Fucking. Wrong.

I walked behind the bar to where the amp for the sound system was and flicked the switch to turn it off. "Not funny, Dee."

"Oh come on, Colt. Don't deny you have a thing for the bitchy redhead. We all know she was at your place last night. We all think it's great that you found someone after—"

I turned and jabbed my pointed index finger in her face. "Shut the *fuck* up, Delilah. You know *shit* about my fucking life so butt out and don't go pulling a stunt like that again, okay?" I barked, before storming over to the stairs.

A deep, male voice laced with concern called after me. "Hey, what the hell happened, Prez? What's going on?"

Aww fuck, not Six too. I held my fists toward the ceiling in sheer frustration. "*Nothing* happened. Now can you all just leave me the fuck alone?"

Finally, I made it upstairs to the end room and slammed the door behind me. Once inside the bathroom I stripped my clothes from my body and turned the shower to the hottest setting. I could still smell her... *taste* her. I needed to get rid of any trace of her that remained.

It was just a shame I couldn't get rid of the remnants of her that had made their way under my skin and into my fucking soul.

CHAPTER THIRTY-ONE

Ellie

Since the Sinners had taken over my dad's hotel, things had gone eerily quiet. Loki's Legion had pretty much disappeared off the face of the earth, and while my parents were celebrating the fact that business was returning—albeit slowly—to some semblance of normalcy, I was uneasy. It was like I was in a constant state of limbo, awaiting the next drastic move by the bastards who made up the Legion.

Colt had kept his distance.

I hated that I was upset by that fact. And I hated that I still couldn't get him out of my head even after the way he'd treated me. But something niggled deep at my psyche, telling me that *that* hadn't been the real him. That something else had caused him to react that way. Perhaps guilt? But there was no way I would be able to prove or disprove my theory, so I was trying hard to let it all go.

Trying hard and failing.

He had firmly lodged himself in my head and was apparently quite happy to hang around and torture me with memories of how good he could make me feel; how caring he could be when he let his guard down. I didn't *want* to miss him. Hell, I didn't want to *like* him. But I was obviously one of those stereotypical women who go for the guys that treat them mean in order to keep them keen.

And boy, did I hate myself for *all* of that shit.

Chloe and Six were loved up and looking at getting their own place as a fresh start, and I was filled with conflicting emotions of envy that she had something so wonderful, and of happiness that my best friend had found the *one man* who made her complete. I, on the other hand, was further than ever from meeting 'the one' thanks to the fact that I could now add a lack of trust of men in general to my list of fears and barriers.

It was around eight in the evening, and I was at work sitting behind the reception desk checking over the guest list, and it felt *amazing* that we actually had guests staying. I'd been busy for the first time in a long while. It didn't matter that the guests were from a Company of Sinners charter in California. They seemed like decent human beings, and they were paying customers, so all felt right with the world.

"Hey, sweetheart, can I get some extra glasses for my room? I got a buddy coming over to discuss some club business, and I got us a nice bottle of single malt for the occasion."

I lifted my chin and was greeted by the bright blue eyes of a grey-haired, bearded man with the word "President" on the left breast of his cut. My mom had checked the Company in, and this was my first time meeting their boss. But after a heads up from Mom, I had made sure to memorize his name by way of courtesy, as I always tried to do.

I smiled sweetly and nodded. "Absolutely, Mr. Carmichael. You're not going to the bar in town tonight?" I realized as soon as the words came out that it appeared prying of me, but I was just making small talk. Since they had checked in two nights before, they had apparently been going out in the evenings.

"Nah. My buddy and I got stuff to discuss that can only be dealt with behind closed doors." He winked at me and a handsome smile spread across his face. I guessed he was in his early fifties and that he would have been a real ladies man when he was younger.

I stood from my desk. "No problem. I'll get that sorted for you right now." I stepped into the back office to collect the glasses, and as the door closed behind me, a familiar, husky voice vibrated through the air and sent shivers down my spine.

Colt was the guy's buddy. How had I not put two and two together?

Not seeing him had been okay. I could *almost* pretend that he hadn't treated me like shit. I could *almost* pretend that I didn't have feelings for him. And I could *almost* pretend that there wasn't a hole in my heart that his absence from my life had created.

But now he was here. And I would have to face him.

I picked out two glasses and forced my legs to move to carry me back through to the reception desk to hand them over to Mr. Carmichael.

"There you go, Sir." My hands visibly shook, and the glasses clunked together as I passed them to the grey-haired man. I fought for control over my nerves and plastered on a smile before I tilted my chin to find Colt's eyes fixed on me. A deep crease etching his brow.

"Thank you darlin'. This here is my buddy, Colt. Colt, I'm guessing you know of Eleanor seeing as she works for you here at this fine establishment?"

Colt nodded, shifting his gaze rapidly between his friend and me. "Yeah... yeah, hi, Red."

My throat thickened with a mixture of emotions that both confused and frustrated me. "Hi."

He grimaced for a moment and then turned to his friend and chucked his chin. "You go on ahead, Slider. Be up in a minute."

Mr. Carmichael glanced my way and smiled. "Sure. Don't be bothering this young lady for too long now." With a last grin and shake of his head in Colt's direction, Mr. Carmichael, aka Slider, turned and disappeared through the door.

I twisted my fingers in front of me. "Why didn't you go with him? We have nothing to discuss."

Colt sighed and rubbed his hands over his face. "Yeah, but I wanted to check on you. You okay?"

How dare he act like he cares? "I'm perfectly fine. You can *go* now."

Ignoring my instruction, he continued. "You had any more issues with Loki's crew?"

"No. And I *said* I was fine and that you can go." I tried to sound defiant, but I could smell his familiar clean fragrance, and my heart skipped at the same time as my determination wavered.

He stepped closer, and I was grateful for the desk that stood between us as a barrier. Shaking his head, he frowned. "Fuck, I really did a job on you, *huh?*"

I thought it was a rhetorical question, but I wasn't sure.

A fluttering sensation took flight in my stomach, and I placed a hand over it as if that would stop the butterflies from dancing. "I don't know what you're referring to."

He raised his eyebrows, clearly annoyed by my reluctance to cave. "I'm *referring* to the fact that you're ice cold with me. And I don't like it."

His eyes seemed to penetrate deep into me, and I inhaled sharply. "But... you made it clear how you felt, so what do you expect?"

Nodding, he rubbed his chin. "You're right. And I deserve the cold shoulder. But it doesn't mean I have to like it."

I had no words. No brain to mouth function. What was I supposed to do with his admission? Should I read between the lines? Should I shrug and walk away with a simple "Yeah well fuck you"? I had no clue.

So I remained silent.

It didn't deter him. "I was an ass. I know I was. And I shouldn't have treated you like that. Not after what you'd been through."

I snorted at his half-assed attempt at an apology. "Is that your way of saying sorry, Colt?"

He shrugged. "I never apologize so I can't say I'm an expert in it but... *yeah*, Red, I'm sorry for the things I said and did. And I... I wish we could go back to the way things were."

I crossed my arms over my chest. "So you'd have a place to sink your dick? I don't think so."

His jaw clenched. "Ellie, you know that's not what I mean." The sincerity in his eyes tugged on my heart strings and once again I was rendered speechless. If I had attempted to speak right then, it would have made no sense at all, and I'm sure I would have cried.

He turned to walk toward the door, and the needy, whiny bitch inside of me wanted more. "Is that it? Are we done?" I asked harshly.

He stopped and turned to peer at me over his shoulder. "I don't *want* us to be done. But honestly, I don't think I can give you what you need."

Oh, so now he's a mind reader? "And what the *hell* is it you think I need?"

He paused for a moment and closed his eyes. When he opened them again, he fixed me with a pain-filled gaze. "I think you need someone to love you. To be *in love* with you. And I... I just can't *be* that guy. My heart belongs to Maria and it always will."

My lip trembled as I searched my mind for words to form a reply that wouldn't make me sound like a desperate mess.

"Am I right, Red?" There was something akin to hope in his eyes. Hope that he was *wrong*. That I could deal with some kind of one-sided, loveless relationship with him just so that I could have *part* of him. I wasn't that desperate. Jeez.

But he *was* right. I *did* want love. I wanted what Chloe and Six had found. I didn't want to play second place to the ghost of Colt's dead wife. And as much as my heart was screaming at me to take what I could get, my head was telling me no. That I was worth more. That I deserved so much more than he could offer me.

I told him through gritted teeth, "You're *so* damn right."

With a sad smile and a defeated nod, he walked away through the door toward his friend's room.

CHAPTER THIRTY-TWO

Ellie

Why the hell he insisted on torturing me with his physical presence at the hotel was something I had several theories about. He'd just 'pop in' when he was passing. Or he'd call in to meet with my dad when he knew he was out with my mom. It was driving me insane. So much so that I called Chloe and demanded that we go shopping for new house stuff. Thankfully she was so damned excited at the prospect of moving in with Six that she jumped at the chance.

She picked me up at ten, and we headed off for the city. I was relieved to be getting away from home, even if it was only for a few hours. As we left town, we passed Colt driving a car I didn't recognize. I avoided eye contact but managed a furtive glance as he passed us. He looked different somehow. He'd had a haircut and trimmed his beard. I figured he was taking the whole hotel business a little too seriously, and he looked kinda weird all business-like. It shocked me to discover that I preferred him unkempt, and at that point, I tried to push the thought of him from my mind, determined not to let him spoil another day.

It was so good to spend time with my best friend again. I knew it was deliberate, but she hadn't talked about Six at all. In light of the shopping trip, I guessed she must be dying to talk about their plans for their new home. Even when we were rifling through bedding designs, and she was trying to decide on a color scheme for their bedroom, his name remained unmentioned. Again when we wandered around Pottery Barn looking at quirky little pieces of furniture not *once* did she say "Six would love this" or "This is Six's favorite color." It was weird, and beginning to get to me that she felt she couldn't even talk about him in front of me. We found a cute little restaurant and went in to grab a table for lunch, and when the waiter had taken our drink order, I decided it was time to let her off the hook.

"Look, I know what you're doing okay? And really you don't need to."

Tilting her head, she frowned. "Huh? What are you talking about?"

"Chloe, we're shopping for linens for your *new* house. A house you're moving into with Six. The man you absolutely adore. Yet his name hasn't fallen from your lips *once* the whole time we've been out today."

She dropped her head and sighed. "Ugh. You got me. I just... I didn't want to rub your face in my relationship status. Not since you told me what's been going on with Colt."

The memory of our long phone conversation after I'd drunk several Jack and Coke's came back to me, making me cringe. "Just because I fall for the douche bags of the world doesn't mean I'm not happy for you, you dumb-ass."

Her hands came to cover her mouth and her eyes widened. "Oh my God. You *have* fallen for him."

Me and my big, stupid mouth. "No, not... that's not what... oh, shit." I huffed and defiantly folded my arms across my chest as I slouched back into my chair.

"When we talked, you just called him all the curse words you could think of, and were angry that you'd had sex with him but... You never mentioned that you'd *fallen* for him. Oh God, Ellie, sweetie." She leaned over the table and reached for me.

Thankfully I was too far away, and I scowled at her. "Nu-uh. Don't go pitying me. I don't need that. And I haven't fallen for him. He just—he gets under my damn skin. And I can't stop thinking about him. But it's the stupid things about him like his smell. His dumb grin. His eyes."

She pressed her lips together and eyed me with a sad, crumpled brow. "Exactly. I'm sorry honey, but that means you *have* fallen for him."

There was no point in arguing. She was my best friend and could see through me like I was a sheet of glass. And what was the point in denying what I'd come to realize myself?

I took a deep breath and leaned toward her. "Yeah. Well, there's no point dwelling on it."

"But you could work it all out. You could tell him how you feel. I bet deep down he feels—"

"No! Fuck no, Chloe. Do you know what he said to me? He told me he can't love me because..." The memory of his words caused my eyes to close and my stomach to knot.

"Hey, whatever he said, I bet he didn't mean it. Guys talk bullshit when they don't know how to handle their feelings, honey. You only have to look at me and Six to know that."

Her voice was filled with so much hope that I almost burst into tears, knowing full well that he had meant every damn word.

I shook my head. "No. He said he *can't* love me because

he's still in love with Maria and will never love another woman. *She* was it for him. And she's gone. Apparently, she took his ability to move on to the grave." My lip trembled.

"Oh no. Honey, I'm so, so sorry. I can't... I don't know what to say to that."

"Me neither. He almost offered me a *kind* of relationship provided I didn't expect him to love me but... I couldn't accept that."

"But he may change. His feelings for you would strengthen, Ellie. I know it."

That useless hope was there again. I smiled, though feeling anything but happy, and swallowed past the tightness in my throat. "No. And I won't do that to myself. I won't. I want a future with a man who loves me desperately. Someone who can't stand to be without me for long." I shrugged, trying not to let my emotions get the better of me. "I want what you and Six have."

Chloe's cell began to ring, and she glanced down at her purse but didn't reach for it. "I say we have a drink and ditch the car in the city overnight. I can get Six to bring me back for it tomorrow."

"Aren't you going to answer your phone?"

She shook her head. "Nope. You and I are going to get drunk. Shopping can wait."

The ringing stopped, and she waved at a passing waiter to get his attention. He didn't see her and the ringing started again.

"Look, Chloe, just answer it okay. It's fine."

She sighed and reached into her purse with an eye roll and a sigh. "It's just Six." She stared at the screen but still didn't answer. "He must need me to pick something up."

"Just go ahead and answer it."

She slipped out from the table and raised her hand. "I'll be two minutes. Promise." She put the phone to her ear and quickly made her way to a quieter part of the busy restaurant.

I managed to grab the attention of a waiter and ordered a couple of glasses of Jack Daniel's, figuring that Chloe had a good point about getting drunk. A little oblivion may just be what I needed.

Chloe was gone a while longer than I expected and I was beginning to think she had ditched me in favor of her beau. But eventually, she returned. Her face was pale and her eyes were bloodshot. She sat down opposite me but her hands were shaking, and her eyes were wide.

I feigned annoyance. "Finally. Did you guys have a fight or phone sex or something?" I tried to lighten the dark mood that had descended on her, knowing that whatever the hell it was would resolve itself quickly. It always did with those two.

She leaned across the table and took my hand in hers. Her skin was clammy, and she squeezed me a little too hard.

My stomach lurched and I shook my head. "Chloe, what's going on?"

"Um... I don't know how... I can't believe..."

"Chloe what the hell happened? You're scaring me."

"I... um..." Her lower lip trembled, and tears escaped the corners of her eyes, spilling down her pallid skin.

"Chloe?" I snapped at her needing answers. Was it my dad? *Oh God, my dad.* A cold shiver traveled my spine and I widened my eyes. "Just tell me."

"C-Colt's dead."

CHAPTER THIRTY-THREE

Ellie

The buzzing in my ears wouldn't stop. As the cab rushed us toward Rose Acres, I stared out of the window, trying to make sense in my head of the news I'd received only minutes before. I was numb. Completely and utterly numb. After Chloe's announcement, I had gone into some kind of trance. A stupor. I had stood and walked toward the exit of the restaurant with the maître d' calling after me that I hadn't paid for our drinks. Luckily Chloe had been more aware of her surroundings and had explained my mistake to the man who had then told her the drinks were on the house.

She had jogged after me and called a cab from her cell seeing as neither of us were thinking straight enough to drive and I'd drunk a couple of JDs. Her hand gripped mine as we rode in silence, but I couldn't look at her. I couldn't move. I wasn't even seeing the scenery outside of the cab as it whizzed by in a blur of color.

None of it made sense. How the hell had things gone from bad to so much worse in such a small amount of time? And *why* was he dead? *How* was he dead? I seemed to remember asking, but Chloe wouldn't reveal that information to me. She wanted me to go with her to the clubhouse and let Six explain. *Why would it be better coming from him?* But all I wanted to do was go home and be by myself. Let the horrific news sink in. Come to terms with the fact that I had lost the man I loved before I even had him.

The cab pulled up outside the compound and Weasel was waiting to open the gates. I guessed Chloe had texted ahead to tell the guys we were almost there. Weasel paid the driver and locked the gates behind the cab after it exited the compound and I watched in a daze. Chloe helped me from the car, and I stood on jellied legs that almost gave way beneath me. Although I'd had a couple of drinks, the drunken stupor I was evidently trapped in was more to do with the surreal situation I was in, and not the effect of the alcohol.

Nausea washed over me, and I retched, a small amount of acidic liquid left my throat and I lurched forward. Weasel appeared and caught me before I fell. I wanted to tell him I wasn't drunk. Although why that even mattered, I don't know.

He slipped an arm around my waist. "Come on, let's get her inside. How has she been?" He asked Chloe behind my back as I concentrated on placing one foot in front of the other.

"How the hell do you *think* she's been for God's sake, dumbass? The man she loves has just been found dead." She spat back venomously.

"Hey, I was only askin'. No need to bite my fuckin' head off, CD." I'd never heard the hard nut guy sound so hurt.

Chloe sighed. "No, you're right. I'm sorry Weasel. I shouldn't have cussed at you. I just... I can't believe it. It doesn't seem real. And Ellie's just disappeared into her own head. She won't talk. She hasn't cried. I don't know what to do."

"Give it time. It'll probably hit her suddenly, and that's when she'll really need you to be there for her. I'm still in shock myself. He's... he's gone. Just like that. Just because of some dumb argument between two groups of adults. It's fucking stupid."

Regardless of the fact they were talking about me as if I wasn't there, I couldn't find the energy to argue. Before I knew it, we had somehow made our way up the stairs and into the clubhouse. The place was eerily quiet apart from hushed voices whispering to each other as we arrived. I glanced over to the bar and for the first time since I had met this bunch of bad-ass bikers, I saw something other than disdain in Delilah's eyes. Her cheeks were glistening, and she had a scrunched up tissue in her hands. Her lip trembled as she peered at me with a pitiful frown and a bizarre urge to hug her washed over me. I guess *that* may have been the alcohol.

Six rushed over and scooped Chloe up in his arms as she burst into tears and I looked on blankly, unable to feel anything at that precise moment. It was as if I wasn't actually there. Like I was watching it from a distance. Or like the people around me were actors in some sick, dark show about my life and I was observing it all playing out.

Six came to me and took my upper arms in a firm grip. He crouched to make eye contact. "Hey, Red. Are you okay? I'm so fucking sorry, sweetheart." His glassy eyes locked on mine with such sincerity but all I could think was that I wanted to tell him not to call me that. That's what Colt called me. But the words wouldn't come, and anyway before I could even think of forming words I was enveloped in muscular arms and pressed to Six's chest in a bear hug.

"Come on and sit down. Dee, get a round of drinks. I think Ellie's in shock."

I ended up sitting on one of the worn out leather couches by the bar with Chloe gripping my hand.

"So what the hell happened? Where is he?" Chloe's voice wavered as she asked the questions *I* should have asked.

Six frowned and rubbed his hands over his face. "He... um... He was driving back into town, and he got a flat. He pulled over to change the tire and one of Loki's crew just... shot him. He was driving by and fucking shot him in the head." He lowered his head, and a pained sob left his chest. I watched as droplets of moisture hit the tile floor beneath him.

"Oh God, no. But... how did you find out?"

"I got a call from Hank at the diner. He saw it all go down. Said that um... Colt had been driving a new car back into town. I didn't even know he was getting a new car. That's how little fucking time I've spent with him lately." He laughed without humor but then something—I guess guilt— caused him to wince.

I remembered seeing Colt in that car coming back into town as Chloe and I left. I remembered thinking how different he had looked. How it was really strange that his hair was shorter, but I couldn't see his neck tattoos. Had he been wearing make-up to cover them? And if so, why? Since when did he care what people thought? My mind was whirring with such incoherent shit. Colt wearing make-up? I really was in shock if I thought *that* was a possibility.

A conversation he and I had had about his family sprang to mind. He had cared what his family thought of him. That's why he had left home. But that's also when all the tattoos had been done. None of it made sense.

Then it hit me.

"It wasn't him!" I blurted.

Six focused on me and leaned over to squeeze my knee. "Hey, I know this is hard on you, Ellie. And I'm sorry but—"

I jumped to my feet with a rush of adrenaline. "Six, it wasn't him. It wasn't *Jacob*. It was... It was his twin brother."

Chloe and Six peered up at me with such pity in their eyes. But then Chloe stood and gripped my hands in hers. "Come and sit down, sweetie. Have a drink. This has hit you hard, and that's totally understandable. No-one is expecting you to accept it all right away." Her voice was soft and reassuring. "I don't know who Jacob is or if he has a twin, but I think you're getting yourself all muddled. Maybe you need to have a nap."

"Chloe, I don't need a fucking lie down. We have to find Colt and tell him his brother is dead!"

CHAPTER THIRTY-FOUR

ELLIE

Six paced up and down the patch of the floor before me with his hands on his head. The crease in his brow was on the verge of becoming a permanent scar due to the depth of the indentation.

He stopped directly in front of me and dropped his hands to his sides with a slap. "Okay, so I knew his name was Jacob, I'll admit to that. The fact accidentally slipped out during a drunken conversation we had, but a *twin?*" He shook his head. "I'm sorry, Ellie, but I'm with Chloe here. I think you're in some kind of post traumatic denial or some psychotherapy bullshit that only Cain's woman could deal with. I would've *known* if he had a brother. *Especially* a twin."

I crossed my arms defiantly. "*Would* you though? How many of these drunken conversations have you had? How much do you *really* know about him?"

His nostrils flared, and his hands came up to rest low on his hips. He wasn't enamored with my accusatory tone and it was evident by the way he gritted his teeth and leaned toward me. "Hey, I know him better than *anyone*, Ellie. I'm his VP for chrisssake. No-one knows him like I do. No-one."

Chloe stepped forward and rested a hand on his chest. "Hey, baby, don't get angry, okay? She didn't mean anything bad by it." Her attention then returned to me. "Ellie, honey, I know this is hard for you to deal with. I totally understand. But maybe once you've calmed down you'll—"

"I'm calm!" I shouted. "Okay, I *was* calm. But you guys need to listen to me. It. Wasn't. Him. I *know* it wasn't him."

Without taking his piercing glare from me, he called, "Hey, Dee, Colt's bike is still in the lot, yeah?"

There was a pause before she replied, "Umm... no?"

His brow crumpled once again. "It isn't?"

We all looked over to where she stood leaning against the bar. "No, it's been gone since real early yesterday."

"And you never thought to mention it?" Six was the one with the accusatory tone now.

She slammed her glass down and pushed herself to a straight up standing position. "I'm not his fucking babysitter, Six. Jeez. And what does that prove anyway?"

Six rubbed the hair on his chin and seemed to disappear into his own head for a while until Chloe pulled him back to reality. "Six, what is it?"

"I guess he must have traded his bike in for the new car. I never thought he'd do that. I... I don't get why he'd do that."

Chloe stroked her hand up and down his arm. "Honey, I really don't understand what you're talking about."

He lifted his head and glanced between us both. "He was found with a totally different car, CD, remember? So that means he must have taken his bike to the place he was buying the car he was in when they shot him and traded it in. But... why would he trade in his bike for *another* car? Why not trade in his other car? He's a biker, not a fucking family car driver.

It's making less sense the more I think about it. Or... If he was buying a new car why didn't he just ask one of us to go pillion and we could've rode his bike back, following him from wherever he picked up the car. But he loved that bike. And he never mentioned getting rid of it."

I made an unladylike growling sound and let my head tilt back. "Urgh! You guys, for the love of *all* that's freaking holy, will you please listen to me? Colt went *nowhere* to pick up a damn car because it wasn't him driving the car he was supposedly found with. It. Was. His. Fucking. Twin." All eyes were on me now. "Has anyone thought to try and call his cell?"

"It was switched off when I called yesterday. I was going to invite him to dinner with me and Chloe. She figured she would invite you too, but I couldn't get a hold of him so..."

I pulled the cell from my pocket and dialed his number. It went right to voicemail. *Shit.*

"Okay, we need to get the guys out looking for Colt. He has to be out there somewhere. I have no idea where but—"

Six blurted, "I do."

My attention snapped to him. "You do?"

He nodded. "There's this place he used to take Maria. Baylor's Point. It was kind of their little romantic spot. He still goes there when he's down and shit. If he *is* still alive and his cell is off, chances are it's because he's there."

In a matter of minutes, I was on the back of Six's bike in the leathers I'd borrowed from Dee, and we were heading at high speed toward Baylor's Point like Six had mentioned. Everyone had insisted I should be the one to go. I think initially they figured that when he *wasn't* there, it would finally sink in that he *had* been killed. But I knew he hadn't. I can't really put into words, and I won't be so twee as to say I could *feel* it. But I knew he would be there at his special place.

I just knew it deep down.

After thirty minutes we pulled off the road onto a dirt track, and the terrain became bumpy and uneven. The bike jerked me around, and I gripped Six with as much strength as I could muster in my fragile state of mind. When he eventually pulled the bike to a halt, I swung my leg over the hunk of metal and climbed off. I quickly pulled off the helmet I had been forced to wear and almost removed my ears in the process.

Six pointed to a place beyond us. "Through those trees. *If he's here, that's where you'll find him.*"

I handed him the helmet and glanced around the place. No bike. *Shit.*

"I guess you're clocking the fact the bike ain't here too, huh?" I heard his tone, and as much I had expected it to be thick with 'I told you so' it was actually filled with sadness.

"Yeah... but I have to check, Six. Can you wait here?" He nodded, and I began to walk in the direction I had been pointed.

I pushed spiky branches away from my path and watched my step as best I could but the light wasn't great in the dense wood, and it was all I could do to stop from falling. Eventually, I came to an opening in the trees, and my breath caught as I took in the spectacular vista before me. Red sandy rocks lined the deep crater, and the sun was beginning to descend below the horizon. The sky was set alight with orange and red hues like a meteor had only just made impact. I could see why Colt loved the place so much, and as soon as the thought of him entered my head I fell to my knees. He wasn't there after all. My heart shattered into a million pieces, and I covered my face with my hands as the tears began to fall, and realization really did begin to sink in.

I had so desperately wanted to be right. I had so desperately wanted to find him here, even if this was the place that reminded him of his dead wife. Just knowing that Loki's Legion hadn't taken his life would have been enough. But now the confirmation I hadn't wanted had smacked me so hard in the solar plexus that I could barely breathe.

He *was* gone, and there was nothing I could do now but grieve. Although I was grieving for a love I'd never even possessed. Why the hell had I fallen so fast and so damn hard for a man who could never love me back? A man who was everything I had never wanted yet couldn't stand the thought of being without. It was stupid and ridiculous, but the truth was that no-one had ever made me feel the way he did. So protected, so desired. Whatever he'd done to me had caused me to love him. Every broken-hearted, smashed up, stubborn-assed inch of him.

I lifted my gaze just as the sun disappeared, and a thick silence fell heavily over the landscape. I knelt there looking out at the breath taking view that had meant so much to Colt, and I could almost picture him sitting there, staring wistfully into the distance and wishing Maria was beside him. My heart ached for his loss as well as my own, and more tears spilled silently from my eyes.

A hand rested on my shoulder and squeezed. I was so glad Six had brought me. There was no way I could have driven home alone. I lifted my hand and rested it on his and trying hard to plaster on a smile I eventually lifted my gaze to meet his.

"Red, what the *hell* are you doing here in my spot, and why are you crying like someone died?"

CHAPTER THIRTY-FIVE

COLT

What the fuck?

Ellie stared up at me, open mouthed for a few moments. Her pink-tinged, tear-stained cheeks rapidly lost their color and I wondered what the hell was going on. I was about to repeat my questions when she leapt to her feet and jumped on me. I instinctively gripped her ass with one hand to stop her from falling into the damn crater as she sobbed openly into my neck. A trickle of warm tears spilled down the collar of my T-shirt, and I stroked her hair trying to console her even though I had no idea what I was consoling her over.

After letting her wail and cling to me for a few minutes, I heard heavy footsteps running through the trees, and I was just about to drop Red onto the ground so I could protect her from whatever asshole had followed her out there, when Six broke through into the clearing.

His eyes widened, and he stopped in his tracks only a couple of feet away. "Fuck me! You *are* alive, you son of a bitch!" He, too, lunged for me, and we ended up in some kind of bizarre group hug. I seemed to be the only one without a clue what the hell was going on. He began to bombard me with questions and so my own had to wait. "What are you *doing* out here? Where's the bike? Why is your cell off? Why the hell didn't you call?"

"What *is* this? The fucking Spanish Inquisition? I felt like a break, okay? And so I rode up here with my tent and slept out last night. The bike is through there." I nodded toward the trees. "And my cell is off to stop you pains in the ass from calling me at all hours of the freaking day and night. You're not my fucking mother, Six, and *that's* why I didn't call. Jeez can't a guy have some damn privacy for a few hours?"

Ignoring my annoyance completely, he slapped me hard on the back. "Well I can tell you this, Colt, I've *never* been so damned relieved to see your fucking ugly face alive and well, man." He squeezed me so tight I expected Ellie to pass out seeing as she was the meat in our weird biker sandwich.

"Okay, can someone tell me what the hell this is? Why would you think I was dead? You're freaking me the fuck out here."

Six pulled away from me, and I released Red's rather fine, leather clad ass, allowing her to slide her feet to the floor. Six rubbed his chin and chewed on his lip, his furtive gaze flitting between me and Red. "I don't really know how to tell you." He stepped back a little. "Maybe Ellie can explain better?" He looked at her and widened his eyes in encouragement.

My attention turned to her once more, and she wiped moisture away from her red-rimmed, puffy eyes. "Oh God, Colt. Something terrible has happened."

I rolled my eyes. "Well, you don't fucking say." There was absolutely no need for the sarcasm dripping from my voice but the longer this went on, the angrier I was getting.

Ellie reached out and squeezed my arm. "I think... I think your brother may have been..." She swallowed hard. "Killed."

Her words didn't really sink in, and I shook my head. "What? How the...? What are you...? What?"

Six chucked his chin at me. "I think we'd better go sit down somewhere."

Even more confused now, I nodded and led the way to my make-shift camp in a clearing through the trees off to the right. It wasn't my usual spot, but the branches had provided some shelter in the storm that had passed over the area the night before. My old one-man tent was past its best, and I hadn't liked the idea of getting soaked to the skin as I slept.

Like I was inviting them into my house, I gestured at a log for them to sit on and I sat on a rock opposite. "Okay. Why the fuck are you talking about my brother?"

Ellie flinched at the harshness of my tone, and I instantly regretted it.

With a trembling lip, she began. "There was an incident. I don't know all the details... but Loki's Legion... um... a man was shot dead on the road into town as he stood by his car. The man... he looked a lot like..."

My head began to spin, and my heart rate increased to the point of sheer panic. *The dead man looked like me.* I knew what she was trying but failing to say. Loki's Legion had shot and killed my twin brother, Jared, thinking he was me.

Those dumb fucking evil bastards have killed my brother? Jared's... dead?

Certain incidents and sensations of the past day began to click into place as my mind raced back to the day before when I was sitting looking out over the landscape. Pain had shot through me like a knife slicing through my skull, taking me completely by surprise and scaring me half to death. I thought it was an aneurysm or something it was so damned painful, and I had almost called 9 1 1. But as soon as it had occurred, it was gone and I had been left with a dull ache in my chest, like a deep sense of grief and sadness that seeped into my bones. I hadn't been able to shake the dark cloud hanging over me since it happened but I'd had no explanation until now.

Now, I knew what it was.

"They shot him in the head," I said the words out loud but to no-one in particular as I stared at an ant carrying a twig along the ground beside my feet.

"H-how did you know that?" Six sounded stunned. Like he expected me to tell him I somehow already knew about the shooting.

"I... think I felt it happen." I shook my head as the ridiculousness of what I was saying reverberated in my brain. Jared and I were chalk and cheese. Light and dark. Day and night. We'd never had the 'twin thing' you read about in magazines. You know, the telepathy and close bond shit. There was no finishing off of each other's sentences. No going after the same girl because our tastes were so alike. No pretending to be each other to piss off our mom. No feeling each other's pain and suffering. We just weren't connected that way. We'd shared a womb, a birthday and an identical appearance but that was it. Yet, for some strange reason, I felt something when his life was taken. I wasn't able to connect the dots until Six and Ellie were breaking the news, but the pain I had felt in my head was no coincidence.

A mixture of emotions vied for supremacy within me but one familiar feeling began to bubble deep within me, and it eventually drowned out the sadness and despair crushing my insides.

Rage.

Building and building until my heart almost beat its way from my chest, and my jaw was on the verge of cracking from the pressure of my clenched teeth. Something tickled at my wrist, and I glanced down to find a trail of blood oozing from where my nails had dug into the skin of my palms as I squeezed my fists into white knuckled, tight balls.

A red mist descended upon me, and I stood, tilted my head back and allowed a guttural, incoherent roar of expletives to leave my chest. As if moving of their own volition my feet began to move, and I rushed to my bike where it leaned beside the tent and swung my leg over the gas tank. Thankfully the keys were in my pocket, and I tugged them free and thrust them into the ignition.

I heard footsteps behind me. "Colt, no! Wait! Please!" Ellie's panic-filled voice rang out and ricocheted off the tree trunks, but I ignored her.

"Hey, Ellie, just let him go, okay? Let him go." Thankfully Six understood me and didn't try to stop me. Loki's Legion had just declared war, and I was very willing to take them up on it. This was the last time they would mess with my club or me.

The. Last. Damn. Time.

CHAPTER THIRTY-SIX

Colt

There's a verse in the book of Exodus in the Bible that folks use to justify getting revenge on people who have wronged them. I'm guessing you will know the verse I'm talking about. In my opinion, this verse can be misunderstood, especially if you read on past it. Now, I'm not a particularly religious guy. What I know of the Bible I learned by accident. I've never been great on forgiveness either, another prominent theme in the Bible. But as I rode toward the Legion clubhouse, hell-bent on taking a life, a million different thoughts ran through my head. I've never considered myself weak. I'm in no way a pushover but what would more death do to improve my situation?

Would killing one of the Loki's Legion bastards in retaliation make me feel better? Possibly. But only temporarily. And taking a life for a life approach would just further the war between the clubs.

I wanted peace.

An easy life. Maybe it was an age thing. I don't know. But

I was getting tired of the fact that the life I was embroiled in was so violent and angst-ridden.

I thought back to when Cain had wanted to leave the Company of Sinners after he'd found out Melody was pregnant and only *now* did I really get it. Although realistically I didn't want to leave the company. The club was my life after all. But I did want things to be different. Maybe forgiveness wouldn't happen; they'd killed my brother for chrissake, but maybe... just maybe there was a way forward.

I found myself at the morgue on the outskirts of town instead of my intended destination, and as I stared up at the stark exterior, I wondered what the hell had brought Jared here to Rose Acres in the first place. Why had he tracked me down?

After parking up the bike, I walked over and pushed through the doors and stepped into the reception area. With its white walls and fancy flower displays it made me think I'd walked up to the fucking pearly gates themselves, until the smell of disinfectant chemicals assaulted my nostrils.

A door opened, and a woman of around fifty, wearing a white smock came to the desk. When she noticed me her cheeks colored bright pink and she patted her hair.

"Oh... hello there, sir. Can I help you?"

I cleared my throat. "Um... I think you have the body of my twin brother?" There was a sentence I had never imagined saying. "Although... um you have him down as me." And there was another bizarre sentence.

Her brow crumpled to a frown and she tilted her head. "May I take a name?"

"Coltman."

"Ah, yes. May I ask what your visit is in connection with?"

Okay, how the hell do I put this? "Like I said, lady, he was my twin brother. I'm here to collect his personal effects and shit."

She cringed. "I see. Well, I'm afraid there is a criminal investigation under way, and the body can't be released nor visited just yet."

I decided to go on the pity offensive considering the way she had blushed when I had walked in. Stepping closer to the desk, I gave her one of my best puppy dog stares, and glanced down at her name badge. "Aww, come on, Sadie. He was my brother. I just want to find out why he was in town. We weren't in contact much, and I figure there was an important reason he came looking for me. Surely you wouldn't make me wait? He was my brother."

Reiterating the last point seemed to do the trick, and she glanced over her shoulder. "Look, my boss goes for lunch in an hour. Can you come back?" Her whispered voice wavered nervously.

I nodded. "Sure, thanks so much, Sadie. I really appreciate your help." I turned to leave the building when her voice stopped me in my tracks.

"Hey, if it's any consolation, it would have been a quick death. He wouldn't have known a thing."

My stomach lurched, and I half turned my face to thank her over my shoulder before leaving. I climbed back on the bike and made my way to my house. I knew full well that the guys at the club would find out soon enough that I was alive, and I just needed some space. Being the center of attention was something I couldn't stomach at the best of times.

I arrived at my empty home and didn't even bother to go into the living room. I made my way up the stairs and into my bedroom and collapsed in a heap on my bed.

I was woken by a loud banging on my door and I leapt from the bed in a panic. When I glanced over at the clock, I realized I had been sleeping for longer than I'd intended and I had missed the opportunity to go see Jared's body. *Fuck it.*

When I reached the door and pulled it open, I was greeted by a couple uniform officers from RAPD. Oh great. Here we go.

"Yeah?" I was aware that my greeting was far from cordial, but then again my prior dealings with the Police had never ended well.

"Jacob Coltman?"

I rolled my eyes. "I think you know the answer to that. Now whaddya want?"

One of the men remained silent as the other continued. "May we come in? I'm afraid the matter we need to discuss with you isn't one that should be dealt with on your porch."

With a deep sigh, I stepped aside to allow the officers to enter my home. It wasn't the first time I'd had cops in my house but this time was probably the worst situation. I knew why they were here, but they probably knew that I wouldn't exactly co-operate. They knew that the clubs dealt their own justice and usually left well alone. But I figured they had to at least appear to be doing their bit.

With a wee, yet snide grin, I asked. "Now can I offer either of you hard-working gentlemen a drink? Tea, coffee? Arsenic?"

They both sat on my couch and glanced at each other. "No, thank you. Please sit, Mr. Coltman."

I sat on the couch opposite. "Well you can't say I wasn't polite," I chuntered under my breath.

"Mr. Coltman. You have an identical twin brother by the name of…" He glanced at his notebook. "Jared. Is that correct?"

I dropped my chin and raised my eyebrows in a "Really?" kind of way.

"Well, I'm afraid we have some very bad news to share with you."

I held up my hand to stop the cop from carrying on further as my stomach knotted with a combination of anger and sadness. "Look, I know what happened, okay? Those bastards killed him because they thought he was me. And instead of letting us deal with it you want me to get involved in the whole charging, imprisoning bullshit. You *know* that won't happen. It's not the way we do things.

"And before you get your lace panties in a knot, I won't be seeking my own revenge. Too much shit has gone down over the years, and I've had *enough*. I want to bury my brother and move the fuck on. But first I need to find out why he was here. I know there must have been a reason. I can't call our mother until I know all the details so I'm hoping you can shed some light on this. He was the apple of her fucking eye, and it'll *kill* her to know he died because of me. It fucking kills me too. I should be the dead one. Not him. Not Jared.

"I appreciate you trying to solve this situation but I think you know you can't. So please... just tell me what I need to know and then leave. If you have to go ahead and press charges, you'll have to do it without my help." My chest heaved after my rushed monolog and the two bewildered guys just stared at me.

"Um... Sure okay. I hate to ask this but would you be able to officially identify him from a photograph?"

I swallowed hard and nodded as my stomach roiled.

The cop handed me a photograph of my brother's pale, lifeless face. They had cleaned him up I guessed as there was no sign of injury to the front but his eyes were closed and circled with purple. I cleared my throat. "Yeah. Yeah, that's him."

"Thank you, sir. I know that was difficult, and I appreciate your assistance. Look, I have a letter for you. It was found in the victim's car, and hopefully that will contain the answers you need." He handed me an envelope, and they stood. "I really hope you will reconsider your stance on helping us, Mr. Coltman. They killed your *brother*. Surely *he* deserves justice."

I clenched my jaw and couldn't make eye contact for fear I may throat punch the ass-hat. "Don't even fucking *pretend* to play the guilt trip on me. It won't work."

Without further words, the two cops left my house and I slammed the door with a little too much force causing a couple pictures to fall off the wall and smash on the floor.

I closed my eyes and took a long, deep breath. What the hell was in the letter? And would it answer my questions or just lead to more? There was only one way to find out.

CHAPTER THIRTY-SEVEN

Ellie

I hated being at the clubhouse. It was like being in a goddamn goldfish bowl. All eyes were trained on me as I paced up and down in front of the bar. But Six had insisted I come back there after our encounter with Colt at Baylor's Point. I, on the other hand, just wanted to find Colt and check on him after what he'd just discovered.

"He won't appreciate you being all up in his face right now, Ellie," had been Six's response.

I just wanted to see him. I didn't have to stay. But I wanted to make sure he was coping okay with the news. And that he hadn't done anything hot headed and stupid like go and kill one of Loki's Legion in retaliation. We'd heard nothing, however, and I was hoping that the 'no news is good news' scenario was correct in this case.

Hours passed, and I needed to know. I pulled Chloe to one side. "Hey, sweetie. Could you take me home? I want to shower and..." My words trailed off as she cocked her head to one side and her pursed lips told me she wasn't buying it.

She grabbed my arm and dragged me out into the yard. "What you *mean* is will I take you to *Colt's* house, right?"

I cringed. "Um..."

"You must think I'm as dumb as a bag of rocks, Ellie."

I sighed in defeat. "Look, I get why Six thinks I should keep away, but the guy just heard that his brother has been murdered. He may think he's strong and doesn't need anyone, but he needs friends right now. I just want to check on him." She momentarily closed her eyes, and her head fell back. Sure signs that she was caving. "Please, Chloe."

Returning to her attention to me, she scowled. "We'll have to go right now. Before anyone notices we've gone. And Six will be so pissed at me, so you owe me big time."

I grappled her into a hug. "Thank you. Thank you so much."

She rushed to her car as I opened the huge metal gates and closed them again once she pulled her car out. I climbed into the passenger seat and slammed the door.

Chloe glanced into her rearview. "Oh shit."

I swiveled myself around to see Six behind the metal gates shaking his head and resting his hands low on his hips.

Chloe pulled the car up outside just as a cop car drove away and I gasped. "Oh god. What did he do?"

"Do you want me to wait for you? He wasn't in the back of the cop car, so chances are he's either not home or they had no reason to arrest him."

"Just wait and see if he answers the door. If not, then I'll come back with you to face Six."

"And if he *does*?"

I chewed on my lip for a moment. "If he does then I need to speak to him. You'll have to pass on my apologies to Six."

She shrugged. "Go ahead then. Go see. But... be careful okay? He may be pissed as hell at you for being there."

I nodded as I opened the door and climbed out of the car. Slowly and hesitantly I made my way onto the porch and raised my hand ready to knock, but the door swung open.

"What are you doing here?" His gruff voice and harsh question was no warm welcome.

"I came to check on you. Are you okay?" As soon as I asked, I realized what a dumb question it was.

He gave a dark laugh without a shred of humor. "What do *you* think, Red?"

I took a deep breath. "I think you're a guy who's had some shitty news and needs a friend right now."

He laughed again. "Oh really? And you're my *friend* now? Huh? Is that it?"

I shrugged. "I—I'd like to be."

He stepped aside. "You'd better come on in then... *friend*."

I wasn't too keen on his tone when he over-pronounced the word, but I glanced back at Chloe and waved with a confident smile. She had to think I was fine, or she wouldn't leave. And I needed her to leave.

She waved back and started her engine. Mouthing the words 'Take care' and 'I love you' she pulled away and drove off down the street. I looked back to Colt where he stood in his doorway; a menacing grin on his face and I wondered what I was about to walk into.

But like a fly walking willingly into the spider's web, I stepped inside his home, and he closed the door.

In a split second and before I could think, Colt pushed me up against the wall and crushed his mouth to mine sucking my breath from my body. His strong hand pulled and pinned both of mine in place above my head, and his other hand somehow managed to slip down the front of my pants and inside my panties.

He pulled away as his eyes blazed, searing into me with

emotions I had never seen in him before. "I'm gonna fuck you raw. And then we'll see if you're my friend. We both know you've got some pretty dark desires baby, and I'm here to make your fantasies a reality."

His mouth was on mine again, and his fingers slipped inside of me. I bit down on his lip.

Hard.

He yowled and stepped back releasing me and covering his mouth with his hand. "What the fuck did you do *that* for?" I knew I'd drawn blood from the metallic tang in my mouth.

My chest heaved as I righted my clothing. "I came to see if you're okay, Colt. Not to be fucking molested. Jeez, why would you *pull* a stunt like that? That's *not* who you are!"

His brow creased, and he lowered his hand from his face keeping his eyes locked on me in silent bewilderment. He opened his mouth to speak but instead he shook his head. "What the fuck is wrong with me?" His rhetorical question hung in the air for a moment before he ran his hands back through his long shaggy hair and closed his eyes. "Fuck. I'm so sorry, Ellie. Please believe me. I didn't mean... I'm so fucking screwed up right now." His voice broke, and I was torn between sucker punching him and holding him.

I stepped toward him and reached out to touch his arm. Speaking softly, I told him, "You've just had the worst news, Colt. I get that. But you can't treat people like shit and get away with it. You know that." His head hung low, and he didn't respond. "I'd better go. Everyone was right. I shouldn't have come." I turned toward the door, but he grabbed my arm which made me jump.

"Aw fuck, Ellie. Don't do that. Don't be scared of me. I said I was sorry, and I meant it. I just... I don't want you to go. Please... stay?"

I swallowed hard, toying with the conflicting voices in my head.

How can you stay after what he just did?

How can you not *stay after what he's just discovered?*

Slowly I turned to face him once more. "I'll stay for a little while. But you need to know that I'm not here to fuck you, Colt. That's not why I came. And sex isn't the answer to every problematic situation you find yourself in. Neither is alcohol. I'll make us some coffee, and we'll talk, okay?" I was impressed with how I had managed to hold myself together and waited with bated breath to hear his reply.

I watched his jaw clench under the hair of his beard and waited some more. Finally, he nodded. "Fine. That's good. Thank you, Eleanor."

Hearing my full name fall from his lips caused my heart to flip in my chest. It sounded so strange, but so good. I closed my eyes briefly to allow myself the split second fantasy of him making love to me and calling my name as he found his release. A twinge of longing tugged at the junction of my thighs.

"You okay?"

His gruff voice pulled me back to reality, and I felt the heat in my cheeks increase considerably. "I'm fine. Just fine."

CHAPTER THIRTY-EIGHT

Colt

Having Ellie in my home again did strange things to me. For starters, I acted like a total dick and hated myself for it. But I just didn't get why she bothered with me. The fact that she was there because she cared about my dead brother and how the news had hit *me,* broke me up. I didn't deserve her care or her concern, but she gave it freely. I fucking mauled her like some animal, and she still stayed. Why had I been pushing her away?

Oh yeah, *guilt.*

She stared expectantly at me, and I tried hard to get my fucking head out of my ass long enough to invite her into my living room. She had seemed to drift off into a world of her own for a moment, and her eyes had glazed over as a pink tinge rose from her chest to her cheeks. What the hell had she been thinking about?

Once I'd checked she was okay, I gestured at the living room. "So. Coffee, huh?"

She cleared her throat. "I'll make it. You come and sit."

Without argument, I followed her to my kitchen and leaned against the counter top as she found her way around my cupboards with ease, like it was the most natural thing in the world.

She peered over at me with a scowl. "I said sit."

I smirked and shook my head as I saluted her. "Yes, ma'am." Pulling out one of the stools from my breakfast bar I sat and continued to watch her in silence. Once she was done, she poured two cups of black coffee and placed one in front of me before sitting on the stool beside me.

"So have you found any more information out? About what happened to your brother? Or why he was here?"

———

My mind returned to the letter the cops had handed me. I had been on the verge of reading it when Red had shown up. "I... I have a letter that they found in his car."

Her eyes widened. "Oh? What does it say?"

I rubbed my hand over my hair and huffed out. "I haven't read it yet. I was about to when you showed up."

"Oh shit, I'm so sorry. Well, go ahead. I can leave you to read if you'd prefer to be alone." She began to climb down from her seat, but I grabbed her wrist.

"No. I don't... um... I don't want to be alone. If you'll stay while I read it, that would be... I'd appreciate that." I felt like a total douche bag. I had never tripped over my own words before but the prospect of reading *that letter* filled me with dread, and I figured I wasn't about to like what was in it.

She sat back down and nodded. "Okay. That's fine. Go ahead."

I slipped off my stool and went to retrieve the letter from the couch where I had dropped it. When I returned, I sat once again, and she smiled at me with that sweet, encouraging smile she has, and a lump of raw emotion jammed in my throat.

I opened the envelope with shaking hands and unfolded the sheet of pale blue paper.

Dear Jacob

I'm writing this in case I can't speak directly to you when I come looking. I'm afraid I have bad news. Our mother passed away last week after a short battle with a somewhat serious illness. She talked about you often, and I think she hoped that you would one day return, but sadly she died before she could see you again. She showed amazing strength after you left and it hurts me to know she went through such pain. She didn't deserve to be left behind like that, Jacob. She loved you unconditionally, regardless of what you thought. I know hindsight is a wonderful thing, but I hope you realize now that you *are* loved. None of us ever stopped loving you. And we never will. But your inability to let love in spoiled things for you. And that wasn't entirely your fault. I know that now.

If you choose not to make contact with me, then I will deal with that. I will have to. But knowing you left because you felt like an outcast in our family makes me feel so bad. You had nothing to prove after dad died. Nothing at all. It wasn't your fault. I know deep down that's what you felt because you had told him you hated him on the day he left for his boat trip. But you were just a kid. Kids say dumb things that they don't mean. And he knew how much you loved him. We all did.

So if nothing else comes of this letter I hope you can at least forgive yourself for that. And make sure you let someone love you, Jake. You deserve to be loved, brother.

Yours,
Jared

———

ELLIE

I watched as Colt read the letter that had been found in his brother's car, and my heart broke for him. His lip began to tremble, and tears spilled from the crinkled corners of his eyes and my own chest began to ache. The huge, tattooed, hulk of a man crumpled and lowered his head to the counter top as the word 'no' fell repeatedly from his lips, dispersing into a faintly whispered plea.

My breath caught in my throat as I observed him falling to pieces before me. The pain filled sobs vibrated from his chest and through the block of wood he leaned on as his shoulders shuddered. His hands came back to cover his head, and the letter was still gripped tightly in one fist.

Tentatively I reached to stroke his arm but flinched as he moved suddenly and lunged at my lap. He buried his head there and slipped his arms around my waist. gripping me so tight I could barely breathe. But I let him cry as I curled over him and enveloped him in my arms. I had no clue what the letter contained, but whatever it was it had broken him. I fought the tears needling at my own eyes as he poured his grief out onto me, but my fight was in vain. Witnessing him going through such pain was too much to bear and eventually I allowed my own tears to fall freely.

We sat there for what seemed to be hours. Just holding each other until he eventually calmed and pulled away to lean on the counter top.

Wiping the moisture from his face he furtively glanced

sideways at me. "Jeez. I'm sorry about that, Red. I never expected to crumble on you like that."

I reached out and squeezed his bicep. "Hey. No apologies. I'm just glad I came. I wouldn't have wanted you to go through that alone."

He turned to me and shook his head. "I just don't *get* you. I mean who the hell *are* you anyway?"

"Sorry? I don't understand what—"

"You're some special kind of woman you know that?"

I felt my face heat as I fidgeted in my seat. "What do you mean, Colt?"

"I've treated you like *shit*. But you've come back for more. I don't get that."

There was a genuine appearance of incredulity on his rugged face. However, anger spiked within me at his suggestion I was a push-over and I snapped back, "I think you and I see things *very* differently."

He rolled his eyes and held his hands up. "Fuck. That came out wrong. It was supposed to be a compliment."

I snorted derisively at his words. "What, that I'm a damn doormat? A masochist? Gee, thanks."

"No. No, I didn't mean that at all. Like I said, it came out totally wrong. What I mean is..." He paused, as if to try and get the right words, so he didn't put his foot in his mouth again. "You don't give up on people. You just... you *care*, whether people have earned it or not. You're... you're selfless, Ellie. And I don't deserve you, not after the asshole I've been. You should run a fucking mile from me and never look back. But instead, you're *here*. For *me*. Whether I deserve it or not."

His voice cracked, and guilt clouded his features and as the stupid—and apparently selfless—idiot I was, I just wanted to hold him. Okay, so he *had* been a dick but he was who he was, and he didn't react to things like most people I knew.

Before I could react he spoke in an emotion-filled whisper. "*Why* do you care, Ellie? I meant it when I said I don't get it."

Wow. The $64-million-dollar question was hanging in the air, and he actually wanted an answer. What the hell could I say? Could I tell him a lie and get away with it or would he see right through me? If I told him the truth would *he* be the one to 'run a fucking mile' as he so eloquently put it?

I took a deep breath and closed my eyes. "Because... because I'm in love with you, Colt." I swallowed as I heard him breathe in sharply. Keeping my eyes closed I went on as if the floodgates had been opened. "And in spite of the fact that you *can't*... or... or *won't* love me back, I can't help the fact that I'm drawn to you. I just feel this connection to you that I've never felt before, and it's like I *get* you. Regardless of the way you act, I *know* you. The *real* you." I clamped my mouth shut and opened my eyes to find him staring at me.

His eyes were wide and blazing, scorching my skin with intensity and my flesh heated merely at the way his gaze was locked on me and filled with disbelief.

My hands became clammy, and I began to shake. "Oh God. Say something, Colt. Please. I feel like a complete dumb-ass."

Without speaking, he slipped from his seat and crushed his mouth to mine almost knocking me over. I gasped for breath in between his passionate assaults, and he fisted his hands in my hair as I wrapped my legs around him.

Confusion, excitement and a spark of hope mingled in my mind until I was a mass of quivering flesh and hormones.

CHAPTER THIRTY-NINE

Ellie

I had been so determined that I wasn't going to fuck Colt.

I hadn't gone to his house for self-gratification. I was trying to be a decent human being, and I'd fought the conflicting sides of myself every step of the way. But even his aggressive outburst, when I had arrived, had done nothing to quell the aching inside of me that I knew only he could sate. I knew that it wasn't him. He was going through some twisted, fucked up stuff and it had to be messing with his mind.

But he was right, I *should* have run a mile, and I had tried to stick fast to my original plan just to be there for him as a friend in his time of need, but my resistance was crumbling; fading fast as my innermost feelings for Colt vied to be listened to. And as he carried me up the stairs and into his bedroom something shifted between us. A crackle of electricity charged the air as it always did when I was around him. But this was different. This was something more. I wanted him desperately, and no amount of inner dialog contradicting my desires was going to change that. So I stopped fighting.

He carefully laid me down on his bed, and I stared up at him as he dragged his clothing from his body but kept his gaze longingly focused on me. Neither of us spoke, and the only sound that could be heard was that of our ragged breathing. As if moving of their own volition my hands began to work too, on my buttons and zippers. Piece by piece I surrendered every item I was wearing, letting them all fall to the floor until I laid there before him; naked, waiting, wanting, aching for his touch. His cock stood proudly, ready to take me, and I wanted nothing more than to feel him filling me again. Claiming me in the way that only he could and only he *had*. No-one before could compare. As he climbed up the bed toward me like a lion toward his prey, I parted my thighs and he smiled, shaking his head as he took a moment to pause and feast on me with his heated gaze. It was a warm, passion filled expression that I had never encountered from him before. His sparkling, silver flecked eyes were usually filled with urgent lust, his touch rough and his kisses demanding, but not this time. This time, he treated me with reverence. Taking his time and savoring each second.

He leaned over my body and reached to his nightstand, pausing again briefly to sheath himself as I watched, greedily licking my lips. Then he lowered himself between my thighs, and hovered, poised at the entrance to my body, teasing me. I held my breath as my heart beat out a rapid rhythm against my ribs and I waited for him to take what he needed. But instead of a deep passionate thrust that caused me to gasp, he entered me slowly as he tenderly cupped my breast in one hand and covered my mouth with his. His kiss was probing and eager but not overpowering and forceful. I reveled in the soft scratching of his beard against my over-sensitive skin as our tongues caressed each other. A moan escaped me at the wonderfully familiar sensation of his pubic bone grinding slowly and purposefully at my clit.

This wasn't fucking. It wasn't just sex. This was making love.

I lightly grazed my nails down his back and smoothed my palms over the hard muscles of his ass as he moved deep within me. I could feel every single, delicious clench as he slid his cock deep and slow and then withdrew with the same amount of assured control. It was a blissful torment, but I relished the way he stroked every inch of my core with deliberately precise movements that sent pleasure radiating through every fiber of my body. As he watched me with awe, the urge to tell him again that I loved him fought for release, but I was too scared to free the words in case it was too much. Too soon after my *first* admission. But the fact was I *did* love him—regardless of every single reason that I absolutely shouldn't.

The muscles of my pussy gripped and clenched him, not willing to let the precious feeling end. But when he lowered his mouth to suckle each of my nipples, in turn, I almost shattered into a million orgasmic pieces. He pulled away and propped himself up on one arm, so he could lock his hooded gaze on me again, and that sexy, sweet smile returned to tug at the corners of his mouth.

He glanced down between us and watched his body slip and slide in and out of mine. "Look at us, Ellie. I fit you so perfectly." His strained voice told me that he was fighting his usual sexual urges so that he could take things slowly. Perhaps to try and express something to me in his actions and with his body that he couldn't or wouldn't put into words.

He maneuvered so that he could raise himself up and kneel between my thighs, spreading me wide as his thick cock still stretched me.

Taking my hand, he moved it to the junction of my thighs. "Touch yourself. I want to see you. All of you," was the simple, whispered command that fell from his lips and I willingly obeyed, rubbing at my swollen, sensitive clit as he gripped my bottom and slowly moved his hips back and forth. I watched him watching me just like he had that time at my apartment only this was more intimate. More intense. More erotic.

My muscles began to spasm and my breathing increased. I wanted to come and I wanted him to join me, but he was evidently enjoying the show too much.

"Let go, Ellie. Come for me while I watch you."

With my eyes open and locked on him I gave in to my urges, rocking my hips in perfect synchronization with his, as the most intense orgasm lifted me, possessed me and took me. I cried out his name and begged him for something I couldn't quite express coherently. But he pulled me up into his arms and cradled me as I repeated my plea over and over.

"You're so beautiful. So fucking beautiful, and I hope you know that, Ellie. I hope you know that," he growled into my ear as I came down from my natural high. My legs were wrapped around him now, where he sat thrusting up into me. This was deeper, and I was able to kiss him and run my fingers through his hair as he gripped me, lifted me and pulled me down slowly onto his cock.

Something changed yet again, and a crease appeared between his brows as his movements picked up pace, and he began to lose himself.

"Aww fuck. Fuck, Ellie, I need you so fucking much. I need you," he told me as his fingers dug into my flesh to the point it was almost painful. But I could feel my core tightening again, and I reached down to tug on my nipples as he slammed me down harder. In a split second, I was on my back again, and he was groaning. His fingers had replaced mine at my nipple. "You make me so fucking hard. So fucking crazy. How the hell do you do this, Ellie? I can't get close enough. I need to be deeper."

Seeing and hearing him so desperate sent me soaring once more, and I lost control of my emotions. "God, I love you, Colt. I love you so much," I cried as he thrust one last time and cried out a jumble of passionate sounds and expletives as he came hard.

CHAPTER FORTY

Colt

For a relatively small amount of time, I was able to forget what had happened to my brother at the hands of Loki's Legion. For a while, I was able to lose myself in something good. And that was thanks to Ellie. I knew she didn't come to my house to wind up in bed beneath me, but it felt so good when it happened.

For once in my life, since I lost Maria, I was able to express something more than just pleasure. More than just the earth shattering sensation of orgasm. For once I also had to admit to myself that I was feeling something other than lust. I hadn't gotten emotional during sex since my wife but fuck if it didn't happen with Ellie.

I couldn't say the words she no doubt wanted to hear because I *didn't* love her. I *couldn't* love her. But the realization that I needed her in my life hit me like a falling building, and the fact that it happened during such an intense experience made it all the more real.

I climbed off her and sat at the edge of the bed. Anger at

myself gripped me inside, and I almost ripped the condom from my dick.

"Colt. What's wrong?" Her voice was small and filled with worry. I couldn't really blame her. I'd just made love to her. That wasn't something I did anymore. So I was definitely giving off mixed fucking signals.

I sat there, with my head bowed staring at the floor as I tried to find the right words. "Nothing, sweetheart. It's all good. Well... apart from the part that isn't. The part about Jared, I mean."

She pulled the sheet from the bed and wrapped it around herself as if for protection. "No. There's something else, I can tell. Is it because I said—"

"No. No, it's not what you said. I *liked* what you said, Ellie." It was true, I did. But something was niggling at me, and I didn't know how to tell her. "It's just..."

Her hand smoothed softly up my back. "Just say it. Whatever it is, Colt. I'm a big girl. I'll handle it."

Her words led me to believe she knew exactly what I was thinking. I turned to find her glassy gaze locked on me; her face flushed the most beautiful, post-orgasm pink, and I hated myself. I reached up to smooth my thumb over her cheek, and she closed her eyes. "Go ahead. Say it."

"I can't tell you I love you, Ellie. Because I—"

"Because you don't." Her lip quivered, and she forced a smile. "I know. And it's okay."

Fuck, she broke me. She surprised me almost every time she opened her mouth, and she disarmed me. Something that no-one else had the power to do. I hated that I couldn't say it. I knew I felt *something,* but love? Nah. It wasn't love. It could *never* be love.

"The problem is, Ellie, I want you. I need you in my life. I realize that now. Just being with you... it helps me somehow and I can't explain it. And I know I'm a selfish dick for saying and feeling it, but it's true. I just don't want you to be... I can't *expect* you to be in a loveless, one-sided relationship. You deserve more and it wouldn't be fair."

She shook her head slowly side to side, sadness emanating from her. "No, it wouldn't. You're right."

Fuck.

Did I just hear her right? No... no... she was supposed to just put up with it. To live with it. She can't say no to me. What the fuck do I do now?

My inner dialog really did show me to be the asshole I already figured I was.

She leaned to kiss my shoulder tenderly. "But I don't want to stay away from you. I... I can't stay away from you, Colt. Not anymore."

Relief flooded my veins like a drug, relaxing every tensed up muscle in my body and filling me with warmth. But this was all too quickly followed by the true sense of how fucked up the situation was. I over-rode the negative shit in my head and grappled her into a bear hug, kissing her with an aggressive desperation that left her gasping for breath.

I pulled away and peered into her eyes. "What would I do without you?"

A sad smile tugged at her lips, but she didn't speak.

"I'll go get us a drink, huh?" I stood and pulled my boxers on, grinning like a teenage idiot instead of the thirty-eight-year-old guy I was.

Once I reached the kitchen and opened the bottle of Jack Daniel's, I stood there going over our conversation in my mind. What the hell was I doing? Was I really going to go through with stringing the poor girl along like that? A resounding yes rang around my head, and I clenched my jaw. I really was a prize asshole. But my selfish need for the peace I felt when I was with her, far outweighed my willingness to let her go for her own good.

I gulped down two fingers of the amber liquid and decided I needed to reread the letter my brother had in his possession when he was found. I needed to let the news sink in. I need to accept that I was alone for real in the world. Even though I had felt that way for the longest time now it was official.

———

ELLIE

I sat there after Colt had left the room with a huge smile on his face and allowed all the pain that was knotting me up inside to flow from my eyes as tears. His confirmation that he could never love me tore my heart to pieces, and I wasn't sure how I could move on from it, regardless of the fact I had told him it didn't matter. It *did* matter. It mattered a whole hell of a lot. I wanted to be loved. No, I *needed* that. What human being didn't? But I was afraid that the strength of feeling I had for Colt would stop me from ever loving anyone else, even if I tried. Which of course I didn't want to.

I knew that I couldn't continue in a one-sided relationship in spite of what I had told Colt. He wasn't in a fit state for me to say anything else at the time and I think I actually believed what I was saying right then as the words fell from my lips. Finding out that his mother had passed away on top of discovering his brother had been murdered was enough for one man to take, however. And so I just let myself cry. Because for at least a short time, I would have to deal with my feelings in my own way. Until he was stronger, or until he had a plan for how to move past it all. Maybe then I could leave. I could move out of Utah and start fresh somewhere. My best friend Chloe had done it once, so why couldn't I?

The world was a pretty damn big place, and there were so many countries out there that I could choose to go to and just blend in. Fade into the background. He'd never find me. Not that he would look. After all, he had admitted he didn't love me, so why would he?

I made my way to the bathroom and splashed cold water on my face. I took a deep, calming breath and went back to gather my clothes, pulling them on one by one in a kind of trance. Unrequited love was a bitch. And I *did* deserve more. Didn't I?

CHAPTER FORTY-ONE

COLT

Walking behind enemy lines was something I had never expected to be doing. And the dumbest part was that none of my own crew knew I was at the Legion's compound. For all I knew, I would actually wind up dead like they had intended when they shot Jared in error.

I pulled the bike up to the metal gates, and they began to open slowly. As I rode in, I spotted the two armed douches in their Loki's Legion cuts standing there waiting for me. I turned off the engine and climbed off my bike as the two men stepped toward me.

"What the fuck do *you* want?" one of them asked with a chuck of his chin.

"You're a little ways out from wonderland aren't you, Princess?" the other guy grinned menacingly. But he didn't scare me. None of them did.

"I'm here to see Deak, dickweed. He's expecting me."

They both stepped closer. "Oh *is* he now?"

"Yeah, he is, Rooster. So shut the fuck up and let him

pass." Deak had appeared in the doorway to the warehouse Loki's Legion called home. Like two guard dogs terrified of their master the men stepped aside and Deak approached me.

He rubbed his chin. "So to what do I owe this most indubitable honor?"

Sarcastic bastard. "I think you already know. You thought you'd killed me, remember?"

He wagged a nicotine stained finger at me. "Oh yeah. That's right. You got a doppelgänger out there... well *had* one at least."

Anger spiked at my guts at his nonchalance over the whole situation. "It's not a fucking joking matter, Deak. My brother is *dead*. That's some fucked up shit. You owe me."

He feigned innocence. "I do? But I didn't pull the trigger, man. Hell, I didn't even know that Caveman was going to pull a stunt like that."

I shook my head, and my nostrils flared as he tried to deny any involvement. "Come on, for fuck's sake. You can't tell me that you had nothing to do with it, that your guy acted of his own free will."

He stepped closer still. "Why don't you come on in and have a drink, huh? We can talk better inside."

"Nuh-uh. No fucking way I'm stepping into another trap of your making. You wanna kill me? Do it here and now."

Once more he acted the innocent. "Hey, man, if *I* wanted you dead *I'd* have gotten the right guy to begin with. Caveman was a dick. Said you'd stopped him from using the hotel for his hook-ups. Wasn't too happy about it. Acted on his own. That's it." He shrugged as if his explanation was sufficient. "And you don't seem too cut up about it all, so I reckon we're even."

"What?" My blood began to boil, and I stepped into his space jabbing my finger in his face. "How in the ever living *fuck* does that make us even? You think I don't *care* that you killed my fucking brother? You think I'm not wracked with guilt that *he* died when it was meant to be me? You think I can go to his funeral and face his fucking wife and explain? What kind of hard-hearted bastard do you take me for? He was my fucking flesh and blood, you dumb fuck."

He smiled and shrugged again. "Like I said, you don't seem too cut up. If it was *my* brother, I wouldn't be standing outside *your* clubhouse arguing. I'd have burnt that fucker to the ground with you all inside it. So I'm guessing you're more relieved to still be alive than you are pissed that he ain't."

I raised my fist and pulled back ready to take a swing when I heard the click of a gun being cocked. "I wouldn't do that if I were you, man. Just let it go and leave. It's not worth it."

I glanced to my right and came face to face with Deak's son, Nate. From what I'd heard he was the most sensible guy in the whole damn crew.

I turned my focus on him. "What the fuck do *you* know, huh? Your father killed my brother."

He bared his teeth like a rabid dog. "It was *Caveman* that killed your twin. And don't forget *your* crew killed my baby sister. If I were you, I'd leave. *Right* now."

Regrettably, he spoke the truth. A while before, the two crews had clashed on a piece of land they had no business fighting over and the girl, *Deak's* girl, had gotten caught in the middle of a gun battle. She shouldn't have been there. She should have been shielded from the shit going on between the clubs. But just like Jared, she had been in the wrong place at the wrong time. I hated that my crew were responsible for that. But until time travel was invented, I couldn't change history no matter how much I regretted it.

And I *really* regretted it.

I held up my hands. "I never intended that to happen and

not a day goes by that I don't fucking regret it, believe me. But all this 'eye-for-an-eye' bullshit *can't* go on." A wave of sadness washed over Nate's face, and I grabbed on to the opportunity to carry on speaking. "Look, I came here today to try and put an end to this damn gang war. It's getting old. Why can't we just avoid each other and get on with our fucking lives?"

Deak folded his arms across his chest. "What? So you wanna be buddies now? You gonna invite me over to play nice? Huh?" His voice got louder and his face redder. "Your crew killed my fucking daughter Colt. She was eighteen fucking years old. So how you think we're gonna just move forward like nothing happened, huh?" Saliva hit me in the face as he shouted.

The pain our two clubs were causing to the people around us truly began to sink in. "That's just it, Deak. I don't *want* any more people to fucking die. Your daughter, my brother. Who next, huh? I'm trying to be the bigger fucking man here. The cops wanted me to hand you over to them, but I didn't. I want an end to it, brought about by you and me, right here, right now. Can we have a fucking end to it, huh? Can we at least agree to that?"

Deak's chest rose and fell at a rapid rate, and his eyes were wild with aggression. I glanced around to find four guns now cocked and pointed at my skull and my sworn enemy grimaced at me, getting closer still.

He growled, "One word is all it would take, Colt. One fucking word and you'd be joining your brother. And the only reason I'm not giving the go ahead is because I don't want your fucking blood on my lot. And I know for a *fact* that the cops don't got shit on us over your brother's death. Caveman made sure of that. So I say you'd better walk the fuck away right now before I change my mind."

I shook my head. "Shall I take that as a no then?"

"Take it however the hell you want, just get off my land."

I turned and walked back to the bike with a sinking sensation in my gut. Would this shit *ever* be over? I was almost ready to step the fuck down as Prez and let someone else deal. But I knew I couldn't do that to Six, not when he was just starting life over. There had to be some way to resolve it. To live without looking over my shoulder every five seconds. To live without fearing for the lives of those I cared about.

I just didn't have a damn clue what *the way* was. But I had some serious damn thinking to do.

CHAPTER FORTY-TWO

Ellie

Colt had been gone all day and hadn't called, but I had fought the urge to message him in case the reason for his silence was connected to my admission of love. The last thing I needed was to hear him tell me again that he could never love me. It's not exactly an ego boost. So I had called Chloe and asked if she wanted to go out for a girls' night, but of course she had plans with Six. I could hear the guilt in her voice as she told me and for a split second, I wished I could be her. That is until I remembered exactly what she had been through over the last year. Perhaps the grass isn't actually greener.

I pulled on my big girl panties and went into town to a bar I had never been in before. I had always thought it was a place for older folks who liked quieter places and actually it was that fact that attracted me for once.

The bar was busy, but the majority were couples enjoying baskets of chicken and fries, and so I took a seat at the bar and ordered a drink from the old guy who was serving. He placed the glass down in front of me and eyed me with suspicion but didn't speak. Drinking alone wasn't something I usually did, and as I sat there at the bar, an uneasy sensation settled over me. Someone was watching me. And even though I had only had two sips of my Jack and Coke the crawling of my skin told me it was time to leave. I decided that I would be better to stop at the liquor store and go home to drown my sorrows.

I paid my tab and left a hand full of dollar bills on the bar and called to the tender to keep the change. As I grabbed my purse, I tentatively glanced around to make sure I was leaving alone. No-one was paying any attention to me thankfully, and I figured paranoia must have been setting in.

By the time I reached the parking lot, it was dark, and I fumbled around in my purse to find my cell. A cab was definitely a more reassuring prospect than walking the mile back to the hotel, but when I eventually located the phone, I found that the battery was dead as a dinosaur.

Great. Just what I need.

A firm hand landed heavily on my shoulder causing me to almost jump out of my skin.

I yelped before another rough hand covered my mouth. "Shhhh, luscious lips. Don't wanna go attracting any unwanted attention now do we?" The heat of my assailant's breath crept over the skin of my neck and I was gripped with fear.

He dragged me into the side alley of the bar as I struggled to free myself from his grip, but he just gave a deep dark, menacing laugh and shoved me against the wall.

"Ohhh, the things I could do to you." He breathed into my ear as he pressed his body against my back. Bile rose up my throat as what was about to happen began to dawn on me.

"P-please... don't do this," I whispered, unable to raise my voice louder through fear. "I swear you can turn and walk away, and I won't tell a soul. I promise. Just please..."

"Oh, don't you worry sweetheart. If I was gonna fuck you, you'd be begging me for more. Nah. You ain't gonna get no pleasure out of what I got planned for you."

My heart rate increased, and I became light headed with panic. "W-what are you going to do?"

"Oh, you'll find out soon enough, *Red*. Your guy thinks he can decide who uses his place for fucking. Well, he ain't the boss of Loki's crew. So you tell him he ain't gonna know what's hit him. He thought me killing his brother was bad." He laughed darkly again, and I scrunched my eyes closed, waiting for the gun shot, the blade of a knife, or whatever the hell else he was going to use to kill me. But instead, he shoved me to the floor and nudged me with his boot. "You have a nice evening now."

I curled into a ball on the wet ground, still waiting for the impact but I heard his heavy footsteps retreating, and I dared to glance up.

"Hey, hey you okay?" A deep husky voice called to me from across the lot.

I lifted my head as I heard more footsteps, but this time they were heading for me and I cowered again. "Just do it. If you're going to do it just get it over with." I cried out before bursting into tears.

"Hey, come on. What the hell happened to you?" A hand rested under my chin and tilted my face upward until I was staring at a black silhouette that hovered over me. "Come on, let me help you up."

His hands came around me, and I was quickly brought to a standing position. I was shaking frantically and shivering.

"You're cold. Here." In the darkness, I felt the weight and smelled the distinct fragrance of leather as his jacket engulfed me. "Can I take you home? Can I call someone?"

"No... no... I just... I need to..." My head began to swim again, and I felt my legs buckle.

"Whoa, hey, steady there. Come on, my car is just across the lot."

My head snapped up, and I stared into the blackness where his face was hidden. "No! No! Please."

Suddenly his face was illuminated and I saw he had a cell phone pointing up at him. "It's okay. It really is. Look, my name is Nate. What's yours?"

Now that there was a little light I glanced down at the leather jacket and saw the patch that read Loki's Legion and my heart almost stopped dead. "It's... it's R-Rae."

"Okay, Rae. You're safe with me, I swear. Can you tell me what happened and whose head needs to roll? Huh? Who did this to you?"

Knowing full well that the man who did this to me was one of Nate's own crew and fearing for my safety if I told him I blurted out a lie. "I don't know. He grabbed me from behind but... Something must have scared him off."

Keeping the glow of the phone on his face he crouched to look into my eyes. "Did he touch you? Did he hurt you?"

"No. Thankfully he left before it got that far."

He clenched his jaw. "Good. That's good. Okay, where can I take you? I want to make sure you get home."

Shit. What the hell do I say? Suddenly I remembered the address on Delilah's driver's license. I had absent mindedly taken notice of it when she had been clearing receipts from her purse a few weeks before and remembered thinking how strange it was that she had a place in such a nice neighborhood yet chose to hang out almost all the time at the clubhouse with its smell of beer and cigarettes.

"I... I'm staying with a friend at... At the apartment block on Barker Street."

"Okay, well let's get you back there." He took my elbow and began to lead me to a black car that was parked across the lot just as he had said.

I nervously climbed in the car wishing I had just asked to borrow his cell and gotten someone to come and get me but my brain was scrambled, and I couldn't think straight. I realized right then that I didn't even know if Dee would be home, and if she was, I had no clue whether or not she would let me in.

He clearly knew where he was going as we headed in the direction of Barker Street in Rose Acres. He kept glancing at me with a look of deep concern etched on his brow, and I managed to force a smile.

"I'm okay, Nate. Really I am. Thank you so much for helping me."

"It's nothing. Really. I've seen a lot of shit happen to women, and I hate the bastards... sorry for my language... I hate the type of men who treat ladies like trash. I feel I should apologize for my whole species."

He seemed like such a nice guy, and I wondered if that could possibly be true considering the fact he was one of *them*. One of Loki's Legion.

He pulled the car to a halt outside Delilah's block and jumped out of the car. Shit. I'd hoped he would just let me out and drive off, but of course, he wasn't going to do that. He was actually a decent human being.

My door opened and he held out his hand. "Come on. I'll make sure you get inside. You were a little woozy back there, and I don't want to risk you taking a tumble." I took his hand and allowed him to help me out. Now that we were in a more brightly lit area, I could see he had dirty blonde hair that was kind of long but not really long. It swept back from his face to reveal kind eyes and ruggedly handsome features. His brow and lip were pierced, and I could see tattoos covering his arms. I slipped his jacket off and handed it back to him. He tossed it into the car and slammed the door before scraping his hair back where it fell forward onto his face.

We walked in silence up to the entrance, and I stopped. "Well, thank you, Nate. I appreciate what you've done for me tonight. I'll be fine from here."

He shook his head. "Nuh-uh. I'm making sure your friend is in so you can get inside, Rae. I want to make sure you're absolutely fine."

I was about to admit to my lie when the door to the block burst open, and I turned to find Delilah standing there. *Shit. My cover will definitely be blown now.*

"Oh... hey Dee. Thank goodness you're home." her brow crumpled as she stared at me in confusion.

"Um..."

"Rae tells me she's staying here with you, and I'm glad you're in, because she's just had a shitty ordeal with some low-life."

She switched her attention between Nate and me and then something seemed to dawn on her. "Oh, right. I was... just coming to look for you... Rae."

"Yeah, sorry my cell died and then some asshole jumped me in the parking lot. Nate here came to my rescue."

She nodded slowly, as if trying to read between the invisible lines. "Okay. Well, thank you, Nate. I'll take it from here." She slipped her arm around me like I was a hobbling old woman and I scowled at her.

"Hey, do I know you?" Nate asked Delilah with a tilt of his handsome face.

She smiled and tucked her hair behind her ear. "No... umm... I don't think I've seen you before."

"Yeah... yeah, sure you have. You used to work at Bad Inc. tattoo parlor in Gainsridge. Didn't you?"

Dee's eyes widened and she smiled. "Yeah. Yeah, I did. Did you go there?"

Nate nodded with a cheesy grin on his face and I suddenly felt like a third wheel. "I sure did. Matlock, the guy who owns the joint? He did most of my work." He held out his arms which were thankfully free of the Loki's Legion patched jacket he wore earlier.

"Oh yeah. I was his apprentice after I worked the desk for a while."

He nodded again and a heavy anticipation filled the air. "I thought I recognized you. Great... great. Well, I should go. But hey, it was nice seeing you again... umm..."

"Delilah." She was clearly fighting the same cheesy grin.

"Delilah." He smiled as he repeated her name. "Oh and Rae. You take care. And if you remember who that bast... who that *guy* was who attacked you make sure and tell someone okay? The cops or... whoever."

I smiled. "Sure, Nate. I will. Thanks again."

"Okay. Well, good evening ladies."

"Bye, Nate."

We stood and watched him walk back to his car where he paused to hold his hand up in a wave, exposing his muscular bicep.

As he drove away, Dee grabbed my arm. "Come on in, *Rae.* You have some explaining to do."

CHAPTER FORTY-THREE

"But you're sure that you're fine? He didn't grope you or hit you or anything?" Dee asked as she handed me a glass filled with amber liquid.

"No, I really *am* fine. Just shaken up. I thought he was going to... well he didn't so I need to just forget it."

"And you didn't get a glimpse of who it was? And he didn't *say* anything?"

I swallowed a large mouthful, playing for time to conjure up my next lie but the burn of the liquid as it traveled down my esophagus made me cough. "Jeez Louise, what *is* this stuff?"

Dee burst out laughing. "Have you never had Thunderbird before?"

Scrunching my face, I shook my head emphatically. "No... I don't think it's *quite* my drink," I informed her as I placed my glass on the coffee table.

"Really?" Her surprise was genuine. "I fucking *love* the stuff. Anyway, stop changing the subject. We need to figure out if he was one of Loki's crew. And if not, we need to call the cops."

I snapped my attention to her, thinking she meant Nate. "Who?"

She rolled her eyes. "The bastard who attacked you, dummy. It sounds like the kind of thing *they* would do."

Relief flooded my veins. "Yeah well they can't *all* be bad."

When I glanced up at her again, she was staring at me with wide eyed incredulity. "You *really* think that?"

I shrugged, remembering how kind Nate had been and wondering what she would think if she knew his true identity.

"So, Nate seems nice, huh?" In order to try and appease her a little, I reached for my glass again and took a tentative sip.

Her cheeks fired up bright red, and she, too, took a large gulp of her drink. "Yeah. I suppose."

"Oh come on, Dee. Lust was written all over *both* of you."

She chewed on her lip. "You think he liked me?"

It was my turn for an eye roll. "Duh, yeah."

She shrugged. "Yeah well, I don't have a way of getting in touch with him, so it's pointless thinking that way."

I know exactly how and where you can get in touch with him. Instead of speaking my mind I stood. "Can I use your phone to call a cab?"

"You may as well stay here tonight."

"But—"

"Ellie, if you go home looking all pale-faced and shaky, your parents are going to know something is wrong. If you go to the clubhouse Six and Chloe will know, and if you go to Colt's... well I think you can guess the theme I'm going for here. And I'm guessing that turning up on *my* doorstep was a last resort because you *didn't* want any of that to happen.

Dammit. She had a point. I slumped back onto the couch. "Can I ask you a question?"

She saluted me with her glass. "Fire away."

I cleared my throat. "Why don't you like me?"

She almost choked on her Thunderbird. "Huh? I... Why..."

Watching her flail around for words made me regret asking. "Come on, Dee. You've disliked me from the start. I just wondered why is all. I'm a big girl, you can be honest."

She placed her glass down and huffed. "You want the truth?"

"It'd be a start."

"I'm jealous."

Huh? "Sorry? Jealous of what exactly?" Her blatant honesty completely floored me.

"All the guys have found someone. And you're all super fucking cute and sexy. I'm alone, and I don't see that changing anytime soon."

"But... you don't have feelings for Colt, do you?"

She laughed. "No way, dude. He's like my brother." She shivered and made a disgusted noise. "And I don't think of Six that way either. Cain, on the other hand, was a different story. But... meh... No point dwelling on shit you can't change."

I suddenly found myself feeling something other than disdain for Delilah, and it surprised me. "Aww, Dee, there is someone out there for you. I just know it. I mean you only have to think of the way Nate looked at you back there." *Ugh, way to bring up the Legion guy again, Ellie.*

"Yeah, well that won't be going anywhere any time soon. Like I said before, I only know of him from what he said about Bad Inc. So I guess that ship has sailed."

The look of despondency on her face tugged at my heart,

and I fought the urge to tell her. "If it's something that's meant to be it'll happen."

She laughed out loud again. "Total bullshit. But thanks for trying, Red. So if you don't like Thunderbird what do you like? And don't say something prissy like wine coolers or I swear I'll kick your ass out right now."

I liked this new side of Dee that I was witnessing for the first time. With a giggle, I confessed, "JD is my poison."

"Ahh. Okay, now you're talking." She stood and disappeared into the kitchen to return a few moments later with a full bottle of my favorite drink.

———

COLT

I was getting Ellie withdrawal.

I hadn't seen her in almost two days, and all I could think about was her tight pussy around my cock and her mouth on mine. Thinking about her body was a great distraction technique seeing as I was being hounded by the cops about info on my brother's murder. I had also been trying to pluck up the courage to go see my brother's wife, now that the cops had informed her what happened. I knew she would need some kind of closure, and some answers, and that I was the only one who could provide that. I'd been given her contact details by Rose Acres PD but hadn't been able to face making the call.

What I needed was a dose of Red. But when I had called into the hotel, her mom told me that she had stayed over at a friend's house. *What friend?* It sure as hell wasn't Chloe because she would've needed surgical removal from Six. And I had never heard her talk about any other friends. The thought that she'd maybe met a guy spiked me deep inside, and I had to fight the urge to break shit. Although that wasn't really her style. She was too classy for the one-night stand thing.

The glaringly obvious fact that she owed me nothing needled at my brain. After all, I'd told the woman I couldn't love her. So what the fuck should it matter if she fucked a whole damn football team? I had no business being all possessive over her. But fuck if I didn't want to find out where the hell she'd been.

I waited in the hotel office for her to show up, and when she did, I reminded myself that I needed to be nice and not act like a jealous boyfriend. Yeah 'cause that was totally me. Not.

But as she walked through the foyer and headed for her parents' apartment, I dove out of the office and grabbed her arm. "Where the fuck have you been, Red? I was worried about you. You didn't answer my calls and you sure as hell didn't come home last night." *Way to go dick-weed. Way to go.*

She glanced around us as her cheeks tinted red then gritted her teeth and hissed at me like a venomous little viper. "Who the *hell* do you think you are? My *husband?*"

I released her arm and stepped back as if she'd punched me in the gut. "No. I just—"

"You just thought you'd check up on me, huh? Well, it's none of your goddamn business what I was doing. You don't love me, Colt, so you sure as hell don't own me. Now I suggest you go crawl under a fucking rock and leave me the hell alone."

She stormed through the door and let it slam closed behind her. I clenched my fist and searched around me for something to punch. On one side I had the glass door Red had just left through, and on the other a very large fake plant. Breathing as calmly as I could, I allowed my anger to dissipate and figured I would go and apologize. I seemed to be doing that *a lot*. Who knew, maybe I'd become a fucking expert.

I walked down the corridor toward the place I knew Red would be holed up with her folks and knocked on the door.

It opened. "Oh, hi, Colt. What can I do for you? Is everything okay?" Eamon looked a little confused and why wouldn't he?

"Hi, Eamon. Yeah... yeah, everything is fine. But I wondered if I could talk to Eleanor please?"

He cringed. "Oh, I'm sorry, but she said she'd had a terrible day and was going to take a long soak in the tub."

Fuck. "Ah, okay no problem. I'll catch her tomorrow."

I turned to walk away, but Eamon called after me, "Is there anything I can help with?"

"No thanks. It was just some... umm... reception booking shi... *stuff* I needed to ask. I can ask her tomorrow." He nodded and raised his hand in a wave before closing the door.

I made my way outside and around to the windows that spread across her parents living accommodation, hoping to grab her attention or catch a glimpse of her at least. I could hear running water and followed the sound until I was standing underneath what I guessed was the bathroom. When the water stopped, I heard it slosh as she climbed in and my dick stood to attention. The bushes to my left suddenly gave me an idea, and I clambered up until I could see through the open window and through a gap in the voile drapes as they shifted in the breeze.

Fuck, she looked hot. Lying there in the tub surrounded by steam and with the water lapping at her bare tits. Her red hair was gathered up in a knot on the top of her head, and her eyes were closed.

Like some dirty pervert, I stayed there watching her as she took a sponge and began to drag it all around her body. Her nipples poked through the bubbles, and she breathed a contented sigh. Watching her from a distance was something I both loved and hated simultaneously. I was stuck on the periphery when all I wanted to do was dip my hands into the hot, soapy water and slide my fingers up the inside of her thighs until I reached her clit. I wanted to sink my fingers deep inside her body and feel her clench around them until she begged me to get naked and join her.

I must have let out a groan as her eyes snapped open and she sat up causing the water to overflow. "Colt? Is that you?" Her eyes widened, and I almost fell from the place I was perched like some peeping Tom.

I cleared my throat and leaned to push the drapes aside. "Guilty."

I expected her to shout expletives at me, but instead she sank back and heaved a defeated huff of air from her lungs. "Are you coming in or are you just going to hang there like some slimy pervert?"

With one hand gripping the branch I was on I reached the other out and shoved the window up. With the grace of a new born foal, I lurched forward and collapsed in a heap on the bathroom floor.

She giggled and for a moment hope sprang inside of me that she might forgive me for being a possessive ass.

"Howdy, beautiful." I tipped my invisible Stetson and spoke in my best southern accent. That accent always got the girls' panties wet. Well, that and the British accent but there was no way I was attempting *that*.

She smiled, but it was gone as quick as it arrived. "What do you want, Colt?"

I shrugged. "To apologize."

"Well go ahead, and then you can crawl back through the window like a bug and buzz off."

Ouch. "Look, I was an asshole and—"

"*Yeah,* you were."

Okay, so she wasn't going to make it easy. I should have known. "And I wanted to make it up to you."

She eyed me suspiciously. "And how do you propose to do that?"

I licked my lips and walked over to the tub dipping my fingers in to test the water I gave a half smile. "I can think of a way to take your mind off your shitty day, baby."

She rolled her eyes. "God! Does *everything* come down to fucking with you?" Her voice raised and her skin flushed a deeper shade of pink than that caused by the hot water. "I don't *need* an orgasm, Colt. I just need you to leave me alone for a while, okay?"

What? Oh fuck. "But why? I know I screwed up earlier but... What you said the other day about not wanting to stay away from me. Has that somehow changed?" *Please say no. Please say no.*

She messed around with the bubbles covering the surface of her skin, and my fingers ached to touch her. But she nodded. "I think... I think I need some time to myself. We both made our admissions the other day, and then with what happened at..." Her words trailed off, and the color drained from her cheeks.

"With what happened?" She didn't answer and refused to make eye contact. I watched as she pulled her knees up to her chest and worry spiked within me at her unspoken words. "Ellie, tell me what happened."

"Some guy. He tried to... mug me. But someone disturbed him, and he ran off."

My fists clenched at my sides, and my stomach knotted. She was hiding something. "Some guy? Did you see who the fuck it was? I'll kill the bastard."

She locked her watery-eyed gaze on me. "That's just it, Colt. You want to protect me, and you want to be with me, but you say you can't love me. I can't... I don't want to deal with that right now. Please, just go." She moved her attention to the bubbles once again, and pulled her knees tighter.

I took a step closer still, ignoring what she had said. "Who was the guy, Ellie? Was he one of Loki's crew?"

She shook her head no. "I didn't see him, and he didn't say anything. He was just after money. Probably a drug addict. But I'm fine so you can go. Just give me some time, okay? Please?"

I wanted to smash stuff. To find the bastard who had scared my girl, and kick the living shit out of him. But then what she had said about wanting me to leave her alone began to sink in. She *wasn't* my girl. And there was a good chance I was losing her. But I was powerless to stop it. I couldn't give her what she needed, and so she was right.

I had to leave her alone.

I stood there in silence as a heavy feeling descended over me and for a moment my legs refused to move. "I'll find out who it was, Ellie. And I'll deal with him. I can assure you of that. And... if you need me... You know where I am."

And with those parting words I walked toward the door, opened it and left, not caring who I might run into in the hallway.

CHAPTER FORTY-FOUR

COLT

Almost a week had passed, and I was acting like a bear with a class A migraine. I had been keeping away from Ellie hoping that she'd miss me, but clearly seven days weren't enough to make that happen, and it was driving me nuts. Eamon and I had agreed to renovate the hotel with the hope of getting things back to normal after all the Loki's Legion crap. I'd been out for long rides on the bike, only driving by the hotel to see if I could catch a glimpse of the redhead to check she was okay. But she was doing a great job of impersonating the invisible man.

Another end to another dull as shit, redhead-free day had arrived and I sat on the floor of the end room upstairs at the clubhouse. I had a bottle of JD in one hand and the remote control for the little sound system in the other. My head was resting back against the door, and I had my eyes closed as "Eleanor" by Biffy Clyro blared out on repeat as loud as I could get it from the small speakers. I was feeling emotions that I didn't want to acknowledge or accept, and when you add to that the fact I was acting like a teenage kid who had been dropped by his crush, I guess it was obvious that the music wasn't really helping. But I let it play regardless.

There was a loud banging on the door. "Hey, Colt. Are you okay in there? That's like the thousandth time you've played that damn song this week."

"Fuck off and leave me alone, Dee." My voice broke as I called out and I knew for a fact she would read shit into that.

"Look, just fucking *call* her. It's obvious you love the bitch."

"I said fuck. *Off*." Okay, so I felt like shit. Red had rejected me, and I hadn't known how to handle it. But *love?* Nah. I wasn't buying *that* bullshit. This was just a case of me being a giant baby for not getting what I wanted. It was because my *dick* missed her. Not me. Nope. Nu-uh.

"Colt, it's okay to fall in love again, man. It really is. And if it *has* to be the redhead then it's okay. There's no accounting for taste, buddy." Delilah was clearly trying to get a rise out of me. But I wasn't biting. Instead, I held up the little remote control aimed in the direction of the sound system and flicked the track forward. An intro I knew she would be familiar with began to play, but I skipped along to the angry chorus lyrics of "One Step Closer" by Linkin Park, and I hoped she would get the fucking message.

"Oh my God, Colt, *seriously*?" she shouted at me through the door. "Methinks the asshole doth protest waaaay too much."

Another raised voice was thrown into the mix. "What the fuck is going on with Colt?" *Oh great. Now Six is joining the 'let's-hassle-the-shit-out-of-Colt' party*.

"Our lord and master won't fucking admit to his feelings for the redhead. She's snubbed him, and he's thrown his teddy out." She was talking in a loud-ass voice deliberately. *Bitch*.

"Fuck. You think that's *really* what's up? He's been in a shitty mood for a week now." I guessed Six was genuinely trying to talk, over the fact that I kicked the volume up a notch.

"Yep. He's showing all the classic symptoms of a spurned heart," Dee informed Six.

That was it. I was done. I switched the music off, clambered to my feet and yanked the door open. "I don't fucking *have* feelings for the redhead! I don't have feelings for any fucker!" I yelled at the top of my voice as they stood there, wide eyed and staring at me. "I love my fucking *dead wife*, okay? I will never, EVER love anyone else. You only get a chance at that shit *once* in a lifetime. And you don't get it again. So shut the fuck up and tell everyone to get the hell out of the place and leave me the fuck alone!"

The disbelief on Six's face almost made me laugh. "Get the hell *out* of the place? You mean like *leave*?"

"That's what I said VP. And as your Prez you'd better do what I fucking say! Out! All of you!"

I slammed the door as hard as I could causing the frame to shatter in several places and then just for good measure I punched the wall. Hard.

———

Ellie

I was kind of grateful that my dad had decided to close the hotel for some renovations. Colt had had a hand in it, and I guessed it was his way of giving my dad a break until the shit over his brother's murder had been dealt with. He didn't want any reprisals, and I could understand that. Plus, it meant that Colt wasn't hanging around. In fact, I hadn't seen him since I had told him to leave me alone a week before. I was missing him, admittedly, but I knew that him staying away was the best thing for me. If I saw him, I would end up beneath him again in his bed, no doubt. My willpower was waning. But I had to save myself for someone who could and would love me. Who *wanted* to love me. And so staying away from Colt and giving my heart time to heal was the best thing to do regardless of how much it hurt.

Several of the rooms had furniture piled up in the center and covered with dust sheets ready for painting, and others were at the stage where the painting was almost complete. The men had worked so quick I was really shocked and very impressed. Although having strange men in the place was putting me on edge, and I was looking forward to the whole thing being over. One of the guys had been flirting with me. He was the antithesis of Colt. Blonde hair, clean shaven and not a single visible tattoo. He was kind of cute in that high school heartthrob kind of way. You know, the kind your mom wants to you to date even though you adore the school thug. I had tried hard to reciprocate his flirty glances but every time I smiled at him I had a voice in my head telling me I was Colt's girl. Of course, I wasn't and it was all wishful thinking, but it was the thinking that was the problem. I guess it's likc trying to give up candy or soda. You know that shit is really bad for you but the more you think about it the more you crave it.

The downside of this kind of cold turkey, though, was the nightmares. They were the stuff of horror movies. On the one hand, I was being assaulted, grabbed and pushed to the ground by faceless men insistent on drilling some message home that I couldn't quite decipher. And on the other, I was being laughed at and told I wasn't worthy of love by Jacob 'Colt' Coltman. The way he looked at me with such deep disdain and told me I could never match up to his wife was like a dagger to my heart but like some faulty stereo system, my brain had it all on repeat and insisted on torturing me. Add to that the pitiful, distorted faces of people watching all this happen, and you could say my head was one fucked up mess.

After waking up in a pool of sweat for what felt like the hundredth time in one night I made my way through to the kitchen to get a glass of water, deciding I may as well give up on any further attempts at slumber. It was uncharacteristically hot. As hot as hell you could say. I figured my dad must have left the furnace on by mistake. I ditched my robe on a chair in the kitchen and walked over to the faucet. Even the floor was warm, and as I reached and touched the metal I realized that it, too, was hot. What the *hell?* I guessed one of the guys working on the renovations must have caught the thermostat or something.

I got some water and took a sip. It was pretty much undrinkable, and concern began to build inside of me. I wasn't sure why, but something was off. Leaving the kitchen, I walked through to the main part of the hotel and keyed in the alarm code before walking through into the foyer, and at that point my heart almost leapt out of my mouth. Right outside the entrance doors, a huge fire was blazing, causing thick black smoke to trickle in through the tiny gaps in the frame.

I ran to the reception desk to hit the fire alarm button that connected straight to the firehouse, but the wire had been cut. The telephone line was down too. My worst nightmare was coming true right in front of me as I began to cough and splutter. I lifted my tank top and covered my nose and mouth as I made my way back through to our living quarters. As I passed one of the guest rooms, I saw more flames outside the window, and I suddenly realized this had been done deliberately. It had to have been. Fire doesn't spring up randomly like that.

Fear gripped me, and my heart thudded in my chest at the knowledge that someone wanted us dead. As tears began to stream down my face, I suddenly missed Colt more than ever. If he had been here, he could have protected us. But he wasn't, and it was down to me to keep us safe.

I had to wake my parents. We *had* to get out. Somehow we *had* to escape.

As I ran toward my parents' room, more and more smoke was beginning to infiltrate the hotel I dropped to my knees remembering that smoke rises, and the floor would have the cleanest air, but it was difficult to see. I crawled along as quickly as I could when I heard a noise behind me, and something grabbed my ankle.

A muffled voice laughed. "Where do you think you're going, princess? Leaving the bonfire party so soon?"

I tried to scream but began coughing instead and grappled at the floor to try and pull myself along. I was flipped over and there, straddling my waist, looming over me was a huge man wearing some kind of gas mask. His wild eyes staring at me in the limited light available. In his hand was an object I couldn't make out. With an evil grin plastered on his face, he raised it up...

CHAPTER FORTY-FIVE

COLT

I was woken up by the faint sound of hollering and an accompanying loud banging sound that seemed to vibrate the whole building, but as I tried to sit, my head began to pound like I was being beaten with a baseball bat.

What the fuck?

I could just make out a male voice shouting, "Colt! Get the fuck down here Colt! Right now!" I was alone in the clubhouse thanks to my insistence on being an asshole the night before, when I had thrown *everyone* out. And someone clearly had a bone to pick with me. I yanked on my jeans and stood too quickly causing a major head rush. When the room briefly stopped spinning, I grabbed my gun and tucked it in the back of my waistband. I figured it was maybe Six trying to get in, but I had bolted the door before I had decided—in my drunken state—that I needed to sleep.

"All right, all right, don't get your fucking lace panties in a bunch, Six." I yanked the door open but instead of Six I was greeted by a pale-faced Nate. Loki's-fucking-Legion Nate. "Hey, how the fuck you get in the compound ass-wipe?"

He was panting like he'd run a marathon. "I'm younger than you dick-head, and I scaled the fence. But never mind that bullshit. You gotta come, now!"

In spite of my throbbing head, I managed a derisive laugh. "I'm going nowhere with you buddy. You must think I'm dumb as a box of frogs."

"Colt, I'm serious, man. The hotel. It's on fire."

———

Never in twenty plus fucking years did I think I would *ever* be trusting one of Loki's crew. And certainly not the son of the President. But after grabbing a shirt, there I was, clinging to the sissy bar of Nate's Harley as we sped through town toward the hotel. My heart was in my mouth and the fear that gripped my insides was almost tearing me in two. But I *had* to keep it together. I had to get to Ellie.

I could see the smoke billowing up from the location of the building long before we arrived, and my stomach roiled. Was she alive? Was she still in there? And what the fuck was I going to do if I couldn't get to her in time? I couldn't save Maria, that was out of my hands, but Ellie, I had a chance to save her. No matter what the cost. Even putting my own life on the line meant shit to me as long as she was okay.

We pulled up across from the building, and I jumped from the bike as soon as it stopped. The street was a hive of activity with onlookers, fire crews and cops taking statements. Blue lights lit the sky, along with the inferno blazing before me. I ran across to where the fire crews were working on putting out the blaze and grabbed the arm of one of the guys. He wasn't one of the Rose Acres Fire Dept. and so I didn't recognize him. The blaze must have been so bad they had to bring crews in from the next town.

He swung around to face me, and I demanded, "Are they all out? Are they safe?"

The guy held up his hand. "It's okay, son. The owner told me he was the only one in there. The place was being renovated. He says he reckons faulty wiring caused it."

"But if Eamon's out, where's his wife and their daughter?"

"He says no-one else was in there. Just him. Said he lived there alone. We did a sweep to be safe but found no-one. It's all fine, sir."

Panic gripped me. Something wasn't right. "Where is Eamon?"

"I'm sorry son, but I need to get back to my team. The owner is... Oh... He *was* over there." He pointed to the small wall at the perimeter of the parking lot which was now empty.

When the guy tried to turn away, I tugged his jacket sleeve. "Sorry, but... what did the guy look like?"

The firefighter scowled at me. "He was about my height, dark thinning hair in a ponytail. Tattoos. Why?"

Oh. Fuck.

"That's not the goddamn owner! Aww fuck!" I lurched forward dodging two cops and three more firefighters.

"Colt! Wait up!" I turned to see Nate taking the same route I had just taken.

When he arrived in front of me, I shoved him hard in the chest. "This was fucking Caveman's doing. You bastards have gone too far this time!"

"Whoa, Colt, this is not *us*. This is Caveman. My dad kicked him out of the club a week ago when he thought he might go the same way as Zak, you know the guy who kidnapped Six's woman? And he was right. Caveman's gone fucking crazy. He mentioned something about getting his revenge, and when I was coming home on the bike I saw the smoke. I knew this was him. I'm sorry, man. I really am. But let's just get in there and make sure everyone is out."

"You can't go in there! You both need to move away from the building right now, or I *will* shoot. This is for your own good."

I turned to see a young cop with his gun aimed at my legs. I glanced at Nate who nodded at me and then lurched at the cop. I set off running toward the hotel again, and a gun went off but I couldn't look back.

I smashed my way through the nearest side window seeing as the fire at the front entrance was way too strong, and I tugged my shirt up over my mouth to help reduce the amount of acrid smoke I was inhaling. Moving as quickly as I could through the obstacle course of collapsed ceilings and ladders left by the decorating crew I searched.

"Ellie! Eamon!" I called out but got no reply. Water began to pour through the hole in the ceiling above me, but I forged ahead. I *had* to find her. I *had* to. "Ellie! It's... it's Jacob... where are you?"

The smoke and lack of light in the place had completely disoriented me, and I pushed through the first door I came to, calling out her name over and over. Before I could move further into the building, I was joined by two firefighters.

One grabbed me. "Hey, get the hell out of here. Leave this to us. You're risking your life."

I shrugged his hand off of me, my eyes now blurry with the smoke and the fact I was coughing my guts up. "You don't understand. The woman I *love* is in here. I *have* to get her out. I *have* to find her."

A loud crashing sound came from behind him as more of the ceiling collapsed and as the firefighter ducked and then turned to see what had happened I used his break in eye contact to push forward. The words I had just uttered rang around my mind. The words I had spoken without thinking. Without fighting them. I *loved* her. After all the time I'd spent denying it and feeling guilty I had blurted out my true feelings to a total stranger.

I love her. Oh my God. I love her, and I'm on the verge of losing her forever.

I heard another firefighter shout, "Two recovered, sir! How many more are we searching for?"

But who? Who had they recovered? And by recovered did they mean bodies? I almost crumpled to my knees and I clutched my stomach. The physical pain was unbearable.

This isn't happening. It must be a nightmare.

The guy nearest me called out, "What you got, Ray?"

"Man and a woman recovered from a bedroom. Maybe early sixties? Still breathing but..."

"Okay, we're looking for a young woman. Red hair," came the reply that crushed me.

They had found her parents but Ellie was still unaccounted for.

A new, panicked voice called out, "We have to get out, Captain. The building is unstable and could collapse at any second."

I couldn't leave.

If she was dying in here, so was I. I was resigned to the fact. I couldn't lose her. Recovering from losing Maria had been the hardest thing I had *ever* done, and I couldn't go through it again. I would just lie down and give up. Now the realization of my true feelings had finally sunk in I knew that living with the knowledge Ellie was dead... that I couldn't save *her* either... I just couldn't do it.

I wasn't strong enough.

A hand grabbed me again. "Come on, son. We have to get

out. I'm sorry, but we have to." it was the guy I had encountered outside. The Captain of the crew.

Once again I yanked my arm from him and gritted my
teeth as the war-zone continued around me with its bangs and
crashes, flames and water and I shook my head. "I *have* to find
her. I have to at least know if she's…"

"Captain! We gotta move out! Now!"

Once again as he turned to connect with his team
member, I made a dash for it. I heard him shout, "Aww fuck!
Get back here!" But I ignored his growled plea. Crashing
through another door with sheer brute force and insanity and
I found myself in Ellie's room. I recognized the cover on the
bed as I staggered forward. But she wasn't there, and my heart
leapt into my mouth. What the hell had he done with her?

The smoke was only just beginning to thicken in Ellie's
room, and I slumped onto the bed. It was getting harder to
pull oxygen into my lungs, and I was weakening; running out
of time. In fact, there was a good chance it was over already. I
closed my eyes to ease the stinging sensation and pictures of
Ellie played in my mind's eye like a movie. Her smile, her
musical laugh. The way she said exactly what she was
thinking and fuck the consequences. Those eyes and how
they seemed to see through me, or at least the façade of me.

My heart was breaking at the knowledge that I would
never hold her again. Never kiss her again. But the one saving
grace was that it would be all be over soon. I wouldn't suffer
for much longer. I just hoped that Ellie hadn't suffered. Not
like Maria had. I just wanted to know that it had all happened
quickly.

But of course, I could never know that.

I could hear loud creaking sounds as the structure of the
building began to give way, and I tried to open my eyes, but as
soon as I did they began to drift closed again. It was too much

effort now. I clambered back onto Ellie's bed, ready to give in and my hand dangled over the other side. Suddenly I forced my eyes open and looked down.

She was there.

It was Ellie.

Urging myself to move and with a renewed determination I pulled myself up and reached to grab her arm. Her skin was still warm, but her body was limp. I somehow grappled her into my arms and began to drag us both toward the doorway, but there was too much debris blocking our path. She lolled to the side, and her head rested on the curve of my neck and shoulder, leaving a wet patch where she had touched me. The metallic stench of blood infiltrated my nostrils and anger at the fact that Caveman had obviously harmed her fired me up. With dogged determination and a rush of adrenaline, I made for the window. I grabbed my gun from the back of my waistband and with the butt end I hammered at the glass with as much force as I could muster until it shattered. Grabbing the cover from her bed with one hand while keeping Ellie close to my body with the other I dragged the cover over the bottom of the window to cover the glass shards.

I tried not to focus on the burning sensation in my lungs as I pulled us both onto the ledge and with her in front of me so I would take the impact of the fall I closed my eyes and pushed off the frame allowing us to tumble backward out of the broken window. Down... down... down...

The impact knocked the remaining air from my lungs, and I couldn't pull any back in but instead of panicking about myself all I cared about was Ellie. Had she made it? Would she be okay?

A familiar voice bellowed out, "Hey! Get the paramedics! They're here! They're fucking here! Aww shit, there's a lot of blood. Something's not right." It was Nate's voice I heard at first. I briefly wondered how he was still standing after his earlier altercation with the cop. But then he was joined by others wearing high viz jackets and crowded around me with panic-stricken faces.

"Is she... is she okay?" I gasped, letting my eyes close.

"Come on man. Don't go to sleep okay? Rae's breathing, buddy. So you need to stay strong for her, okay?"

Who the hell is Rae? What about Ellie? I fought to get the words out, but I was sapped of every ounce of energy.

If there is a God... and if you haven't given up on me yet... please let Ellie live. You can take me, but it's not her time... please.

Soon everything began to echo. The world began to recede until all that remained was blackness and the comforting cloak of silence.

CHAPTER FORTY-SIX

Ellie

I attempted to open my eyes but it was such a massive effort, and I almost gave up. But spurring me on was the fact that I wanted to know where I was, and I needed to know what the hell was going on. My limbs were as heavy as lead, and I was pretty sure I'd been drugged. There was a cool breeze covering my nose and mouth, and I eventually realized it was coming from an oxygen mask that was attached to my face.

Scrambling around my brain, I tried to remember what the hell had happened to bring me to this point. And then like a barrage of scattered photographs it came rushing back. Every horrific second. Though the image that stood out the most was the evil grin of the long haired man whose tattoos I could only just make out just before he struck me in the head. I should have been in pain, but there was none. Confusion began to take over, draining me of what little energy I appeared to have and the continual lulling beep of a machine close to my bed did its best to pull me back into the depths of slumber.

"Ellie? Ellie honey, are you awake?" The shaking, hope-filled voice of my best friend Chloe came from my right side, and I battled to open my eyes again. "Hey, sweetie. You *are* awake. Oh god, it's so good to see you open your eyes," she sobbed and clung to my hand. "Don't try to speak. You're in the hospital. You're going to be okay."

The hospital? Okay, that actually did make sense. After all, I'd had a blow to my head. And the mask... oh yeah the mask would be to help my lungs after the smoke inhalation.

There had been a fire.

Oh god... my parents.

The bleeping of the machine beside me picked up speed and suddenly my eyes were wide open. The terrifying memory of sweltering heat, smoke and flames assaulted my mind, and I began to gasp. It was as if someone was sitting on my chest. I stared up at Chloe, who covered her mouth with her hands as tears streamed down her face. Suddenly the room was alive with movement, and I was surrounded by people wearing scrubs. Nurses? Doctors? I wasn't sure, but they were all talking in rushed voices about IVs, BPs and sedatives.

I began to relax once more, and I felt Chloe grip my hand again. I turned my focus to her. "My... my mom and dad... are they..." It turned out speaking was painful and even more effort than keeping my eyes open.

"Please, try to rest honey. You *need* to rest."

Okay, so she wasn't answering my attempted question. Did this mean she hadn't heard me? Or maybe that she didn't *want* to answer me. Tears escaped the corners of my eyes as I closed them again, trying desperately not to think the worst, but failing miserably.

———

The next time I opened my eyes, I was with Colt and we were at Baylor's Point. I had no clue how we had gotten there or why I appeared to be wearing a long, flowing, white gown I didn't remember owning. It was kind of like a wedding dress or something an angel might wear. The sun was blazing down on us, casting an almost ethereal, golden glow on our surroundings and when I inhaled through my nose I could smell the fresh pine scent of the trees behind us.

Turning my attention to Colt, I noticed his clothes were dirty and his arms scratched and bruised. He was standing with his back toward me at the edge of the precipice with his head bowed.

"Colt? Are you okay?" I was relieved when my words were coherent this time, and it was easier to speak.

He turned to me, but his face was really dirty too with what looked like soot or coal or... What struck me more though were the streaks of moisture that had made clean trails through the black marks on his face.

He was crying. Why was he crying?

I tried again. "What's wrong, Colt? Are you okay?"

He simply shook his head, sadness emanating from him and an almost palpable heaviness hung in the air between us.

He brought his fingers to his lips, kissed them and held them out toward me as his lip trembled. "I'm so sorry, Red. I had to save *you,* not *me*. It *had* to be you. But it's over now. I'm so sorry I can never love you now."

Suddenly the sky grew dark and ominous; a swirling black cloud surrounded us, and my heart began to hammer at my ribs as fear gripped me. Before I knew what was happening I was in his arms and we were falling backward into the blackness of the rocky chasm but my back was to his front, and so I couldn't see his face.

What did he mean he'd had to save *me not him*? What did

he mean he could never love me *now*? And why were we here at Baylor's Point? None of it made sense. I tried to speak, but my voice became trapped in my throat again causing me to panic. I *needed* to speak to him; to ask for an explanation. But the farther we fell, and the more I tried to turn to look at him, the tighter his grip became, restricting my movement even more.

At last, my panic ridden voice was free. "Colt! Please Colt! Tell me what you mean! Please!"

"Shhh. It's okay Ellie, dear. You're safe now. It's okay, sweetheart," a familiar, soft, feminine voice assured me, and my escalated heart rate and the rapid bleeping began to calm.

Someone stroked my hair, and I opened my eyes to find myself back in the hospital once again. Glancing to my side I was filled with immense relief to see my mom's face. *She* had been the one stroking my hair. So the meeting with Colt had been what? A dream?

As soon I made eye contact with my mom we both began to sob. She reached up and cupped my cheek with her hand. "I thought I'd lost you too, Ellie. But *he* saved you. He made sure you got out. He saved me too. If it hadn't been for *him*... I'm so grateful. So very, very grateful."

As I let the tears fall, her words began to sink in. She thought she had lost me *too*?

"Mom... mom, where's Dad? Did he save us?" I croaked, my throat was sore and the pain in my head returning.

Fresh tears trailed down her pale skin. "Oh, sweetie. No, it was Colt. Colt saved us. But... your dad... I'm so sorry. So, so sorry. He... he didn't make it."

CHAPTER FORTY-SEVEN

ELLIE

It was strange and surreal being surrounded by bikers at my dad's funeral. Everyone was very respectful, and he was given an honorary MC send off. Motorcycles lined the road that led to the chapel and seeing the men all bow their heads as we passed in the car made my throat tighten, and my lip tremble. He would've liked that they were there. I know deep down he always wanted to ride a motorcycle, and I saw the way his eyes lit up when Colt arrived on his. I reckon my dad was a biker at heart.

But the weirdest fact of all was that members of both CoSMiC and Loki's Legion were present. Everyone from Nate and Deak to Six, Dee, Chloe and the new prospects from each club. All there for *my* dad. The fact tugged at my heart, and I had to fight to keep it together. Everyone had put their differences aside to say goodbye.

Everyone except Colt.

During the service, although I was falling apart on this inside, I was fighting to be as strong as I possibly could for my mom's sake. But as soon as everyone had gone home and mom and I were left alone in our rented house—her in bed, sobbing and me clutching a glass of Jack Daniel's in the silence of the living room—I crumbled.

My dad was gone.

The man I considered a hero; invincible. The man who had protected me for so long and loved me more than anything would never hold me again. My heart had shattered into a million pieces, and I felt sure I would never be the same again.

With Colt gone too, I was struggling to cope with it all. Everything had imploded around me, and there had been nothing I could to stop it. I could have blamed Colt and his crew, or Deak and his but really it was pointless laying blame. Where was the healing in that? It wouldn't bring Colt or my dad back to me.

I had been plagued by nightmares again when I did sleep, but most nights I lay awake crying. My doctor had prescribed me something to help me sleep, but I hadn't been taking the medication. I wasn't ready to let go of the pain. The pain *meant* something to me. It was like I was feeling it for those who could no longer feel.

———

In the weeks that followed the fire and my dad's funeral, everything changed. Both of the biker crews met on neutral ground and called a truce. Six had stepped into the role of President and he and Deak—with Nate as mediator—had come to an agreement that enough lives had been lost and enough time had been spent fighting. That it was time to move forward together. They agreed that they could start to work collectively on local community projects to try and repair some of the damage that they had inadvertently caused to others, simply by their war with each other.

The police had even been involved, and Caveman, aka Larry Cavan, had been arrested on suspicion of first-degree murder, assault and arson. It turned out he had a pretty heavy drug and alcohol problem as well as anger management and control issues. He had even attempted to bite the ear off of one of the officers who arrested him. Psycho.

So what of Colt?

I too wanted to know the answer to that question. He had been taken to a hospital out of town on account of the severity of his injuries after falling from the window with me in his arms. Although I hadn't been informed what those injuries were. There was a shroud of secrecy surrounding Colt's disappearance and when I managed to locate the hospital he had been taken to, I was told by his doctors that they couldn't give me any information as I wasn't his next of kin. And there was no-one to ask, seeing as he no longer had any apparent living next of kin.

So I was left in limbo. I didn't know whether he lived or died. It was as if he up and vanished off the face of the earth.

At first, I was sure that CoSMiC were hiding something from me. Surely they knew his fate. But the longer I hung around Chloe and Six the more it became clear that they knew just as much, or as little as I did.

After two months of searching in vain, while hoping and praying he would return, I gave up. After all, if it's apparently clear someone doesn't want to be found, there's no point looking, right?

———

Knowing I would never recover from losing two people who

were so very important to me, and knowing my mom and I had lost everything in the hotel fire we made the difficult decision to move away. To start afresh in a new place. There was a hole in my heart that I knew would never and could never be healed.

I had my memories of growing up with the most wonderful dad a girl could wish for, and that was okay. I had so many to cling to.

The memories of Colt, however, were a little more difficult to live with. I had fallen for a broken man. A man who thought that every person only ever gets *one* shot at real love. When deep down I knew he was wrong. Part of his problem had been the inability to *let* himself love and *be* loved. Reading the letter that his brother had intended to leave for him, told me that this was something he had struggled with all of his life, and that broke my heart. Letting Maria love him must have been so very hard for him. But loving her back must have taken all he had. After all, he lost his father whom he had worshipped, as a hero, and he had always blamed himself. And so in loving someone so passionately, he was allowing himself to become vulnerable. And that was something he saw as dangerous.

He also blamed himself for losing Maria. But cancer knows no boundaries. It's such an unpredictable illness with so many possible outcomes, and it was in no way something he could have altered. Maria's death had crushed him, and the guilt he was still carrying when I met him must have been overwhelming; not only from his dad's death but also from losing the love of his life. My heart ached for him. And for me. For what could have been if he had only let me in.

I had never been in love until I met Colt. Jacob Coltman was an enigma. Such a hard, brash exterior but with a heart so big that the pain filling it would have killed most people. Not

Colt though. His heart may have been broken, but it was inherently good.

I discovered, from Nate, that he had gone to the Loki's Legion compound to try and appeal to Deak's better side for a truce. For some kind of unwritten agreement that they could get along. And in spite of the murder of his brother, he chose not to retaliate. He chose to be the bigger person. To try and make amends. If only it had happened back then, maybe the fire wouldn't have happened, and Colt and my dad would still be with me.

Every time I thought about Colt, I fought back tears. When he disappeared, he took pieces of my heart with him. But it was the not knowing that hurt more than anything. At least with my dad, I knew what had happened. I only wished that Colt had cared enough about me to somehow let me know if he had lived or died.

I was plagued with life-like dreams much like the one I'd experienced in hospital. The touch of his fingers caressing my skin; the sensation of his mouth on mine. Only I would wake to find myself alone in a strange, new house in a strange, new place.

I would eventually have to move on. But the dream of Colt at Baylor's Point preyed on my mind. Was it some kind of other-worldly meeting? Did I really know he had passed away after we fell, and I was in denial? No-one would talk about it with me back in Rose Acres. Every time I tried to broach the subject, the conversation was rapidly turned around in a different direction.

So as time went on, I worked hard to let it sink into my head that I had lost him. I was thankful that I had my mom, and Colt was responsible for that fact, so at least I had something amazing to remember him by.

That was something.

CHAPTER FORTY-EIGHT

One year after relocation

E L L I E

My feet were killing me. But I couldn't complain. Not really. My mom had been amazing in giving me the day off to shop for clothes, and I had lost count of the number of times I had asked if she minded. But of course, she didn't. Looking after her grandbaby was her favorite hobby now she was officially retired. And looking after a five-month-old didn't seem to faze her in the slightest. She never ceased to amaze me and had far more energy than any woman her age.

I tried on outfit after outfit, but nothing seemed to be just right. And the fact I was going on my first date in over a year meant that I was a walking disaster of nerves and butterflies. But it felt good to be getting back out there. At least that's what I was telling myself. Settling on a pretty grey dress with a subtle white floral print, I stood at the register ready to pay my bill.

"Oh hey, Ellie. You found something at last?" Boo, the

shop's owner asked as she rang up my dress complete with staff discount.

I giggled and rolled my eyes. "Yeah. You'd think finding something myself would be easy after the number of clients I've dressed working here."

"Oh honey, *that* part never gets easier. I always see things I want for me, but then someone always comes in and tries it on and it looks better on them than it ever could on my squidgy derrière."

"Oh seriously, Boo? I doubt that." Boo was one of those beautiful curvy women who would look great in a garbage sack tied up with twine. It was just a shame she didn't see herself like others did.

My part time job at Boo-teek had been a way of getting out and being active. I had worked right up to the birth, but Boo had insisted I took six months off afterward to get used to being a mom. She was a wonderful friend who had taken a chance on a puking young woman who was dealing with the devastating news that she was pregnant to an absent father.

"So how's that little bundle of joy doing?"

"Oh you know, eating, giggling, pooping and sleeping. In between scaring us half to death trying to crawl."

"Oh my goodness, you're going to be exhausted running around moving stuff to higher surfaces and closing cupboards. I remember it all so well. But it's fun."

I nodded with a smile. "Oh yeah. Never a dull moment that's for sure."

"So, what's the occasion that warrants such a pretty dress? Is the lucky town of Schofield getting painted red tonight?"

I felt heat rise in my cheeks and found myself glancing around to check who was listening in. "Umm... I have a... umm..."

Boo clapped her hands together. "You've got a date?"

Suddenly she was around my side of the counter and hugging me so tight I could barely breathe.

"Y-yes, I do."

She held me at arm's length. "And who is the lucky fella?"

"His name is Jonah Watson."

"Jonah the mechanic? Oh, he's a looker." She winked.

"Yeah. That's the guy. You know him?"

"I take my old station wagon there for fix-ups, honey. If I'd known you liked him, I would've set you up months ago."

"Oh no, it's fine. Really. I'm still getting used to the fact that I have a date. It's taken me a while to accept." I began to back away and head for the door. I was ready for this conversation to be over.

"Well, you're going to look beautiful. That gorgeous red hair of yours will look stunning with that pretty dress, honey. You go and have a wonderful time. And I want all the details."

I waved as I left the shop and breathed a sigh of relief as the warm June air touched my skin.

———

Jonah had wanted to pick me up from home, but I wasn't ready to do the whole introducing-the-baby-to-a-new-man thing. I needed to see where things went first. Jonah was a nice guy and seemed trustworthy, but I needed to experience him for myself first. Explaining this to him had been difficult but thankfully he had been great. One positive checkmark.

I arrived a little after eight at Barclay's Steak House and made my way apprehensively to Jonah.

He stood as I approached. "Wow, look at you." A handsome grin spread across his face and my confidence increased a little. It had been a while since a man had reacted in such a way to me and I liked the buzz it gave me.

I tucked my hair behind one ear and felt the burning in my cheeks. "Thank you. I loved the dress but wasn't sure if it was me."

He took my hand and kissed the back of it. "Oh believe me when I say it's definitely you." My stomach fluttered at his words, and I was unsure if that meant something.

He held out my chair and I smoothed the dove grey fabric underneath me as I sat. "So, how was your day?"

"Busy as always. Yours?"

I smiled at the fact we were making such lame small talk. "About the same."

A waiter came over and handed us a couple of menus and I began to browse two long lists of delicious sounding items. My stomach growled, but I knew I would struggle to eat anything, thanks to my insides being taken over by a swarm of crazy butterflies who appeared to be learning Zumba.

Jonah placed his menu down on the table decisively. "Well, I think as we're in Barclay's Steak House it'd be wrong to go with anything but the rib eye."

Unable to choose I placed mine down too. "Yeah. I'll go with that too." He waved a waiter over and placed our order along with a portion of fries and a pitcher of beer. It stung a little that he hadn't asked for my drink choice. But I decided to let it go as he was more than likely nervous too, and trying to be a gentleman.

He folded his hands and rested his elbows on the table. "So, Ellie, tell me about yourself. I mean something I don't already know."

Was this an interview now? Jeez. I shook my head. "There's nothing else to tell really. I moved here a year ago with my mom after we went through a difficult time. Got a job, had a baby, rented a house. Not in that order, exactly." I shrugged. "That's really all there is. I don't have anything exciting in my past." Okay, so that was a slight lie. "How about you? What made you want to be a mechanic?"

He took a deep breath. "Well... I have *always* been fascinated by how things work. You know? When I was a kid, I was regularly getting in trouble for deconstructing stuff. I loved clocks mainly. But as I got older, I got interested in bigger things. Engines and what not. And I was always the go-to-guy when things needed fixing. My dad wanted me to go into finance. But it just wasn't me. And so I dropped out of school and got an apprenticeship at the garage and the rest, as they say, is history."

The waiter placed our drinks in front of us, and then soon after, the food arrived too. Jonah began to tuck in right away.

"What's your favorite thing to work on now?" He placed his cutlery down and chewed thoughtfully. "Definitely bikes. The bigger the better." *Oh great. Another bike fanatic.* "In fact, I got to work on a beautiful black Ducati Monster yesterday. It was only a flat and he stopped in because he didn't have any equipment, but it was nice to see a 2010 model in such great condition. Man, what I wouldn't give to ride one of those things. I have to have a pickup for work, you know? But what I really want to own is a Ducati. The way it clings to the road..."

My mind was carried away as he talked about something that was clearly a passion of his, but the talk of motorcycles took me back to place I didn't want to revisit. Memories that were just too painful to recall began to surface, and I shook my head in a bid to dislodge them.

"You okay, Ellie? You drifted off there for a second."

Oh, shitty shit. "Oh, gosh, Jonah you must think I'm terrible."

He held up his hands and smiled. "Oh no, hey I guess you're tired a whole lot, with having a kid and all. I hear they can be demanding little critters. Anyway, you didn't answer my question."

I racked my brains trying to figure out what the hell he had asked me, but I couldn't call it to mind. Cringing, I apologized. "Jeez, I'm so sorry, what did you ask me again?"

He chuckled. "Nah, no biggie. I just asked if you'd ever ridden a motorcycle that's all."

I picked up my beer glass and took a long pull. "Yeah. Just pillion. But it was a long time ago. I'd... I'd rather talk about something else if that's okay?"

A crease appeared between his brows. "Ah yeah. Okay, that's fine. I can see from your eyes you're real tired. I don't mind doing the talking. I mean, you're gonna want to know everything about me if I'm going to be getting to know your kid." Jonah launched into another monolog about cars and bikes and oddly enough managed to omit all facts about himself.

My kid? This guy hasn't asked a single question about my baby and here he is assuming he's going to be introduced? And boy can he talk.

"Oh and I forgot to say. You wanna know something weird about the guy with the Ducati?"

Not really. I shrugged. "Sure." The night was already starting to feel long, and we hadn't even gotten through the main course.

"He... wait for it... you're not gonna believe this..."

I forced a smile. "I'm waiting."

"Okay... this is no word of a lie. He only had *one* leg. *One.* Can you imagine? One darn leg and he was still riding. Crazy."

Now I was impressed. "Wow. That's incredible. Was he okay?"

"Oh yeah. He was fine. Obviously loved his bike. I mean the dude could ride. *Really* ride."

My mind shot back again to my time with Company of Sinners MC and I tried to imagine how any of them would've coped in that situation. And it dawned on me that they would have never given up riding either. My heart lifted as I felt a sense of pride for the amputee I didn't even know and wished I'd had a chance to meet him. He had clearly overcome adversity and had laughed in its face. I liked the sound of that guy.

Jonah carried on with his story. "He was a really cool guy. Older than us, you know? Tons of ink. I mean *tons*. Shit, I couldn't even imagine having *one* tattoo, but the ones he had were amazing."

I smiled to myself as I remembered the inked friends I had left behind in Rose Acres and something akin to homesickness overtook me.

Jonah oozed enthusiasm as he continued. "Funny thing was his bike was black, but it *clearly* wasn't his favorite color." He shook his head and chuckled for reasons only known to himself.

I scrunched my brow. "How the hell could you tell his favorite color from one meeting? And how did you get onto such topics at a workshop when we haven't even covered that over dinner?"

He either didn't get my snide reference or he just ignored it. "He had this tat on his forearm. Huge fancy lettering with kind of broken hearts and wings all around it. Real beautiful. You could see he really went to town on getting it just right."

"Again, how could you tell his favorite color from *that*?"

"The word he had tattooed—one single word—and it said 'Red'."

CHAPTER FORTY-NINE

ELLIE

Red?

It was as if I had slipped into some parallel universe. Jonah kept on talking as the restaurant began to spin and my heart tried to escape through my ribcage. It had to be a coincidence. Surely it was a coincidence.

Jonah reached across the table and touched my arm. "Hey, Ellie. You've gone awfully pale. Are you okay?"

"The... the man with the bike. Did he tell you his name?"

"Umm... probably... why?"

"Jonah what was his name?"

"I... I can't remember. Why?"

I shook my head. How the hell could I explain? "Nothing. Was he just passing through town? Or is he staying here?"

He sat back in his chair and scowled at me. "I thought we were on a date, Ellie. But all you're interested in is some old dude with a flashy bike."

I gasped. "Oh really? Has it occurred to you that you called my child a *kid* on more than one occasion but haven't even bothered to enquire about its gender or name? And that you have talked non-stop about cars, bikes and the shop, but you've told me *nothing* about yourself in spite of the fact that you said that's what you were doing?"

He opened and closed his mouth like one of those dumb coin games at the amusement arcade where you try to flip the penny in.

He held his hands up in surrender. "But I don't know shit about kids. Hell, I don't even *want* my own so I have no clue what to ask about them."

Okay. That iced the huge shit cake that had been baking throughout the short but awkward evening.

I stood. "Look, Jonah, I think we both know this isn't going to work out. Thank you for inviting me and for saying I looked nice. It really boosted my deflated ego. And it's been a long time since anyone has done that. But I think I'm going to go home and cuddle my baby and relieve my mom of her babysitting duties." I reached into my purse, took out a couple of twenty dollar bills and placed them on the table. "I'm really sorry, Jonah."

He stared up at me for in disbelief for a moment and then nodded. "Okay, sure. Do you umm... want me to walk you home?"

"No, it's fine. It's not far."

"Well... I'm sorry it didn't work out. Take care okay?"

I smiled. "Thanks. You too."

I turned to walk away and he called after me. "Ellie." I stopped and turned to face him one last time. "That guy. The guy with the bike. I think he's staying over at O'Flannigan's Inn."

My heart leapt, and I made for the door as quick as I could, knowing full well that I had to walk by O'Flannigan's on my route home. Could I simply walk past without giving into temptation to go in and see for myself if the man was Colt? I doubted it.

I began to walk at a fast pace that matched my heart rate. The lights of O'Flannigan's Irish Inn were like a beacon in the distance and without really considering the consequences I headed right for them. What would I find there? If it was Colt how the hell had he lost a leg? Why had he run away and played dead? Why did he not want to be found? I had so many questions I wanted to ask him. But I had so many things I wanted to tell him too.

With my heart pounding, I pushed on the door with two shaking hands and walked in. The place was buzzing with what would have been a wonderful atmosphere under normal circumstances. But this was anything but normal. A trio of musicians played in a corner and the majority of the patrons sang along.

As the song ended the place erupted with a loud raucous cheer. The singer, a bright-eyed, white haired man addressed the audience. "Thank you, thank you. Now I think we'd better calm things down a wee bit. Seeing as closing time is upon us as we don't want to be sending you on your way in too high spirits we're going to sing an old Irish love song. This one's called 'Red is the Rose'."

A round of applause ensued, and the two other band members placed their instruments down to join their leader in an acapella version of the song. As they began to sing a shiver traveled the extent of my spine and emotion tightened my throat. The song my dad used to sing to me as a child began to drift across the air and into my heart. As they sang, memories of my dad began to play like a film reel in my mind and my sense of loss deepened inside of me.

As I trailed my gaze around the bar of silently swaying

couples, I was suddenly locked on a pair of very familiar grey eyes that were wide with disbelief and I gasped.

As the song reached its crescendo, I watched as Colt pushed his way through the crowds of people making his way toward me. When he reached me, he scooped me up in his arms as the crowd cheered once more for the wonderful rendition of the beautiful song.

―――――

Colt

It hadn't been a dream. It really had been her walking down the street the day before with a pink tote bag emblazoned with the words 'Boo-teek'. I had watched that familiar mass of flame red curls bounce along, but I hadn't been able to see her face. Although something deep inside me knew it was her. I would know that hair anywhere.

And there she was in some Irish Inn I happened to be staying in as I passed through Schofield on my way back to Rose Acres. What the hell was she doing here?

I fought my way through crowd of alcohol-fueled revelers, ignoring the sting of my prosthetic rubbing against my tender skin, and prayed that she wouldn't turn and run. Although I wouldn't have blamed her if she had. It was what I deserved. But she stayed. Frozen to the spot as if she had been rendered immobile. Her chest heaved, and her eyes stared, unblinking, directly into mine.

When I reached her, my initial urge was to kiss her. Right there in full view of every fucker in the place and hang the consequences, but I didn't want to give her any excuse to leave. And so I hauled her into my arms and held on for dear life.

I clung to her and inhaled the scent of her hair as emotions I had learned to push deep down began to resurface for the first time in over a year. The trio on the small corner stage fired up another Irish folk song and the people in the place began to jump around and dance. I needed to get her out of here so we could talk.

I pulled away and cupped her face in my hands. "Follow me?" Please say yes. She hesitated and my heart beat out a frantic rhythm.

She closed her eyes and tears escaped the corners. "I can't. I have to get back." She tried to pull away, but I couldn't let her go. What if she was passing through, too, and she left without saying goodbye? *Just like you did, asshole.*

"Eleanor, please. Don't go. Not yet."

"Colt, you don't understand. I can't stay here. I can't be near you." She turned to go, and I panicked, grabbing for her arm and tugging her close to me again so that our bodies were flush together. "Ellie, please. Please don't go. Not yet."

"I only came here to check if it was you. And I see it is. So now I know to avoid coming near this place until you're gone. I thought I could do this but I... I can't."

She pulled herself from my arms and walked toward the door. I started to follow her when a guy I recognized stepped in front of me. "Let her go, dude. I don't know what went down, but she said she doesn't want to talk to you. Why don't you get on your bike and take your one good leg back to wherever the hell you came from?"

I clenched my jaw. "Look, buddy, I get that you're trying to look out for the lady, but she and I have shit to deal with. So just step aside and let me go to her." I tried to step around him when his fist collided with my face, and I staggered back a few steps but managed not to fall.

I righted myself and stepped up to him. "You got a death

wish, huh asshole? Coz you just signed your fucking death warrant." I raised my fist to retaliate when a scream halted me.

"Colt!" Red must have seen what happened, and she was standing by the door in her pretty little dress, her body looking all kinds of fucking sexy but with a look of horror on her face. "Jonah, no!"

The mechanic had his fist held aloft ready to strike again, but when he heard her call out to him he lowered it and leaned toward me. "You're one lucky son of a bitch. I hope you know that." And with that final comment, he shoved past me and walked in the opposite direction to Red. I chuckled to myself. It was he who was the lucky son of a bitch. If it hadn't been for Red shouting, I would've put the prick in hospital. I glanced around me and realized the music had stopped and every set of eyes in the damn place were trained on me.

"Come on. Let's get out of here." Red was beside me again and gripped my hand, tugging me toward the door.

"You know I have a room here. We could talk. Just for a little while."

She stopped in her tracks and turned to face me again. Her green eyes blazing with an intense fire I hadn't seen in far too long. "Fine. You have ten minutes."

CHAPTER FIFTY

ELLIE

I followed Colt up the stairs to a room on the first floor. He paused and turned to face me. "I can't believe you're here."

I glared at him and folded my arms across my chest. "Just open the goddamn door, Colt."

As requested he unlocked and pushed it open, and we both stepped inside. If I'd had a proverbial cat to swing, I couldn't have swung it the room was so damn small. But it was kind of cute and cozy at the same time with scenes of Irish landscapes on the wall.

He stood at the other side of the room staring at me. "You look so fucking beautiful." His deep, husky voice still gave me shivers.

I took a moment to look him over. His hair was shorter. Shaved underneath and kind of floppy at the top. He wore a long-sleeved black shirt with a plaid lumberjack-style shirt over the top. As I watched, he shoved his sleeves part way up his forearms and suddenly the tattoo was visible. The one Jonah had mentioned. I swallowed hard as my lip began to tremble. It was so beautiful. An intricate font spelled out his name for me and surrounding it were broken hearts. The words trust, hope, love, and respect were scattered around in smaller fonts and with each word was a complete heart.

He stepped the short distance across the floor toward me and slipped his hands into my hair. "Please don't cry, Ellie. Not over me. I don't deserve it." Pain was evident in his eyes, and his face was dangerously close to mine.

"Your tattoo... it's beautiful."

He smiled shyly. "You spotted it then, huh?"

I reached out and traced the edges with my fingertips. "Why are the hearts all broken?"

He paused as if the collect his thoughts. "Because that's how I felt when I left you. And... see they're not all broken." He gestured to the ones accompanying the other words.

"And what do those mean?"

His smile widened. "They're all the things you gave me Ellie. And I'm so grateful for that."

I gazed up into the eyes of the man that stole my heart and subsequently broke it, and a moment of clarity occurred. He was too close to me. Much too close.

I stepped back a little. "What happened, Colt? After the fire? I thought you were dead. You broke my heart, and I have no idea why."

He gestured toward the bed. The only seating area in the room. "Come on, let's sit, huh?"

He held my hand as we sat but I pulled mine away. "What happened, Colt?" I asked again with more insistence but without making eye contact.

He leaned forward and heaved a deep sigh, resting his elbows on his knees. "When I realized you were in danger ... Something became very clear to me, and it scared the shit out of me."

"W-what became clear?"

He turned to face me. His eyes were glassy in the dim lighting of the room. "I realized I was in love with you, Ellie."

I gasped. Of all the things I was expecting to hear it wasn't that. "But... you... you left."

He nodded. "I also realized that I couldn't have a relationship with you. Regardless of my feelings. It felt like a betrayal to Maria. And... I didn't deserve to be loved. I was responsible for the death of my own father... Well, I told him I hated him as he left for a boat trip and he never came back. Maria died, and I couldn't save her. And then you were in a damn fire because of some dumb fucking feud between me and a rival MC. You deserved to be loved by someone better, Eleanor."

A cascade of warm tears trickled down my face. "Don't you think it would have been good to ask me how I felt about all of that?"

He nodded slowly. "Yeah. I see that now. But also... there was something else."

"What else?"

"When I pulled us out that window, on the night of the fire. I landed on a pretty huge shard of glass. Severed the nerves in my right leg. I thought I was going to die, but even then all I could think was about you. And all I wanted to know was if you'd made it. If you were going to be okay. Once I knew you were, I made my peace with dying. But then... Then I awoke in a hospital to be told that my leg had been amputated to save my life, and I was so fucking angry, Ellie. So fucking angry. I should have died, but instead, I was facing an uncertain future. What the fuck use would I be to anyone with one damn leg? And then I thought about you again and the fact that I knew how good you were. How good your heart is. And I knew that you'd tell me I was no less of a man. That you'd love me regardless. But I didn't want you to have to lie to me."

Anger spiked up from deep within me, and I wanted to slap him. I wanted to shake him. But instead, I stood. I had to leave. "How *dare* you presume anything about me? You never gave me a chance. You just stayed away and played dead, you bastard. You left me wondering and worrying. All because you didn't want to appear to be less of a man? My god, you really are an idiot. People go through these things, and they get on with it. They cope. That's exactly what we would've done. And why would I have been lying to you? Do you know me at all?"

He bowed his head and stared at the floor. He didn't even bother to defend himself, and I felt cruel. He had saved my life after all, and for that alone he deserved my respect and my gratitude.

Lowering myself to the space beside him once more, I took his hand in mine. "Do you not realize that my love for you was unconditional? Dumb as *ass,* of course, but unconditional, too." I smiled, and he smiled in response. I reached up and stroked his face. "Colt, you saved my life. You saved my mom's life. You are a brave, strong man with a good heart. And it doesn't matter how you changed physically. I would have loved you, regardless. More so even for what you did. With *all* my heart. I just wanted you to love me back. But you couldn't."

He reached up and slipped his hand into my hair again. "But I did love you, Ellie. I still do. It took me a long time to let myself believe I could love again but when I did it was too late... I was on my way back to Rose Acres to find you. To ask you to forgive me. I know it was a long shot and that I didn't deserve your forgiveness, but it was all I needed. And then I was going to leave and let you get on with your life. I knew you would have moved on. Your boyfriend is certainly protective of you, and I can understand that."

"My boyf—Oh you mean Jonah. He and I are…" We were nothing. So why couldn't I admit to it? I changed the subject rapidly. "So what made you decide to look for me after all?"

"I had a long rehabilitation period. It was the hardest thing I've ever gone through. Or at least I thought it was. But as part of my physical rehab I had counseling too. Apparently losing a limb is quite life-changing." He chuckled and rolled his eyes. "Another thing I wasn't willing to believe, but of course, they were right. It changes *everything,* and not just physically. My therapist was this feisty brunette." He laughed lightly. "Reminded me a lot of you. In fact, we ended up talking about you a helluva lot. She made me realize *I* had been responsible for losing you. That I'd had a chance at love again and that I'd pushed you away. And that in doing so I caused *you* so much unnecessary pain. I needed to say sorry for that. I needed to tell you how I truly felt. How much I loved you… *love* you."

The sincerity in his eyes almost broke down my defenses, but there were other things he needed to know, and I wasn't sure how he would react. I couldn't let myself be distracted by him. Not again. Not ever again.

"I've missed you so much, Red," he whispered as he leaned toward me and before I could resist his mouth was on mine. His hands were in my hair, and my fingers clung to his shirt as his lips and tongue took mine in a passionate and familiar kiss. My body ached for him. The need was so strong, it took me by surprise. I had been kidding myself thinking I could just move on. Thinking I could get over him. I never would.

Even if it was just for one last time I had to feel him inside of me; his skin next to mine. He groaned, and desire spiked at the junction of my thighs. My body responded to him just as it always had. I craved his touch like we'd never been apart.

He pulled away from my mouth and his hand moved slowly downward until his thumb traced my lower lip. "How could I have been so wrong, but with such good intentions, Ellie?"

"I honestly don't know. I thought you knew me better than that."

"I did. I know I did. But I want to know you again. Will you let me? Will you let me love you?"

His words were my undoing, and we tumbled backward, a tangle of limbs and teasing, probing kisses. I was aware there were things I had to tell him but being in his arms again felt too good, and I didn't want to break the spell. I reached for the hem of his shirt and dragged it from his body. He responded in kind and when my dress was cast aside I lay beside him giving him the chance to explore my body as he had, only a year before.

His breathing rate increased as his fingers found my erect nipple. Yanking down the lace, he freed my breast and lowered his mouth to draw the sensitive bud of flesh between his teeth. I moaned my pleasure and scratched my nails down his bare, muscular back.

"Colt, I need you. I want you to fuck me." The words shocked even *me* as I heard them fall from my lips but they were spoken in the heat of desire and they were true.

He stopped moving and pulled away from me, moving to the edge of the bed and running his hands roughly through his hair. "Fuck. *Fuck!*"

What had I said to anger him? "Colt?"

He turned his head and gazed at me over his shoulder. "I want to. I really do. But... I don't... I haven't..."

Fearing he was regretting being with me, I reached out to

touch him. His skin was warm and soft, but the muscles underneath tensed. "You haven't what?"

He closed his eyes. "This is gonna sound really pathetic, but I haven't been with anyone since... well, since this." He gestured to his right leg and relief flooded me. "I'm worried about your reaction to it. The way it looks... I..."

Okay, this I can deal with.

I climbed from the bed and stood before him as I removed my panties and bra. He watched my every move, lips slightly parted; eyes hooded. Next, I tugged him to a standing position and smoothed my hands over his chest. "Remember what I said about unconditional?" He nodded, and I smiled. I reached for his waistband and flicked the button open, followed by the slow trail of the zipper until it could go no further.

His eyes were fixed on me as I lowered myself to my knees and pulled his jeans and boxers down, revealing the thigh socket of the partially metal, mechanical looking prosthetic he wore. "You're a hero, Colt. *My* hero. Don't ever forget that. Even if tonight is all we have, don't ever think this makes you less attractive to me or less of a man. If anything, it makes you more of one. This happened when you saved lives. When you sacrificed yourself for the lives of others. And that in itself makes it beautiful." I leaned forward and kissed the scarring that was just visible below his groin. When I gazed up at him again, the expression on his face had changed. It was unreadable, and that bothered me. He had to know that of course what he had been through *mattered* but not because it made him hideous. Quite the opposite. And I was determined to make him realize that.

With one hand on each thigh, I sucked his beautiful, thick cock into my mouth and he almost overbalanced. Letting his rigid flesh slip free from my mouth again, I began to pepper kisses over every inch of him. And I could sense his muscles tensing. I licked my way along the edge of the casing and back, until I could suck him into my mouth again.

His head rolled back, and he sighed deeply as the tension left his body. "Okay. You've made your point. Now can I make love to you?" *Make love?* But he didn't make love. I snapped my focus up to his eyes, and he smiled lovingly. "Let me love you, Ellie."

CHAPTER FIFTY-ONE

COLT

Once I was free from my jeans, socks and shoes I stood there, unabashedly naked, prosthetic and all as she trailed her hungry gaze over my whole body. She didn't cringe or flinch. There was no pity in her eyes only lust and adoration. Hell, she told me I was her *hero*. My physical appearance didn't faze her in the least, and I really was stupid to think it would have. But I still needed to prove my love for her. This was all about *her* now. I wanted to express with my body how much I missed her touch, her smile, every single thing about her.

Without her, I wasn't me. Or at least I wasn't the me I wanted to be.

Her naked curves were just as beautiful as I remembered. Her figure was a little fuller, but it only served to make me want her more. I lowered myself to the bed and rested between her open thighs. I wanted to taste her. To feel her body envelop mine. I had wasted so much time trying to figure out who the hell I was now, after the fire, when the truth was staring me in the face.

I was hers. That was all I needed to be.

She kept her eyes locked on me as I sunk myself deep into her tight, wet pussy, and she moaned a sexy little sound that told me it was exactly what she wanted. Withdrawing again, I held myself up on my forearms as I dipped my head to pull her nipple into my mouth again. Her breasts were larger than I remembered but again that meant there was more of her to feast on. More of her to love. And I had missed the feel of her beneath me so damn much. I hated myself for the separation I had forced on us and wished so much that I could go back and change the way I handled everything. Instead of being a coward who was stuck with ghosts in the past I would have told her I loved her on the night she first said it to me.

———

ELLIE

Colt's weight on me felt so good. So right. The way he could make me quiver with lust hadn't changed. I wanted to come from the second he thrust into me, but I was determined to make this last. In my mind, I was sure this was the last time. This was goodbye. Especially once he knew the truth. And so just for those moments, I wanted to block out the world around and all the shit that went with it and just let him love me. Because that's what he was doing. Every deliciously slow grind of his pelvis against my clit brought me to the brink of the abyss, but I wouldn't let go. Not yet.

"Ellie, oh god, Eleanor," his mumbled plea against my neck sent a shock wave of shivers right to my core. My clit throbbed, and my body was desperate for release, but he pulled away and locked his gaze on mine.

A crease between his brows and his bottom lip momentarily held between his teeth. "What did you mean when you said 'even if tonight is all we have'?"

I didn't answer. Instead, I pulled him down so his mouth connected with mine and I kissed him like it *was* goodbye. Like he would be leaving again, only this time I would know he *did* love me after all. And that meant more to me than any apology he could offer.

I was losing the ability to hold back. His hips circled and with every single connection my muscles began to tense. He tugged on my nipples desperately and his thrusts increased in speed. Pleasure radiated through every cell in my body, and I was getting close. His cock filled me and stretched me as it always had and the memories of every time we had been like this came flooding back. A cascade of tears escaped my eyes and I cried out as the overwhelming sensations of the most intense orgasm catapulted me out into the stratosphere.

"Oh god, Ellie, I love you so much. I love you, baby," Colt cried out too as he came.

We laid there, still connected, still breathing each other in until our hearts calmed and we had floated back down to earth.

He tugged me close and wrapped his muscular arms around me as he kissed my forehead and then rubbed his nose down the length of mine. "Eleanor Cassidy. Who would've thought that you'd melt my heart and make me love again. I'm just so sorry it took me so long to accept that love was what I was feeling. Can you forgive me?" He lowered his head until his eyes locked on mine. "Hey, why are you crying?"

Shaking my head, I tried to turn away but he wouldn't let me. "I just... I don't understand what changed that's all."

He smiled and kissed the tip of my nose. "I took my head outta my ass and grew a pair of balls."

In spite of my tumultuous emotional state I giggled. "Only

you could put it so eloquently." I swallowed hard, as I knew there were serious conversations to be had. Pulling myself free from the warmth of his embrace I grabbed the comforter from the end of the bed and wrapped it around me. "We... we need to talk, Colt."

When I turned to gauge his expression, he was frowning, and tension had re-appeared in his jaw. "Yeah. I guessed we would. And I'm guessing the comment you made about tonight being all we have is connected. I'm not stupid, Red. I knew you wouldn't stay single. I'd be an idiot if I thought you wouldn't have met someone new." He moved quickly and began to pull on his jeans. "Anyway, you don't have to worry. I'm only passing through, so..." He stood. "Well, Jonah won't find out about this from me." His voice broke, and he stopped moving to face me. He stood there shirtless with his hands resting low on his hips, his bare, tattooed chest heaving. "I just hope he knows, Ellie. I just hope he knows how lucky he is. I hope he tells you he loves you every fucking day, and that you are the center of his universe. I never had the chance to make you feel that way, and I *hate* myself for that. I hope he puts a diamond on your finger someday, and gives you babies and... I hope you can love him back. I hope I haven't ruined that for you, Ellie. I want you to be happy." He closed his eyes briefly, and when he opened them again, I could see defeat reflected back at me. "And I hope he doesn't leave it too late, like I did."

The pent up emotion inside me fell in damp trails down my skin. Here was my out. I could go along with this, and he would leave, and he would never know. Our little family could move on. And although I knew that was wrong, I struggled to speak. To correct him about Jonah and I.

He turned his face away and lifted his hand briefly to his eyes. "You know, the hardest thing I ever did was to not come back to you. After I lost my leg, I felt completely fucking useless. And I see now that all I really needed to resolve that was you. But I just couldn't expect you to love me. And I didn't want you to. But now. Now when it's too late, it's all I want, Ellie. It's all I need, but I get it. And now I guess the hardest thing I will ever do will be to walk away and admit to myself that it's really over. How do I do that? I don't have your strength, Ellie. Not anymore."

I knew at that moment that my words wouldn't help. I had to take action. And I had to act immediately.

CHAPTER FIFTY-TWO

Ellie

Walking out of Colt's hotel room after his heartfelt admission was one of the hardest things I had ever done. But I had to get home. There were things I needed to do. He had sat silently on the bed as I had dressed, readying myself to leave while guilt needled my insides.

Before I walked out of the door, I leaned to kiss his head. "You'll be happy again. You'll see." I just hoped I was right.

Once I arrived home, the sun had begun its ascent, and I showered quickly and dressed in jeans and a T-shirt. I made a quick explanation to my mom that I had to take the baby for a check-up appointment, and she accepted my lie without question. My stomach knotted and I felt queasy at the thought of keeping the truth from her, but I had to wait and see how things panned out later that morning with Colt.

Once I was ready, I checked my appearance and smiled. This would be a monumental day. I just hoped it would be so in a positive way. Although if I was going on gut feeling, everything was going to be wonderful.

———

Colt

"You'll be happy again. You'll see." Her words repeated over and over, and my heart ached like she had stabbed me. It was over. She hadn't said goodbye as such, but her words were final. She was basically wishing me well. It was a kind of "Let yourself be happy someday" kind of brush off. The kind of thing you say when goodbye hurts too much. And fuck did it hurt. I felt like a prize idiot for hoping for more. For hoping that making love to her would make her realize she still loved *me* and that she could let Jonah go.

Like I said, prize idiot.

As soon as I had showered, I pulled on clean clothes and stared at my reflection. Grey peppered my sideburns and beard, and the lines around my eyes had deepened. I was a forty-year-old guy with no wife, no real home and nothing much to show for my time on earth. Quite a catch. Ellie was young with a whole life ahead of her. A whole life in which she could take the time to find the perfect guy. So why would she have chosen me?

So where the hell should I go now? Rose Acres would be a quick stop off to see the guys at the club and apologize for my unexpected departure and disappearance. I had heard on the grapevine that Six was doing a great job as President but that he was only considering it a temporary thing. Rumor had it that he was soon to be headed for Scotland to be with his best friend who had set up his own business and offered Six a job out there. It kind of felt like the end of Company of Sinners in a way. And that made me sad but simultaneously relieved. So much shit had gone down that maybe it was time to leave all of that behind.

"Get your ass in gear, man. No point hanging around feeling sorry for yourself," I told the despondent-looking guy staring back at me. I grabbed my keys and my ratty old backpack and walked out of the room and out of O'Flannigan's Inn.

I straddled my bike, and as I turned the keys in the ignition, I glanced around me. Somewhere in the back of my mind, I clung to the hope that she'd show. And it'd be like the movies where she'd beg me not to leave. But of course, she didn't, and so I set off toward the town limits. Figuring I should stop off and make an apology first.

I pulled to a halt outside Mel's Motor Mechanics and turned off the engine. Jonah walked toward me wiping his hands on a rag.

"What do you want?" he hollered at me with a look of disdain.

I climbed off the bike and headed in his direction. "Hey, man. I wanted to apologize for last night. You kinda got caught up in the middle of something that goes back a while, and I had no business threatening you like that."

He gave me a snide curl of his lip. "I can look after myself."

"Oh, I'm sure you can. But, well, I'm not known for my patience. None of the CoSMiC guys are."

At hearing the news I was connected to an MC, his skin paled and he dropped his rag. "Aw fuck. Aw man. I didn't... I had no idea. Are they gonna come for me?"

I laughed lightly and shook my head. "Nah. You're good. Don't sweat it. Anyways, I just wanted to wish all the best to you and Ellie." Before I choked on my own words, I turned to leave but decided to make one last comment. When I faced him again, his brow scrunched, and he appeared confused. Ignoring that fact, I told him, "You'd better treat her right though. Or CoSMiC might just pay you a visit after all."

"B-but... why would you say that about me and Ellie? What did she say?"

Now *I* was confused. And when I thought back to the conversation we'd had I realized that she had never actually said she and Jonah were *anything*. "Aren't you guys... you know... an item?"

He sighed dejectedly and shook his head. "Sadly no. We dated. Well, we had *a* date. Last night actually. But then she heard that you had showed up in town, and she was outta there like there was a fire. I don't think we're what you could call a perfect fit, if you know what I'm saying."

"So she's not your girl?"

"No, sir. Not even close."

I smacked myself in the head. "Fuck."

After I scrambled back on to the bike, I headed back to the Irish pub as fast as I could travel. *What the hell had she meant, if not goodbye?*

I eventually pulled to a halt in the parking lot of the pub and clambered off my bike forgetting for a moment that my prosthetic didn't quite work in the same way as a real leg and I almost face planted onto the gravel.

"More fuckin' haste, less fuckin' speed, dumb ass," I chastised myself aloud.

Once I had pushed through the door, I made my way to the bar. "Excuse me, Fergus, has there been a red haired woman in here looking for me at all?"

"Oh, aye there has, Mr. Coltman. She arrived just after you left. But I thought you'd gone for good, and I told her so. She wasn't too happy at the news, I can tell you."

"Fuck! Okay, where did she go?"

He cringed and shrugged. "I'm sorry but I have no clue.

She just left without another word."

"Okay. Okay, thanks."

I shoved the door open again, and when I reached the parking lot I grasped my hair and looked skyward. "Okay. So I know I asked you for something once, and you came good. But now I'm asking again. If you're up there, I need to see her, okay?"

I glanced to my right, and an old couple were staring at me as I made my plea to a god I wasn't sure even existed. When they realized I was now focused on them, they scuttled away with panicked expressions and I couldn't help laughing.

I walked to the front of the pub and glanced up the main street and then down but there was no sign of my red head. I *had* to figure this out. I *had* to see her. But how the hell could I do that when I didn't know where she lived?

A squeaking noise from across the street began to irritate the hell out of me, and it distracted me from my train of thought. Peering in its direction, I realized it was a kids' play park and the squeaking was a kind of basket baby swing. And beside the swing was the most vivid shock of familiar, long red curls.

Ellie.

I jogged across the street in her direction, and my thigh hurt like a bitch, but I didn't care. As if she felt my presence she looked over toward me. When her gaze rested on me, she stopped the swing and lifted her hand to her chest.

When I got even closer, I began to slow my pace and stopped only a few feet from her. "There you are." My throat tightened with that damned emotion shit I was suffering from more frequently than I liked.

Tears escaped her eyes. "But the man at the Inn said you'd gone. Gone for good."

I stepped toward her again and lifted my hand to cup her

cheek. "I thought you were telling me goodbye, Ellie. I thought you and Jonah... And you didn't correct me."

She nodded. "I know. I'm so sorry." She flung her arms around me, and I held her tight to my chest.

Pulling back, I gazed into her shimmering green eyes. "So it wasn't goodbye?"

She shook her head. "No. I needed to do something, but I *was* coming back to you. I should have said that. I should've been clearer. I also should have told you that Jonah and I were never a thing."

"Yeah, I know that now. I saw him and he told me. But I don't understand what you meant, Ellie. It all sounded so final."

She turned away from me and lifted the child she had been pushing from the baby swing. "I had something to show you."

More riddles. More vague comments. "Okay, what is it? What do you have to show me, Ellie?"

She held the child toward me, and my heart almost stopped as I looked into familiar grey eyes. "Colt... this is Jacob... He's... he's your son."

The ability to stand, something I had been working on since getting my new leg, was suddenly one I didn't possess, and I dropped to my knees but my eyes stayed firmly fixed on the little dude in Ellie's arms.

She lowered herself to the ground too, a cascade of tears relentlessly falling down her pale skin. "*This* is why I wanted you to come back. For *him*. Not just for me. Now do you get it? Now do you understand why I was so hurt?"

I tried to speak, but along with the ability to stand, the ability to form words evaded me too. The little guy in Ellie's arms gurgled and giggled as the June breeze ruffled his shock of dark hair. Hair like mine. Eyes like mine.

Mine.

"I'm... I'm a daddy?"

She clung to her baby and fixed me with her hope-filled expression. "Do you *want* to be a daddy, Colt? That's the question in need of an answer."

"Oh god, yes. I want that so much. So, *so* much, Ellie. I never thought this would happen to me. Can I... Can I hold him?"

A sweet smile spread across her face, and she held him out to me.

I turned the baby boy toward me and grinned in spite of the fact my eyes appeared to be leaking. "Well hey, there little buddy." I whispered softly as he reached out for my hair. "Hey there *Jacob Coltman, junior*. I'm... I'm your daddy." My voice broke as I uttered words I never expected to say.

Ellie cleared her throat. "Ahem... It's Jacob *Cassidy*, actually."

I lifted my face until our eyes met. "Well then, Eleanor Cassidy will you marry me, and make our little family complete?"

Her eyes widened, and she covered her mouth with her hands as a sob escaped. Then she lunged forward, and the three of us ended up in a heap on the sandy ground of the play park.

"Shall I take that as yes?"

Her laugh rang around me, and I held my breath until she said, "Yes, Jacob *senior*, I *will* marry you."

My arms came about her and my baby son, and in that moment I heard the wind rush through the trees and a little butterfly fluttered above us for a few seconds.

And I knew.

Maria had given her blessing.

EPILOGUE

COLT

I look up at my woman as she straddles me, rocking back and forth, head back eyes closed as I tease her clit. Her gasps and moans make me even harder if that's possible. She rolls her hips in time with my movements, and I can feel her tightening. She's getting close. I reach up to toy with her nipple, and she explodes around me, and I follow, whispering how much I love her as we both calm down.

The little round bump of her belly is getting bigger, and I can't wait to meet my second child. A girl this time. This is a fucking huge day for me, and making love to Ellie is the best way to calm my nerves. Today I will be giving away a bride. Cain's... I mean Cameron's bride, Kelly, to be exact. It doesn't seem so long ago since I was sitting there at Baylor's Point, talking to him on the phone about his engagement. And here we are now, in a little hotel on the Isle of Skye on the morning of his wedding.

Jacob is down in the garden with his Aunt Chloe and Uncle Six while Ellie and I have some alone time. That little guy is the center of our world, but I must admit it's great to have stolen moments when I can remind Eleanor just how much I love her.

We take a long, lazy shower together, and I wash her hair. I can tell she's aroused again, and so I drop to my knees and give her what she needs with my tongue. She tells me her orgasms are so much more intense now she's pregnant, and I'm only too happy to oblige her insatiable, if hormonal, increased sex drive.

Once we're dried off, I go and dress in my suit, ready for the wedding. Cameron is wearing a kilt but the rest of us guys decided to skip that part of the traditional Scottish wedding. He did well to get us in morning suits. After all, we are bikers deep down in spite of the fact that the club may be winding down.

Ellie steps out of the bathroom in a pale blue summer dress that skims her hips and shows off the beginnings of our new bump. And now *I'm* aroused again.

"Don't you look at me like that, Jacob senior. We don't have time, and you know it."

I step toward her and slip my arms around her waist. "Can't help myself. You shouldn't be so darn beautiful."

I lean to take her mouth in a kiss that hints at what later will bring, and when I pull away she's smiling; her pupils are dilated too. "Maybe we could make it quick?" She bites her lip and gives me those sexy, come to bed eyes.

"Nah-uh, Miss Cassidy—soon to be Mrs. Coltman. I have a bride to give away. And a bunch of bikers not to piss off."

She sticks out her bottom lip. "Spoil sport."

———

We arrive at the little church near a place called Broadford on

Skye, and I'm taken aback by how fucking beautiful this place is. Everywhere you look, there are mountains and so many shades of green. There's this range called the Cuillins and it's like something from a sci-fi movie set. I can see why Six and Chloe are moving over here.

The Scottish accent is so hard to understand sometimes, but I could still listen to it for hours, regardless. Although Ellie keeps on slapping my thigh when I ask Kelly to pronounce certain words for me.

I leave my fiancée with her best friend and my MC brother, and head off to collect the bride. Kelly's understandably nervous, and keeps thanking me for making the long journey to give her away. I make a joke that it only took five minutes in the wedding car. She giggles, slaps my arm and tells me in that cute accent that I'm such a kidder.

A half hour later, Kelly and I enter the church, and all eyes are on her. She looks so beautiful in her gown. But I only have eyes for the stunning redhead and the little dark haired boy standing beside her in jeans, a shirt and a little clip on tie. That kid fills my heart with so much love I can't express it in words.

As I lift my face I lock my gaze onto familiar green eyes. She smiles.

And I'm done for all over again.

The End

ACKNOWLEDGMENTS

Thank you to every single reader who insisted I continued with this series. Your love of my stories is what makes this all worthwhile.

Thank you to my beta readers Lou H and Christine F. Your comments and encouragement throughout the writing of this book were a huge help and I'm so glad you fell for Colt.

To my wonderful street team. I have been bowled over by the number of you who continue to stick with me and get my books out into the world. Thank you from the bottom of my heart.

What would I do without all the amazing bloggers out there? I have so much gratitude for each and every blog who has helped to spread the word about this series. There are far too many to list but please know that your support means the world to me.

ABOUT THE AUTHOR

Lisa is happily married to her best friend and together she and her husband have one child and two daft dogs. Writing has always been her passion although it has only been in recent years that she has taken the plunge to try her hand at novels. Back in 2014 her debut *Bridge Over the Atlantic* (later republished by *Aria Fiction* as *A Seaside Escape*) was published by an American company and was shortlisted in the Romantic Novelists Association RONAs for their prestigious Romance Novel of the Year.

Lisa is now the proud author of both self-published *and* traditionally published titles since being signed on a four book deal to *Aria Fiction*, an imprint of award winning *Head of Zeus Publishing*.

Originally from Yorkshire, Lisa now lives in bonny Scotland, a place that features in many of her titles. And when she's not writing, reading *or* editing she can be found being taken for a walk by her energetic dogs.

ALSO BY LISA J HOBMAN

(Please note these titles are not erotic novels)

A Seaside Escape

A Year of Finding Happiness

Christmas Presence

(*A Seaside Escape Christmas Novella*)

What Becomes of the Broken Hearted

Reasons to Leave

Reasons to Stay

Duplicity

Through the Glass

The Girl Before Eve

Last Christmas

(*A TGBE Christmas Novella*)

The Worst of Me

In His Place

\And coming soon:

Zara Bailey's Summer of New Beginnings

Lightning Source UK Ltd.
Milton Keynes UK
UKHW040155191121
394190UK00013B/515